QUEEN OF ALL

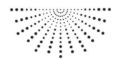

Queen of All

ANYA LEIGH
JOSEPHS

Supervising Editor: Emily Oliver
Associate Editor: Aleshia Scogin
Cover Designer: L. Austen Johnson, www.allaboutbookcovers.com

ZENITH PUBLISHING

CONTENTS

To all the kids out there who've been told there's something wrong with how you look, or who you love, or who you are: this book is for you. You deserve to be the hero of your own story and to have the chance to tell it.

PREFACE

After all these years, it's you.

How I have waited.

How I have prayed.

How I have—forgive me—begun to doubt that you would ever come back to me again. To stand before me, in a new guise but still so certainly yourself. To love me as I love you. To hear this story.

My dearest one, you must understand my doubts. You must forgive them. For even when I doubted, I never gave up the last of my hope. I never gave up waiting for you.

I have waited like trees, having shed their leaves, wait for spring to come and breathe new life into their cold roots. I have waited the way flowers wait, their faces upturned to the sky, for rain to drown them in life. I have waited as a bird waits, tenderly watching her unhatched egg, keeping that sweet seed of life in perpetual possibility for one day longer.

I have waited as patiently as the Earth. And as long.

You slept, unknowing, and I waited, counting every breath like an eternity until you would return. How fast and slow at once the time went, perhaps I can never tell you. Perhaps there are no words, in this tongue or any other, that can tell you how I ached to see you again. How I longed to hear your voice. How I loved you, all alone.

And now here you are. With me again.

When I had all but given up on the dream of ever seeing you return.

But then, a part of me knew this was how things were meant to be for us.

My mother once told me that the Goddess made the Earth round because that shape shows us the nature of the universe. The Earth, like a womb, circles back in on itself, holding us within the warm embrace of Her body. Time, she told me, is a circle too. Everything we lose comes back to us again.

Everyone we lose comes back to us again. Just, she said, as I lost you, and just as you returned to me. As, one day, your father will return to me, too, in this life or in some other.

Everyone we lose comes back to us again.

These words are all that has sustained me while I have waited. Not the knowledge, for not even I can pretend to know such mysteries, but the hope: that time would flow back into itself like waves returning to the ocean, like blood pumping through a heart, like a child curling up to sleep.

It is not vanity when I say I know more of the Earth's secrets than anyone else who has ever lived, with the exception, perhaps, of the Goddess herself. I know the rhythm of the passing years as only She and I could, each season no more than the pattern of breath in and out of my eternal lungs. I know the names of Her most hidden children, the zizit in their mountaintop retreats and the tannim on their forgotten isles and the behemoth in the breathless depths of the sea. I know love and loss more deeply and feelingly than anyone who has ever lived.

But I did not know that it was true. I could only hope, not ever be certain. Not until I saw you here, again, at last.

My own...

Oh, I know you don't remember. You don't even know me, not yet.

That's all right. That's all right, my love. I have told myself our story again and again, so that even the vastest expanse of time could not wear the memories thin. I have readied myself for this, for the day when I could finally tell you everything.

Would you like me to start with our story, or at the very beginning?

PRELUDE

She pushes the Sending away for as long as she can. For days it haunts her, whispering to her in her dreams, standing behind her at the loom while the morning sun through the window turns her skin golden in its gentle light. It murmurs her name as she smears a thick layer of rich schmaltz onto her bread at breakfast, touches her shoulder with ghostly fingers as the baby nurses at her breast, follows her to the stream as she carries the washing down, calls her name aloud as she and her husband join together at night.

At first, she means to accept or ignore it. Others have been haunted before and lived a number of happy years before the madness set in. Better to do that and let her life come to an almost natural end than to hear what this voice has to say. Her man will bury and mourn her, and maybe, if she can hold on long enough, the baby will be old enough when her mind goes that it will remember her as something other than the sickly shadow that she will no doubt become in the end.

She's ready to endure a whisper in the night, a face reflected in the stream, a disembodied rage bristling behind her. She's ready to lose her mind in the fight to keep the life that, though destiny and her mother may have sent her to, she ultimately chose for herself. She should have known that would be only the start.

The great ruak arrives with a storm. She's still unsure, even at her great age, if all the thunder and lightning is really necessary, or if it's just for show. Her mother still keeps some secrets to herself. To yield them up would be to yield her power, and the great Adirialaina will never do that—not until the Goddess Herself comes to claim her.

Yet she doesn't fear her mother's might, even as the sky flashes sickly white with a bolt too powerful to be of any natural origin. She does not weep, or scream in frustration, or call out for mercy. She takes a single shuddering breath and goes inside from the garden to clean up for supper.

Her sister-in-law has made a rich dish of lentils and rice—*mujadra,* they call it, in their Common Tongue that is still so strange to her—and the whole kitchen smells of frying onions and braised herbs.

She washes her hands and sits at the table next to her husband. She's quiet throughout the meal, but then, she's often quiet. No one notices. And no one is much surprised when she urges them all to go to bed early.

"The storm will be bad. Best get some rest," she says, and they take her advice, as they are wont to do.

A strange girl, but a clever one, they say about her. *She knows things, and sure enough it's best to listen.*

If only they knew.

Her husband locks the cottage's shaky door against the gusts of wind. She watches as the rest of the family goes into their bedrooms, shutting themselves away. She could do the same, she supposes, but a locked door is no refuge against what she knows is coming.

Instead, she hands the baby to its father and murmurs an excuse before ducking back into the main room of the house, quickly, matter-of-factly, as though she's going to douse a pot left on the fire and not as though she'll never see the little one again. The baby knows, though, its fat fist tangling in her hair before it settles its heavy head against its father's chest and returns to sleep.

Its magical intuition is already powerful for a child not even a year old. The ruak in its tiny, perfect body will grow as it does. One day, it will be strong enough to shake the Earth.

She is proud to think of such a bright future for this child, for the only child she will ever have. She tries not to think of the suffering that the weight of destiny will demand from this soft and helpless babe. She does not yield the child up to her mother's machinations, not in her own mind, though it was by Adirialaina's will that it was conceived and born and will go on to save their people.

I will see you again, one day, she promises the child

fiercely. She wonders if its ruak is already strong enough that it can hear the words of her mind. She hopes so. She hopes that the dream she cannot put into words will settle into the babe's consciousness; that, somehow, it will remember this moment—not as an abandonment, but a temporary separation.

She strokes the baby's dark hair and kisses her husband briefly so that he won't realize anything is wrong, and then she readies herself.

Of course, her mother still makes her wait. She sits down at the kitchen table as though anticipating a more ordinary type of family visit, and carefully does not allow herself even a quick glance at the empty door behind which her husband and child are now peacefully sleeping.

She knows she'll never see them again. One last look will spare her nothing. It will not unwidow her husband or give her child a mother's love to remember. It will not let her keep her family. Nothing will.

When it arrives at last at the stroke of midnight (for Adirialaina has never been accused of lacking a flair for the dramatic), her mother's voice comes in like a crack of thunder. It has been three long years since she heard her mother speak, but the power in that voice still makes all the little hairs on her arms stand at attention, makes her stomach churn, makes her jaw set with something like fury.

You know what you have to do, Adirialaina's voice tells her. *You know who you are. You have played this game long enough, and your part in it is finished.*

She could rage at the unhearing sky. She could scream and wail out her grief until the timbers of the cottage shatter around her and break as her heart is breaking.

She could even refuse. That's never happened before, and there's no knowing what would come of it, but she could try, for the sake of her small family, her *real* family.

Instead, wearily, obediently, she walks out into the night. As the single lighted window of the cottage where she has spent the only two happy years of her long life disappears into the gloom of the night, over the heavy pounding rhythm of the storm, she hears the baby start to cry.

CHAPTER ONE

The most beautiful girl in any of the Four Corners of the Earth kicks me awake in the middle of the night.

Through my half-open eyes and by the light of the moon, I can see her perfectly sculpted face looming over mine. Her ruby-red lips, so entrancing that a passing bard once wrote a lengthy ode in their honor, blow hot air directly up my nose. The bard, for obvious reasons, did not mention the stench of her morning breath. As she begins to wake up, I cough, try to turn over, and fumble for our shared blanket with the intention of pulling it over my head and going back to sleep. It's gone.

As I reluctantly blink my way awake, our bedroom comes into focus: the white-washed walls, the low rafters, the ladder down into the main room, the trunk where we keep our clothes, and then Sisi, grinning triumphantly, holding the blanket over her head.

"What do you want?"

1

"And good morning to you too, my beloved cousin," she says, her dark-rose cheeks dimpling in an extremely winsome fashion. Most people can't stay mad at beautiful Sisi for long. Luckily, I've had plenty of practice. I was still only a baby when Sisi and her brother came to live here, so for fourteen years, she and I have been making each other, and driving each other, mad.

"No, you see, morning happens *after* the nighttime. Which is what we're having now. Nighttime. Morning is later."

"Well technically, it's after midnight. Thus, good morning." She smiles at me again.

"And before dawn. Thus, good night." I make another futile grab for the blanket, but Sisi has a good six inches of height on me and is quicker than I am even when I'm not drowsy from sleep. Defeated, I slump back against the frame of our bed. "Come on, you didn't just wake me up in the middle of the night so that we could debate the finer points of timekeeping. Are you up to something? You already know I won't want to be a part of it."

"Listen." She points down at the floor of our bedroom. Because we sleep up in the attic, I can just barely hear a low rumble of voices through the floorboards, coming from the main room below. "What are they doing awake at this hour? There must be something interesting going on." Question and answer, all in one. As usual, I seem to be altogether unnecessary in this conversation Sisi is having with herself.

"Yes. I'm sure the price of grain has gone up fifteen milar a tonne, or something."

"You have no spirit of adventure," Sisi accuses.

"Another of my many faults."

"Fine, then I'll go by myself, and I shan't tell you what I find."

"Have fun. Do try not to get caught," I advise.

She turns to face me fully, batting her long, dark eyelashes at me. It's a trick that would certainly work on any of her many admirers among the local boys, but I'm immune to that kind of flattery. "*Please,* Jena? Sweet cousin, my dearest friend, it'll be ever so much better if you just come with me."

"Come where? Down the stairs? It's not much of a valiant quest, even if I were inclined to be your brave companion." After a moment's thought, I add, "And I'm reasonably sure that I'm your only friend."

But Sisi has no trouble continuing her conversation with herself, with or without input from me. "I'm sure you saw that carriage coming up the drive today?"

"I thought that was a delivery of new cider jugs from the potter." We ran out two days ago, on Fourthday.

"No, it was a horse-drawn carriage!"

Now, that's a decent bit of news, I must admit. People around here use pushcarts, or occasionally mules and donkeys. Horses are unofficially reserved for the Numbered, as anyone without noble blood is unlikely to be able to afford their feed and upkeep. I carefully arrange my expression so Sisi won't see that she's caught my interest, but she continues on unabated. "Anyway,

Aunt Mae might have said that, but I know for a fact that wasn't the potter's lad."

"So, Daren's finally got himself fired, and the potter's found someone new. I don't see why that's such a big deal." The potter's apprentice is famous around town for his clumsiness, and it would be no surprise to anyone if someone more suited to such a delicate profession replaced him. Daren is a good-hearted lad, as Aunt Mae always says, and he does work hard, but he likely breaks more pots carrying them in from the kiln than he sells in one piece. This is especially true when he delivers jugs for the cider press on our farm, since his infatuation with Sisi makes him nervous. Of course, everyone fancies Sisi —he's not alone in that, just a little more hopeless than most.

"It wasn't anyone from the potter's. Nor anyone else from Leasane. It was a man around your father's age. Better dressed, though, in some sort of gold-and-purple uniform. He gave Uncle Prinn a sheet of paper. I couldn't quite see what was on it, but it was stamped with a golden seal and I'm sure it was the Sign of the Three Powers itself. So, I can only assume that your father has been given a message from the Royal Court in the Capi-tal. How often do you think a messenger from the King's own home rides across half the Earth to seek out an apple farmer? And what could be in such a message?" She looks about ready to faint as she finishes her speech, her cheeks flushed with the effort of having so much to say so quickly.

I have to concede that this is indeed a good point—

but I have a few good points of my own to make. "Sounds too good to be true. Which means it probably is. Perhaps this messenger just wanted a cup of cider and directions back to the High Road. If it was anything more than that, we'll hear about it soon enough. In the meantime, why not go to bed? Or at least lie here and speculate so as to spare ourselves the inevitable results of snooping into what's none of our business: we sneak out, we get caught, we get beaten, we get sent right back where we started no better off but for sore backsides."

"You are becoming frightfully dull lately. Ever since that incident on market day—"

"Which was all your fault, I might add, though it was me who took all the blame. *Here's an idea, Jena, let's not do our chores today! Oh, let's steal the apple cart and ride it into town! It'll be fun! We'll meet boys! We'll buy candies at the market! We won't get caught! And when we* do *get caught, I certainly won't run away home and pretend never to have left my sewing and not say a word when Jena's getting thrashed for it!*"

"Bruises heal. Unsatisfied curiosity never does."

"I don't know, I'm still a little sore..." To be honest, my feelings were hurt worse than my backside. Aunt Mae is strict, but she'd never thrash us so hard that bruises dealt out a week prior would still hurt. What stings isn't the beating, now, as Sisi points out, healed and mostly forgotten. It's the fact that I'd gotten one, and Sisi hadn't. As usual, I got stuck taking all of the blame and the pain while Sisi got away scot-free, since she's too pretty and charming for anyone but me to stay angry with.

"A half hour, that's all. Won't you give your poor dear cousin, near to you as a sister, your closest kin in affection if not in blood, a half-hour's worth of your rest, when I would wake a thousand night's watching for you?"

I roll my eyes, but I must confess—even just to myself —that I do quite want to know what's going on down in the kitchen. As usual, Sisi is, infuriatingly, right. "Just half an hour?"

"Thirty minutes, to the *instant,*" she promises, smiling with all the innocence she can muster.

"Shake on it, you scoundrel. I can't trust you."

She spits in her hand and offers it to me, and I take it. Sometimes I think Sisi wouldn't have made a very good Lady of a Numbered House, even if her brother hadn't left the Numbered for his unsuitable marriage with my cousin Merri. Sisi and I shake, and then she yanks me out of the bed by our joined hands.

"Come on," she says, and I sigh. I'm really in for it now, whether I like it or not. I might as well make the best of the night's adventure, since there's no way I'm getting back to sleep. Silently, I bid fond farewells to the comfort of my pillow and the joys of sleeping on an unbruised backside.

As reluctant as I profess to be, I'm the first one out the casement. There's an opening just wide enough for us to fit through if we're careful, meant to let light and air into the attic room. Sisi and I are both big girls, and it's an uncomfortable squeeze as my stomach presses against the wall. Unlike Sisi, at least I have no bosom to contend with as of yet.

For a moment, I'm dangling in the air, kicking into nothing, but then I find the first rung of the ladder perched on the outer wall and begin to climb down. By now the path is familiar after years of such midnight escapades, not to mention all the many more ordinary times we've climbed up to our shared attic room. The small size of the farmhouse means this is a fortunately short journey. Soon enough, I'm making my mostly silent landing against the soft earth of Aunt Mae's precious flowerbeds.

It's pitch-black out here, but I know that Sisi is beside me because I can hear the soft thump of her feet landing next to me and feel her warm hand against mine. As we tiptoe along the outside of the house, I see the candlelight leaking out from the single glass window. That window is my father's pride and joy, the only addition he'd made to the house after his own father died and left both farm and farmhouse to him. A real glass window is a luxury far beyond what we could really afford, even when times were better. Yet it's an addition that makes my father happy—as little enough does—and right now it certainly serves Sisi and I well. It marks the front of the house clearly and means we can see into the candlelit room, though no one in there can see out into the darkness. I hope.

All the adults in the family are gathered around the table. Nearest us is the back of my father's head, recognizable from the way his brown hair is shot through with grey. He worries, my aunt always says, with so many people counting on him. *Grey before thirty, dead before*

7

fifty, I've heard others say in town. I try not to think about that. We've never been close, my father and I, but I can't imagine life without him.

Next to him is his only sister, my Aunt Mae. Unlike the rest of the family, who are in their nightclothes, my aunt is fully clothed in her light-blue daytime dress, though she has her arms stretched over her head in a yawn. Aunt Mae usually rises early to cook breakfast for the whole family and likes to be in bed by an hour after sundown. I wonder whether she's up late or rising early.

My father's brother, Uncle Willem, and his wife, my Aunt Sarie, are across from them. They face the window, meaning we can clearly see that they stand side by side as always, arms identically crossed over their identically narrow chests, looking down at whatever is on the table with identically sour expressions.

Their grown daughter, Merri, too thin and pale in her nightgown, has her hands on her stomach. She's been with child for nearly eight months now, her belly growing even as the rest of her seems to fade away. Merri used to be an exceptionally pretty girl, her good spirits and twinkling eyes enlivening the otherwise plain features of our family. That beauty has faded away, though, over the course of her difficult pregnancy.

And yet, that has not diminished the love that her husband has for her. Jorj, Sisi's only living blood relative, is next to Merri, one arm around his wife's frail shoulders. His eyes, however, are glued to the table. He's a handsome man of thirty, with the same rich dark skin and finely sculpted features as Sisi. Like his sister, he was born into a Numbered family. He was once One Hundred and Twenty-Third in the Kingdom—that is, one hundred and twenty-third in line for the throne. Fourteen years ago, he'd given up that claim, and the fine palace in Easthame-by-the-Sea, after his parents' untimely deaths. He'd come with nothing but his love for Merri, who had been a serving maid in his parents' palace, and his four-year-old sister in his arms. Since then, he's been a doting brother, cousin, husband...and soon, a father.

The only members of the family missing are Merri's three little brothers. The boys, as they are universally called in our family, range from a few years younger than me to nearly Sisi's age, and so perhaps, like us, they weren't deemed adult enough for this conversation. They pick on us girls regularly, so we don't feel any need to wake them up and warn them of our plans whenever there's a mystery afoot. Besides, they sleep in a single shared room just off the kitchen—the logistics would be impossible.

As I'm feeling momentarily guilty, nonetheless, about leaving the boys out, Sisi nudges me sharply with her elbow, drawing my attention back to the matter at hand.

Everyone inside is looking down at the table, and as my father shifts to the side to say something to Aunt Mae, I finally see the subject of everyone's attention: a single piece of paper.

Sisi was right. This *is* more interesting than being asleep in bed. Annoyed with myself for having admitted as much, even in the privacy of my mind, I scowl in the darkness. I think I can see Sisi smirk back at me.

Unfortunately, the thick oak of the door covers the voices of the assembled adults—the conversation, and so the context, are indistinct. I can see letters on the page, but they mean nothing more to me than the indistinguishable murmurs coming through the walls of the house.

"Can you read that?" I whisper to Sisi. Unlike me, she got a Numbered Lady's education from her brother, even after they moved to the farm. She can read and write in Common, and even knows some words of the Old Tongue. I can't even scratch the four letters of my byname.

She shakes her head and whispers back, "Too far away."

I instead turn my attention towards trying to understand the barely audible noises from within. After a moment, I can make out what Jorj is saying, the task rendered somewhat easier by the fact that he is hollering at the top of his lungs.

"Absolutely not!" he shouts. "I won't hear another word about it. I am her only kin, and it is my word that decides!"

So Sisi was right, and this mystery does revolve around her. How annoying. For once, I'd like to have a fascinating incident center around *me*. Or at least get the satisfaction of Sisi being wrong about something important.

I can't hear what happens next, but from the way his hands move, I can tell that my father is saying something soothing, slow and steady and quiet as ever, and yet as unshakeable as stone.

Jorj shakes his head, backing away and frowning. Clearly, whatever my father has said, it hasn't been heard.

Now Merri jumps in, one hand on Jorj's arm, as if in support. Uncle Willem cuts her off. He grabs something off the table—a small, black velvet sack, obviously heavy with coin from the way he holds it—and brandishes it at her.

Sisi nudges me again, as though I need the hint. Whatever's happening, there's money involved. Maybe a lot of money. If that's the case, then we certainly need it. The farm isn't doing as well as it had when I was younger, though my father works hard to hide it from us children. The only reason I know that is that Sisi helps Aunt Mae with the farm's accounts, and she relays everything back to me.

Whatever Uncle Willem says about the purse, it makes Jorj turn to his wife. He looks at her carefully. Though it's a warm summer evening, she's shivering and pale in the night air, her face and hands bony. She stays silent and still, not meeting his eyes. Instead, she looks down at her own swollen stomach, at the rise of her dress stretched tight across her middle even as it falls down her shoulders and arms, too big for her increasingly scrawny frame.

Jorj's shoulders slump, almost defeated. He shakes his head again, but weakly now, a token protest.

My father speaks again. Whatever he says makes Jorj

look up in surprise, and then there is a great cacophony of noise, like everyone is shouting all at once. The loudest voice—as usual—belongs to Aunt Mae, but I can't understand a word over the tumult of different sounds.

Sisi and I look at each other in the intervening chaos. It's so dark that I can't read her expression, but nonetheless I know her mind. It's starting to seem less and less likely that we'll ever find out precisely what the contents of this mysterious letter are. I can almost hear Sisi's thoughts at work—I imagine she's trying to figure out how she might steal the letter out of my father's possession and find out what secrets it holds. That probably means tomorrow night will be no more restful, nor less perilous, than tonight.

Suddenly, the blur of noise inside is interrupted by the sound of footsteps, and then, just by the door, a voice speaks clearly: "Why not settle it now?" The kitchen door flies open. I jump backward out of its path, just in time to miss being clobbered in the face and see Aunt Mae standing in the open doorway, her arms crossed. "Girls? I think you can come in now," she calls while the other members of the family stare out at us.

Sisi and I just look back at them. I imagine she's as terrified as I am. Aunt Mae's voice is so calm, like the air before a terrible storm.

"Don't just stand there staring at me like a couple of startled cats, I heard the both of you coming down the side of the house. You're just lucky you didn't break your necks in the dark. Now come on in, your elders want to speak to you." Her tone is almost cheery. I recognize a trap when I hear one.

Sisi at least has the decency to lead the way into the house, while I follow a few tentative steps behind. After all, this was her idea, and now it ought to be her problem. With any luck, I can take my trustworthy and familiar tactic of sliding beneath everyone's notice, though I briefly consider the alternate possibility of running for it. In spite of my size, I'm quick, and as always, it is Sisi who's the center of attention, not me. Yet, I am, for all my denial, desperately curious to find out what is going on here, and I know my stubborn cousin. She'll cross her arms and lock her lips and never say a word if I don't follow her in to face whatever's coming, for better or for worse.

So, as always, we stand together now as everyone turns to look at us. Jorj is flushed with anger, his black eyes flashing as he looks at his sister. Sisi stares back at him, unafraid. Of course, it's easy to never be afraid of trouble if you know you can always get out of it.

"*What* are you doing out of bed?" he shouts, and I've never heard him talk to Sisi—or anyone—like that before.

"I wanted to know what was going on," Sisi mumbles quietly. "I heard voices in the middle of the night, and I knew it must have something to do with the carriage, and I just wanted to know."

"Oh, you *had* to—"

"Jorj," my father says calmly. "It doesn't matter. The girls are here now."

13

I wince at the plural. It seems like my father has noticed me too, not just Sisi. How unusual.

"They should be safe in bed," Jorj insists.

"I'm not sure of that, as I've said," my father replies, his voice as calm as ever. He looks at both Sisi and me. For a brief moment, his warm brown eyes meet mine, but then he turns back to Sisi. "After all, the letter was addressed to Sisi. She's practically a woman grown now, and clearly she wishes to know its contents. Is there any reason we should keep them from her?"

"She's too young," Jorj grumbles. "Nothing good can come of it."

Merri pipes up. "You were younger than she is now when your parents died, and then you had to act the man. You found a home for yourself and your sister, you arranged your own marriage, and you took care of Sisi. Is reading that letter so much worse than all that?" It's not like her to contradict her beloved husband, but we're all acting out of our accustomed characters tonight, it seems.

Defeated, Jorj raises his hands in a posture of surrender. "Fine. Tell her. Let's see what she has to say."

The silence that follows is deafening. Sisi looks expectantly around the room as each of the adults, in turn, shifts uncomfortably. It seems that, although they may have agreed that it's time to talk, no one is quite certain what to say.

Aunt Mae finally begins, cautiously. "Sisi, we received—that is to say, you received—a letter today. Earlier."

"I gathered as much," Sisi replies. There is just

enough sarcasm in her tone that Aunt Mae gives her a sharp look for her disrespect, but not enough so that she doesn't continue. Sisi is always so much better at managing such things than I am.

"It was from His Highness, Lord Ricard, Second in the Kingdom."

"The crown prince sent me a letter," Sisi says blankly. It seems even Sisi can't summon up a joke in response to *that* news. Her tone is flat, revealing none of the surprise that she must be feeling—that I certainly am. It seems like something out of one of Aunt Mae's tales more than from my real life: A letter all the way from the City! From the Prince himself! And for our own Sisi! I always knew, in some distant part of my mind, that she was one of the Numbered and therefore not like us, but this seems too strange to be true. Even if she had stayed a fine lady, she certainly couldn't have expected to hear from the Prince, the King's own brother, Second in the Kingdom!

"Yes, he...well, he—oh, just read the letter," says Aunt Mae, finally thrusting it into Sisi's hands.

I sink down a little where I stand as Sisi takes the paper. I'd been hoping Aunt Mae would reveal the details aloud; if she doesn't, there's no way I can read the letter myself. I'll have to get the story out of Sisi later, if I can persuade her to share it.

Sisi scans the letter quickly, her beautiful dark eyes darting across the page. From where I stand at her side, I can see the thick black lines on the white parchment. I try to decipher Sisi's expression, but for once I can no more read her face than I can read the words on the page.

She stares at the letter for several minutes, though it is only a single page long, and then looks up, meeting my father's gaze. I hold my breath, waiting for her words. The anxiety in the room is so intense I can feel it around me, as though I'm soaking up everyone else's fear.

"You said it was up to me, Uncle Prinn?"

"Yes," my father says, firmly, although I can practically see a denial on the tip of Jorj's tongue.

"I choose whether or not to go?"

"Up to you."

"And everyone will accept my choice?"

My father looks around the room. Aunt Mae is the first to nod her agreement, then Uncle Willem and Aunt Sarie, then Merri, and then finally, reluctantly, Jorj.

Sisi holds the letter up and rips the paper cleanly and deliberately in half. Then she throws the two halves back down on the table. "Then I won't. I won't," she says. She closes her eyes, shakes her head slightly, and falls silent. Everyone stares at the discarded letter, at Sisi's trembling hands, waiting for her to say more. But when she speaks again, all she says is, "May we be excused to bed?"

"Of course," Aunt Mae says, before anyone else can answer, and Sisi turns on her heel and walks back outside to the ladder leading up to our loft. She climbs up first, without another word or a backward glance. I follow her, in her shadow as always. I can't help sneaking a look back at the main room, and at the shaken adults who are gathered around the fallen scraps of paper, still staring at them in silence.

When we're back in our quiet little room, Sisi turns away from me wordlessly, nestling into her half of the bed and hiding her face beneath the covers.

"Sisi?" I ask.

There's no answer.

"Aren't you going to tell me what's going on? Sisi?"

Still, she says nothing. I sigh and sit at the corner of the bed beside her, gently laying a hand on her hip to try and get her attention. She turns away again.

"You know I can't read. I don't know what it said—"

"Jena, please," she says heavily. "Let me sleep."

"But Sisi..."

She only sighs. It's not like her to keep secrets from me unless she's angry with me, which she doesn't seem to be. It's even less like her not to be sympathetic to something I've missed out on because I didn't get the same education she did as a Numbered lady. But she seems as unmovable, and as distant, as my father was tonight.

"Sisi, please. Tell me tomorrow, then, but don't keep this from me."

"There's nothing to tell. It's late. We should go to sleep."

"So, I've said from the start."

She doesn't even laugh at that, or lean over to ruffle my hair and call me a silly little bird. She doesn't say anything at all.

CHAPTER TWO

*W*e're dragged out of bed with the dawn. As promised, there is no sympathy for us weary nighttime adventurers. As soon as we stumble down the ladder, bleary-eyed and half-awake, Aunt Mae puts Sisi to work kneading dough and has me run down to the well for the day's full supply of water, a particularly arduous task.

We're sent off to our separate chores so early that I don't get a chance to talk to Sisi at all. I find myself wondering if that's a deliberate maneuver, if Aunt Mae is trying to keep me from having a chance to ask Sisi about the contents of the letter. That seems silly, since Sisi and I sleep in the same bed. If she wanted to tell me anything, she'd have plenty of opportunity to do so.

But Sisi is clearly still determined to avoid me. During the morning meal, Sisi sits straight across the table from me, between Uncle Willem and her brother Jorj, picking at her portion of breakfast. I tear my slim slice of dark bread into crumbs, watching Sisi's face as she carefully avoids my glances. Once we've eaten— slowly to make the meager portions last a little longer— Sisi remains inside, helping Aunt Mae clear the plates, as I follow Uncle Willem, the boys, my father, and Jorj out to the orchard to begin our day's work.

As we cross the garden, I see the pahyat-house that Sisi and I built when we were children, rotting peacefully under the shade of a blackberry bramble. The tiny house was meant to look like our own, though made from twisted branches and bits of grass. I remember how we used to steal bits of food from the kitchen and even some of the offerings Aunt Mae leaves out for the Goddess to put in the house. Milk, when we could get it, in a thimble because some of the smallest tribes of the pahyat people supposedly loved to drink it along with bits of sweets. We'd check every day to see if the food had been taken, though it never was.

"Jeni!" Jorj snaps at me. "You're walking right through the peppers."

I realize he's right. Lost in my thoughts, I've dragged my feet right through the tender seedlings, uprooting a few. I stop to try to fix the damage I've done, conscious that we can hardly afford the waste of good food, and then hurry to catch up with the men.

My father has set us to work in the furthest corner of the orchard today. I climb up the first of the trees. It used to be Merri's job, before she was with child, and her slim frame seemed better suited for the task. No matter how scanty our meals get, I'll never be slender like most Third

Quarter folk. I'm built more like Sisi and Jorj, but without Sisi's appealing curves. As Aunt Mae sometimes laughingly puts it—much to my dismay—I have the body of an apple: round in the middle... and in all the other parts too. In spite of my size, though, I've always been the best at climbing to the top of the trees, whether to pick fruit from the branches in autumn or to check how they're growing and to prune the extra branches in summer.

Uncle Willem and Jorj do the bulk of today's work, tying off the thick, heavy branches further down on the tree. My father inspects each trunk to see which parts are healthy and which need to be removed then sends each of them where we're needed most. I'm left on my own to take care of the small, dry twigs at the top branches—less important, perhaps, but still a danger to the growing fruit as they can block the sunlight if allowed to remain throughout the season. I sit on a branch and pull out my small belt-knife, trimming away whatever feels brittle or dry to the touch.

As I work, I let my mind wander. I love my task, not just because I'm good at it but also because of what I can see from here. I move from branch to branch throughout the long morning, getting glimpses of every corner of the farm. Over the course of the day, I see the sky changing, from the orange and pink of dawn to the bright shining blue of the late summer's midday sky. I can see the rolling hills that surround our farm, and the long dirt road that goes from our front door out through those hills, and onwards, to the rest of the Kingdom.

That road leads to the center of Leasane, our town, where the market is. It leads to the other small houses owned by the other small farmers with small lives like my own. It leads to the forest surrounding the town, and, just a little off the road, all the secrets that lie there: Kariana's abandoned cottage, the old stone circle that must have been made centuries ago by the adirim, the huge bones in the wood that Jorj used to say belonged to a ziz, those mythical birds with wings big enough to blot out the sun. It's the road Merri walked down to find work with Jorj's parents, and the road Jorj followed her back here on, carrying the baby Sisi in his arms as they fled the ruin of their childhood home. It's the road my mother walked down when she came to live with us, and, I assume, the one that carried her away again on the day she abandoned my father and me.

I wonder if Sisi will find herself back on it one day, walking away from us, and where it will lead her.

Her brother Jorj has been able to fit himself into life here. He's respected—even my father sometimes defers to him, and the men in town treat him well, not so much for his high birth as for his friendly ways in spite of it. Besides, he's so entirely in love with Merri that nothing else seems to matter much to him.

Sisi, on the other hand, has never quite found her place. It's hard to imagine her settling down as a farmer's wife in a little house like the one my grandfather built for our family, having children, growing old, and dying here in Leasane. She knows too much, thinks too much, argues too much. She doesn't fit into the pattern that is set out for girls like us.

I wonder what I'll do with myself if she goes.

Then again, I may have little choice but to accept that things are changing—even the farm, the land itself, is different than it was when I was young. My father tries to hide it from us, but it's plain to see. The heavy lines on his face, the hours Sisi spends with Aunt Mae poring over the account books, trying to figure out where the money is going, and the state of the trees themselves all tell the story of our struggle to get by.

So, too, does my daily work here on the farm. There are a few early-season fruits on the branches already. Though still green, not ready to eat or press for cider, most are already shot through with the dark mushy patches that indicate worms. I slice into one with my knife and cringe as I see the white squirming masses slide out of it.

Five years ago was the first time that the rotting disease affected our crops. That season, we lost a tenth of the growth to rot and the bugs that follow it. The year after, despite my father's careful efforts to remove fruit at the first signs of disease and to bring in fresh water often, just as many again were lost. Three years ago, one in four had to be carted out to the woods so they wouldn't infect the rest. Two years ago, it was nearly half, and last year, most. This harvest it seems like little healthy fruit will grow at all.

When I was a small girl, it was different. For leagues around, people said that Gaia blessed my father's farm.

In the summertime, on the longest day of the year, he would invite the witch-woman Kariana to come from her little cottage in the woods. Aunt Mae would make a special feast for us all, and afterward we would go out into the orchard and hold hands and dance as Kariana sang something in the Old Tongue. Ours wasn't the only house she came to, but she'd always whisper to me before she left that we were her favorite—probably because of Aunt Mae's famous apple pie, for which she'd carefully preserve the finest fruits of the previous harvest to be enjoyed on the holiday.

Within a few weeks of Kariana's visits, the trees would bloom white and lovely, and in autumn they'd be so heavy with fruit that even the thickest branches bowed low to the ground. We couldn't harvest it all, leaving some in the fields for the poor to take if they were hungry, or to fatten the birds. *Out for the go'im,* Aunt Mae used to say. I was never sure if she believed it or not, but in those golden childhood days it seemed possible to reach into a bedtime story, to believe that peoples other than humans might still walk the land in secret, that the old tales were faded histories, not fantasies.

Now many of the trees' limbs are bare, and still more of them hold nothing but a few shriveled fruits, or sickly green ones that will never ripen. In recent years, we can afford to leave nothing for those less fortunate—we are poor ourselves, and everyone we know is poor. And the magic, I hear people whisper, has all gone out of the Kingdom as though it were never there.

Times are hard, and only getting harder. There are

too many mouths to feed. I suspect Jorj and Merri put off having children on purpose. The child they're expecting now is only their first, even though they've been married fourteen years. Perhaps they hoped that things would improve, but they haven't. Or perhaps barrenness curses more than just the land, and they weren't able to have this child they both want so badly until now.

Aunt Mae is stretching what food her garden grows as far as she can, and I think my father has taken out a loan out from one of the larger farms to get by. They try to hide all this from us children, but from my vantage point in the trees, I see everything. Up here, hidden by the leaves, I'm easy to forget about.

Not that I need to be up in the sky for people to forget that I exist.

Sisi, at least, has every reason not to fit in here. She burns too brightly for our little town and I've always known that, known that she would one day find her way out. It might be because of this letter, it might be something else still to come, but she'll have a different path through life than the one that's set out for me.

Unlike Sisi, I have no special secret past. Other than having no mother, I'm an ordinary girl. I was born on this farm and, in all likelihood, I'll die here or in some other spot half a league away. My days will be filled with work like this. I'll pick apples when I'm young, and then by the time I'm Sisi's age, I'll marry one of the boys she doesn't want, and I'll have children and a room of my own in the house. Or I'll stay unmarried like Aunt Mae, and I'll nurse my aunts and my uncle and my father when they get old. Either way I'll die and be buried in the back garden like my grandparents are, and perhaps if I'm very lucky, someone might think to tell my nieces and nephews stories about me. Otherwise, I'll be forgotten.

I don't like the thought, but it's the truth, and I may as well accept it.

I hear Merri's voice in the distance, calling us all in for supper. After we eat, it's straight up to bed, to face Sisi's cold silence. I try to press her to tell me the contents of the letter, but I'm faced with nothing but her stern and stony face. She claims to be tired, but, though she lies wordlessly and motionlessly in our shared bed, it's hours before either of us fall asleep. Still, the message is clear: if I press her about the letter, we won't talk at all. Given the small space we share, and my otherwise limited social life, her silence is an effective punishment.

This becomes our new routine, not so different from the old one. The days are filled with hunger, hard work, and anxiety about what will come of our little farm, of our futures. The only difference is that now, I don't have Sisi to laugh with at the end of a hard day. At mealtimes, she sits as far away from me as she can manage, and at night she pulls the covers over her head and pretends to be asleep as soon as her head hits the pillow. It's as though we haven't shared a bed for nearly all our lives. I know she tends to toss and turn for hours—she's just faking sleep to avoid talking to me, and she'll do it for as long as I insist on trying to get her to tell me what was in that mysterious letter.

Curiosity plagues me but not as much as knowing

that my best, and *only,* friend is vexed with me. The mystery of the letter starts to seem less pressing than earning Sisi's forgiveness.

So, as I always do when Sisi is concerned. I give in, letting her fill the evenings with third-hand gossip from the aunts and updates on how the boys are growing and how Merri is coming along. I stop asking about the letter, but I don't stop hoping. Maybe that's why she decides to trust me, on the fifth evening after it arrived, with the secret it held.

It's only been a few days since our fateful nighttime trip, but it seems like much longer, the monotonous mornings and silent evenings fading into one another. After I return from the orchard for supper, as plates emptied of too-small portions of hashed vegetables are being cleared away, Aunt Sarie hands Sisi a basket filled with dust-stained work clothes.

"Take this down to the stream," and then, with a glance outside at the oncoming evening, "and take your cousin with you."

It had begun to seem as though the adults were conspiring to help Sisi keep her distance from me. Perhaps that was mere paranoia on my part—or perhaps they had been, and in the busy rush after supper, Aunt Sarie had simply forgotten. Like as not, I'll never know. But it doesn't matter as long as Sisi and I are back on the same side.

The two of us walk out together in the cool, pleasant air of the late summer evening. The sun is low in the sky but still just visible above the treetops. We head into the woods together, where the trees cast long, dim shadows, nearly blocking out the sun's lingering light. The route to the stream is familiar, though—after a lifetime of taking a weekly turn at laundry, I'm sure that I could find the way even in total darkness.

At first, our walk is entirely silent, as so much has been between us lately. A half hour passes before Sisi stops suddenly, pointing into a clearing just off the road. Through the trees, I can see where the setting sun turns the bare ground golden. "Do you remember that?" Sisi asks.

I squint, trying to think what she could be referring to. There's nothing there, just the featureless and dusty ground, not even a single small flower poking through. Then I realize where we must be, the only spot in the woods where nothing will grow: "That was Kariana's house."

We stand there in silence for a moment, looking through the trees at the emptiness left behind. I was only eight years old when Kariana's cottage was burned to the ground with her inside, but I still remember what the little house looked like. She was the only person I knew who lived alone. She was also the only person in Leasane who knew anything about the mysterious power she used to call ruak, and that, in the Common Tongue, we called magic.

To look at her, you would think she was an ordinary woman, with a square, lined face and brown hair shot through by a long white streak. She always had a smile for the children and a special word or two for me. That might just have been because I was always interested in what she had to say. One night, my cousin, the younger Willem in the family, had had a bad fever, and she'd come to help him. As she laid out strips of willow bark and pressed cool water-dampened cloths to his sweaty brow, she'd carefully explained to me what she was doing and why, all while I watched, wide-eyed.

I hadn't been there the day the soldiers came for her. Other children in the village got to go, to see the spectacle. The soldiers even encouraged it. A proclamation went up the week before: that magic was to be done only by the konim, sacred mages trained in the Royal School, and that a witch practicing experimental ruak was a danger to us all. I remember a whisper, those words that finally condemned her—*blood magic*. The worst accusation of all, a crime I didn't even understand. After that, Kariana was confined to her house. I saw the soldiers guarding her there, those purple-and-gold uniforms standing out brightly against the dark trees while I was up working in the orchard one day. I didn't see what happened when they burned it down. Aunt Mae ushered us all inside and kept us there, out of sight, so we couldn't see or hear anything.

Still, looking at it now, I can imagine what it must have been like: purple-and-gold uniforms, red and gold leaves on the trees, yellow and gold flames leaping from the soldiers' torches to the top of the hut. I imagine Kariana shut away in her little house, the small, peaceful place that had been her refuge, her domain. So many times I'd walked down this path—Aunt Mae always sent me on any errand to Kariana's that came up, perhaps because she knew the witch-woman's fondness for me. We'd sit in that house and enjoy a cup of tea and she'd have a few words or an old riddle for me. Strange that such a lovely home could become no more than a prison. And then a pyre.

My mind flashes back to the fire. I shiver, as if I can almost feel the hot wind blowing in my face, making me jump. I was far too weak to stop them or save her. I was only a child, and I still am. An ordinary, powerless girl.

"He did this," Sisi says softly. "Lord Ricard, the Second in the Kingdom. Everyone knows that he commands the Golden Soldiers. He's the one who ordered them to do this. And I'm supposed to—" She cuts herself off with what I realize is a sob.

I want to ask, but I don't. Instead, I reach out my hand toward hers, lacing our fingers together and gently squeezing our hands palm to palm while she starts to cry.

"This is what he does. Here and all over the Kingdom. He burns, he *destroys*—so what does he want from me?" Her voice is trembling, strained. "What does it *mean?*"

I don't know, since I don't know what the letter said. I consider it wisest not to point this out, however. I just stand there at her side, trying to imagine what's going on inside her mind, until the sky grows dark and the crescent moon rises, and I know we must get on with the washing-up or risk the wrath of our aunt.

"We should go," I say, but she shakes her head again.

"Wait. Jena, I..." She turns, looking me clear in the

face for the first time in what must be days. "I need to know what you think. That you think I did the right thing."

"All right." I'm taken aback at her words. It isn't like Sisi to doubt herself, not ever, and certainly not to turn to me for reassurance. She usually plows ahead with whatever she thinks is right, and I follow—that's always been the way for us.

Nonetheless, now, she seems almost stunned into silence, like she can't find the words to say what's on her mind.

I prompt her gently. "Just tell me what the letter said, Sisi. Maybe then I can help."

She squeezes my hand affectionately. "How like you, my dear. You needn't always be worrying about me, you know."

If I weren't worrying about Sisi, I don't know what I'd do with myself. But I don't say that. Instead, I just give her a moment while she gathers her thoughts.

When she does speak, what she says is so staggeringly unbelievable that my ears can scarcely process what they hear. "The letter from the Prince—he was inviting me to come to the City, to the palace itself, on Midwinter's Day. The King hosts a ball then, apparently, and I've been asked to join him. As the Prince's personal guest."

"But why?" I ask, which is possibly a stupid question. "I mean, why you?"

"It was in the letter," she says, her voice quiet. Then she begins to recite. Clearly, from the flat, bitter tone in her voice, she's reading back the words on the letter. She must have turned it over and over in her mind so many times that she has every word memorized. "To Lady Sisi of Eastsea, Four Hundred and Fifty-Third in the Kingdom, from His Most Royal Highness, Lord Ricard, Second in the Kingdom, greetings. Rumors of your beauty having reached even the capital City, I write to invite you hither. My brother, the King of all the Earth, hosts a great ball on Midwinter's Day, and I hope you will do me the honor of being my guest. Kindly send word of your decision by dint of one of my servants, who await your reply. Monies will be sent for your travels."

"Wow." I blink at her. "That's a lot."

"You say that like I don't know it already."

"But..." I have a thousand questions, and I know she won't suffer them all. I have to choose my words carefully. "How did he even find out you were here? I mean, *rumors of your beauty*...How do rumors of your beauty, or anything else for that matter, get all the way from our little town in the middle of nowhere to the City? To the *palace*? And the Prince?"

She sighs. "I don't know. I always thought no one knew, or cared, that Jorj and I were out here. But after what happened to our parents..."

As far as I know, her parents were killed in the pox that swept the country that year—nothing that the King's own brother would take note of. And it's not like they were particularly important, though they were Numbered and therefore technically in the line of descent to the throne. Only technically, though—Sisi's Number, which she's just recited and I have, of course, promptly forgotten, is somewhere in the Four Hundreds. Jorj's is lower, and therefore nearer the throne, because he was technically the heir to their House when their parents passed away, making him, in pure theory, the Lord of Eastsea.

The thought is positively baffling, as the last time I saw the Lord of Eastsea he was scratching his rump at the breakfast table since we've got a nasty case of fleas going around. Sisi and Jorj are just like the rest of us now, part of the life of the farm, and that's how they want it. It shouldn't matter how they were born, and I really thought it didn't. They're *our* family now, just ordinary people, for all their high birth and all Sisi's beauty.

"I always thought we'd gotten away from that. Jorj certainly told me often enough how lucky I was, that I was going to grow up with none of the pressure, none of the danger that was our birthright as those Numbered so close to the throne...but it seems like that wasn't true. Even though my family was never in the first Hundred nor likely to inherit, we're still not safe. Even here, far from the palace, they want something from us. Or worse, from me."

"Why would that be worse?" I feel foolish for having to ask so many questions, but, on the other hand, Sisi seems to be almost deliberately avoiding telling me what is actually going on.

"Because Jorj has the name, he's the heir to the title, he's the one in line for the throne. There's only one thing I have that he doesn't."

"And that is?"

She only shakes her head in response to that. Clearly, then, I've asked the wrong thing, although I still don't understand why. I don't dare any more questions. We fall back into silence as we walk together to the stream, where we scrub the dirty rags against the rocks using a hard cake of soap. I keep my eyes on my work, watching my hands redden as the lye foams around them. We return home without any more conversation. As we once again pass the ruins of Kariana's house, I can't avoid seeing how Sisi's eyes linger among the ashes for a long time. I wonder what she's thinking—what she, the bravest person I know, could possibly be so afraid of.

CHAPTER THREE

On the day Sisi changes her mind, we receive two visitors. The first comes to see my father in the middle of the day. The second enters our bedroom in the dead of night.

Because I'm high up in the apple trees working, I'm the first to spot the town's innkeeper, Zenel, as he hurries up the narrow path to our house. Zenel is a stout man, usually cheerful, but today his quick pace and hunched shoulders make him seem a stranger to me. I call down to Uncle Willem, letting him know we have a visitor, and he and my father stride toward the house.

As I start to climb after them, though, my father orders, "Stay here. Work needs to get done."

Of course I'm stuck here while they go off to swap secrets. *Work needs to get done*—more like *Jeni doesn't get to know anything interesting*. As usual.

The three men are gone for over an hour. I keep

careful watch, hoping to be able to piece some of the truth together from what I can see from my high vantage point. I spot Zenel first, storming away from the house, his round face red with rage. My father and Uncle Willem return to their work perhaps twenty minutes later, their heads bent close together in counsel. They fall completely silent as soon as they're within my view, so I can't even try to eavesdrop.

My best shot at getting the full story is from the most reliable source of gossip around, so I volunteer to help Aunt Mae get dinner ready. The rest of the family sits around the table, relaxing after a long day's work, while Aunt Mae and I are alone in the kitchen. It's the perfect opportunity to get some answers.

"What did Zenel have to say?" I ask, trying to sound casual, like I'm just making conversation.

"He wanted to talk to your father. Stir those beans faster, or they'll stick to the pot, and I'm not going to be the one to scrub 'em out."

I do as I'm told, though my arm is growing sore from the task after a long day of pruning the trees. Sisi and my aunts, who don't work in the orchards, usually take care of the cooking while we rest. Today, though, I'm willing to trade my evening respite for a little news.

"Just about some troubles they've been having down at the inn, is all." Aunt Mae says, not meeting my eyes.

"Why would he need to talk to Papa about something going on at the inn?"

"He thought your father might be able to convince

the—er, the customers that are giving him trouble to go on their ways."

I dare to push a little further. "And Papa can't? Or didn't want to?"

"Stop asking foolish questions and start serving up that stew."

No luck with Aunt Mae, then. Disappointed, I do as I'm told. We eat quickly and silently, as we usually do after a workday, and afterward Sisi and I head out the door and up the ladder to our loft.

"Do *you* know anything about this Zenel business?" I ask as I close the shutters behind us, without much hope that she'll either have the answer or care to share it if she does.

"Hmm? Oh, aye."

I decide my wisest course is just to wait, hoping she'll explain on her own. Lately, it seems like I can't talk to Sisi at all without annoying her, and pushing gets me nowhere. My ploy works, though, as she continues.

"I was in the garden when he came. There was lots of shouting, so I heard most of what passed between him and Uncle Prinn. It's the soldiers."

"What?"

"The Golden Soldiers. You know, Lord Ricard's men?"

"I know who the Golden Soldiers are, Sisi, I'm not *stupid*." Everyone knows them, with their neatly choreographed marches, their beautiful shining uniforms. They're the first standing army the Kingdom has had in living memory—King Balion's rule stretches across all Four Corners of the Earth, so what would he need an army for? There's no one to fight.

But Lord Ricard insisted a threat could arise. He trained, maintains, and pays the troops out of his own pocket. Uncle Willem says he's a genius, keeping the people safe from the go'im, especially the powerful ruak of the adirim, and the threats they might pose if ever they return. On the other hand, Aunt Mae, like many of the other women in town, spits on the ground whenever the army is mentioned.

"What in Gaia's name do the Golden Soldiers want with old Zenel?" I ask.

"Well, they were sent to bring me that letter. The invitation to the ball that we saw them reading that night we snuck out. You remember."

"Yes, I remember all thirty seconds of conversation we had about that letter quite clearly." I regret my sarcasm right away, afraid it might drive her back to silence, but fortunately Sisi has more to say.

"Apparently they didn't leave."

"What?" I'm bewildered.

"They've been staying at Zenel's since they brought the letter here."

"The soldiers?"

"Aye. All four and twenty of them."

"But it's been two weeks!" I exclaim.

"So it has. And—well, you're probably wondering what all that screaming was about? Well, because they're royal servants, they technically don't need to pay for their rooms. Apparently, they're eating Zenel out of house and home while they 'wait on their answer,' and there's nowhere for him to put his paying customers, since he can't even tell them to leave."

"But you gave them your answer already. Didn't you?"

"Not one they like."

I frown. "I still don't understand what Zenel wanted from Papa. Does he think Papa can make the soldiers leave?"

"No." A shadow passes over Sisi's face. "No, he wanted Uncle Prinn to make me change my answer. So that the soldiers will go away."

"What? That's ridiculous."

"Apparently I ought to be made to think about others and not myself. As if that isn't what I'm expected to do every day of my life!" She seems to realize that she's nearly shouting and, catching herself, continues in a whisper, neither of us wanting to attract too much attention to ourselves. "I wouldn't do it when the family asked, and I'm certainly not going to go just because the *town's innkeeper* wants me to. But this...it makes me furious. No one cares what I want. I'm only a girl. I'm expected to think of everyone else in the family before myself. And I don't know if I can ..." She trails off into silence at that.

"Sisi?"

"Forget it. It doesn't matter—your father promised, and we both know Uncle Prinn would never break his word. He isn't going to make me go, so it's not worth getting upset over."

Well, there is a sentiment I never thought I would hear my cousin express on any subject.

"It's going to be all right," she says, and I'm not sure if she's talking to herself or to me. It doesn't seem like a statement that invites a response either way, so I say nothing, letting her brood while I change out of my day dress and into my nightgown. I resolve to ask her about it tomorrow, when she's had a little time to calm down. That's usually the way to handle Sisi's moods.

We climb into bed together, and I tuck the quilt up over both of us. Sisi reaches over, squeezes my hand gently, and then goes to blow out our candle.

Just as the flame begins to waver, there's a knock on the wall by the casement. I assume it's our most frequent visitor, Jorj, who once in a while comes to tuck Sisi into bed like she's still a baby, or perhaps Aunt Mae coming to remind us of some forgotten chore that must be done before we can sleep.

"Come in," Sisi calls, and a face appears in the dim light of our room, rising up the ladder. But it isn't Jorj or Aunt Mae—it's Merri.

As she climbs up into the room, she looks like something out of one of my aunt's old stories, a haunted dibuk from a myth. Her cheeks are pale, as though she's exhausted from the effort of climbing even that brief distance. Her cheeks are sunken and her pregnant stomach casts a shadow on the floor in front of her, distorting her appearance even more.

Sisi reacts at once, almost leaping out of the bed to offer Merri a seat there, but Merri shakes her head. Her long brown hair hangs over her face, obscuring her features.

"I won't bother you for more than a moment or two, Sisi. I know it's late, and you both have to rise early and work hard in the morning."

"You're never a bother," Sisi replies, smiling warmly at her sister-in-law.

"Well. I've come to ask you something I fear may change your mind."

"I'm sure it can't be so terrible."

"It is. I hope...I hope even if you can't agree, that you'll forgive me for asking. Sisi, I've come to ask you to reconsider your answer to the Prince."

I turn toward Sisi, waiting for her response. If I didn't know her so well, I might think she had none, for she steadies her expression carefully to prevent Merri from noticing. It's nothing like the shouting rage from earlier, but for a split second I see her eyes flash with an anger so bright and cold that it almost frightens me to see her capable of it. When she speaks, though, her voice is perfectly calm. "May I ask why?"

"Of course. I would never just—I know how you feel, believe me, maybe more than anyone else I *understand*. I had to leave my home too, to go work for your mother and father. It could have been a lot worse for me, I know, and I know how hard it is. I just...there's no other choice. There's no other way. I'd never ask, if it weren't for—" And her voice breaks. "For the baby."

"I don't follow," Sisi says, and there's a flat note to her voice that makes me flinch.

"We're barely making do as it is," Merri continues. "And I'm about to bring a little tiny person into this life, someone entirely helpless, who will need to be nurtured with the utmost care for years to come, and I don't know if there will be enough to keep the farm going till the baby's grown. If things continue the way they have been, then..."

"It's going to be all right," Sisi soothes. "I know you're nervous about the little one. Of course you are. But we've always made ends meet before—"

"But not now!" Her voice is raspy and intense, and in the dim light there's something almost frightening about it, almost supernatural about sweet, quiet Merri whom I've known all my life. "We have to face it sooner or later, even if Uncle Prinn doesn't want to. The fact is, the farm is failing. We're going hungry already. And I'm about to bring a child into this house, into this family, into this life, when I know that what we have isn't enough."

"We have the house. We have a farm. We have a family. What more could any child need?" Sisi asks, the slightest waver in her voice.

"I want Jorj's son to have the best life he can. I want him to be raised like...like one of the Numbered. The way his father was, the way you should have been."

"You don't need that to be happy. If Jorj has taught me anything, he's taught me this—we were lucky to escape that life. There are things more important than silken sheets and Midwinter balls. Like family, and caring for others above yourself, and being able to choose," Sisi says, but there's something hollow in her voice.

"Yes, and yet there are some luxuries you cannot be happy without. You cannot be happy if you don't have enough food to eat, if you don't have a bed to sleep in, if you don't have a roof over your head in winter. If I need to go back into service, wear out my hands and my back washing dishes in some Numbered lord's scullery until I'm bent and gray so that I can send a few zuzim home, if Jorj ends up one of His Royal Highness' Golden Soldiers because we need a little of that gold, then what kind of life am I offering this child, who never asked for any of this?"

There is a long pause while Sisi considers. Finally, sounding small, she asks, "You really think all of that is going to happen?"

"I think it could. And it is not a risk I am willing to take with my child's life, when there is any hope. When there is any other way."

"You think I'm being selfish," Sisi says quietly. "To refuse, when it could do so much for us. Not just the Ball. There could be much more where that letter came from, and we'll never see a bit of it unless I do as I'm told by the Second in the Kingdom."

"No. I had hoped you wouldn't think—that you wouldn't feel I'm judging you. You have a right to be afraid, or resentful, or whatever it is that you feel. I understand what it is like, to be young and a woman and to fear, to know that you are at the turning point and think it can all be taken away from you. That at any moment you'll be pushed into the arms of some man and it'll matter to no one at all whether you like it or not. I would never think less of you for not making that sacrifice."

Merri pushes on. "I know what I'm asking for, Sisi, sister, I do know. But still, still, I am asking. Please. Tell Uncle Prinn you've changed your mind. You'd like to go, you'd be willing to try, you want him to take the money and you want to know what Lord Ricard wants. Say it's your curiosity. Say you just want to see the City. Say you're a young girl, and your head is turned at the prospect of a royal ball. Say you have a plan to murder His Royal Highness in his bed. Say what you have to, *do* what you have to, Sisi, just...go, please go."

Sisi can't meet her eyes. She looks down at the floor, at the wall, even briefly at me, but she doesn't look at Merri. "I'll think about it," she says.

Merri looks as though she wants to thank her, fall to her knees and kiss her hand, but she knows my cousin well enough to understand just how unwelcome that would be. Instead, she nods once and says, "Thank you," then goes without another word, disappearing as suddenly as she came.

In the moments that follow, I expect Sisi to fall silent and cold again, the way she did when we first learned of the letter. Instead of pushing me away again, though, she picks up the candle from the bedside table and sits upright next to me, holding the light between us. Her face is barely illuminated as she says quietly, "Do you think I'm a good person?"

"What?"

"Do you think I'm a good person? Kind? Compassionate? Caring? Even just nice?"

"Of course. You're my best friend, I like you more than anyone."

"But do you—" Sisi cuts herself off. "Never mind. You don't understand."

The word "obviously" hangs off the end of her sentence, unspoken but present. I hate when she treats me like this, like I'm a stupid baby who can't keep up with her. She never used to do it when we were little, and even though I've been four years younger than her every day of my whole life, suddenly when she got her breasts in and her monthly bleeding started, it became a divide between us, like there are some things I can't understand just because my parents didn't have the courtesy to bring me to this Earth half a decade sooner. "Try me."

"I want to be...I want to be someone worth admiring. Not just someone *you* like, because, darling cousin, as much as I love you, I feel I must tell you, that's not a very high bar."

I feel as though I ought to be insulted, although I'm not entirely sure why. "What does *that* mean?"

"Well, you just don't know all that many people. I'm not sure you would know if I really were the kind of selfish, heinous monster who would..." Falling silent, she seems possessed by some feeling I don't understand. Too upset to go on speaking, she covers her face with her hands. "Jena, what am I going to do?"

I've gotten what I asked for. She is talking to me, about this, whatever it is. But I still can't really understand what she's saying. Our life was so simple, so ordinary, so much the same every day, and now this letter has changed everything. It has changed Sisi, which is what really shakes me. My cousin, confident and brilliant Sisi, seems so torn now, asking questions I can't answer nor understand. Nonetheless, I try my best to respond. "The right thing. I know you'll do the right thing."

She composes herself. "Thank you, Jena." She leans over, kisses my forehead, and smiles a strange half-smile. "Thank you, little bird."

I stick my tongue out. "Don't call me that. I wish you'd call me Jeni, like everyone else."

Her odd look turns into a grin. "I know, cousin. That's why I do it."

It's nice to see her smile, so I don't object, as much as I don't like being called by my True Name. "I thought it was because you're a true believer. You know, Old Ways, True Names, Blood Magic, the Will of the Goddess—"

"Shut up!" Sisi hisses. At first I think it's just because she hates being teased, but then I see the expression on her face, all the more frightening for the shadow that is cast over her features.

Either she's not in a mood to be joked with tonight, or she takes all this far more seriously than I would have suspected. Whichever it is, I decide it's wise not to poke the angry ziz, as the old expression goes, and that the most prudent course of action is just to go to sleep, where no one can be annoyed by me. I turn over onto my side, away from Sisi. I hear her sigh, but she says nothing. Some time passes, and then she blows the candle out.

In the morning, my father tells me that we're going to the City.

CHAPTER FOUR

$\mathcal{I}$t seems like those words should reshape my life the instant they are spoken by mere virtue of their existence, the way a witch is supposed to be able to speak the Old Tongue to change the Earth. However, we don't set off at once, or even soon, after Sisi has made her decision to accept the Prince's invitation. There are still weeks of planning and preparation ahead.

The Golden Soldiers leave the inn at last, off to bring Sisi's answer to the Prince, and give us another fat purse of golden shekin to pay for the voyage. Aunt Mae and my father carefully portion them out, splitting out the smallest possible sum that can get us safely to the Capital and leaving the rest to restore the farm. I'm not sure exactly how much money it is—I've never seen a coin larger than a milar until this began—but I get the sense that it's a small fortune. Certainly, we seem to have given up on this year's harvest and the whole family have turned their attention and their working hours toward preparing for the journey to the City. A donkey is purchased, some repairs are made to the old apple cart, and Sisi and I are set to endless sewing as we try to turn our shabby wardrobes into something fit for the royal court.

Merri keeps us company on this task, her advanced pregnancy preventing her from taking on any other work around the farm. She's good with her hands, though, and much better at sewing than I am, so we're more than grateful for her help. She's almost finished turning one of Sisi's old dresses into something that fits me. I usually end up wearing Sisi's hand-me-downs, as the other women in the family are slender like most Third Quarter folk. No amount of skill will ever make one of my aunts' old dresses fit Sisi or me, and Merri has been comfortably wearing my clothes for the duration of her pregnancy, much to my embarrassment.

Sisi and I are much closer in proportions. Still, I am flat where Sisi has womanly curves, and the dress needs to be pinned around my chest and hips to make up the difference. She's also a good half-foot taller than me, and no one wants me to show up to the City in a dress spattered with mud from trailing on the ground. Hemming the straight bottom of a dress takes less skill, so I can work on that while Merri cleverly tucks the garment's bosom so I won't be swimming in it.

And so, it is Merri and I who are alone in the kitchen one rainy afternoon while Sisi and Jorj are in town gathering supplies and everyone else is in the orchard, when Merri suddenly doubles over.

I drop to my knees next to her, barely noticing as the pins in the dress we were both working on jab into me. "Merri?"

"Ah. Goddess, have mercy," she gasps, and her face is pale, her breathing strained and heavy.

I know what's happening, of course. I was barely old enough to remember little Will being born, but I've been called to help with other Leasane women as they labor. Her pains mean that her baby is coming. I scream for Aunt Mae, for anyone.

Merri grabs my hand. Her fingers clasp painfully around mine. "Help me, Jeni."

I don't know what to do. I was too young to remember much of what happened when the boys were born, though I do remember trying to follow Kariana into the birthing chamber. I know Merri is going to have her baby, but not how to help her, how to protect her from any of the dangers that may be coming. I know they are many. I know women die while bearing children, and often, if they must do so without expert help. I know I am the wrong person to be with her, that she ought to have a witch, like Kariana, or at least a more experienced woman who has helped with other births, by her side.

But Merri is grabbing at me, her eyes wide, wild, and desperate, and the fact is that I *am* the only one here. So, I do what seems right, the only thing I can think to do—I try to soothe her.

"Why don't you try to take a breath with me? Go on then. In, and out." I count her through several long breaths, and her pain at first seems to be easing, until another sharp contraction ripples through her body and she screams again.

Goddess, where is everyone? They shouldn't be out of earshot—the farm is hardly so large as to require them to be far away enough that they can't even hear Merri shrieking at the top of her lungs. I can't do this on my own. I need someone who actually knows what they're doing to help Merri. Someone like Aunt Mae, or Aunt Sarie, who is Merri's mother and would no doubt bring her comfort, or even Sisi, who at least has confidence to get her through this ordeal.

But the only person here is me.

"Um. I think you should...we should get you into your bedroom. See if you can lie down."

Merri nods at me and takes my offered arm. She leans heavily on me as we make our way into the small room she and Jorj share. Despite her slight frame, it's difficult to walk with her leaning on me. I manage, with difficulty, to get her settled onto the bed, and help her strip off her day dress so it won't get ruined. She still has a chemise on underneath for a bit of privacy, though that might have to go too at some point. It's hardly worth worrying about.

I shed my outer gown as well, lest it get dirty and ruin our hard work in tailoring it to fit. I have only the slightest idea of what childbirth actually entails, but I don't think it's the tidiest of activities.

"Thank you, Jeni," Merri says, looking a bit clearer-headed. That lasts only a moment before another wave of pain overtakes her. Then she's doubled over again, as though she's going to be sick. I take her hand back in mine, letting her squeeze till my bones ache. It seems to give her some small measure of comfort, at least, and that may be all I can do for her.

I talk her through another set of deep breaths, and a few more agonizing contractions, before someone *finally* comes to see what's going on. It's Aunt Sarie, looking frazzled. "I heard screaming. What's wrong?"

"I think Merri's going to have her baby soon," I reply, letting my own nerves show now. "I tried to get her in here, I don't know if I did right..."

Aunt Sarie looks over both of us. I see her take a slow breath, trying to steady herself, as she looks at her daughter, gasping and sobbing on the bed. It's a long moment before she finds the words, and she doesn't have to say anything for me to read the truth plainly on her face.

Something is wrong with Merri. She shouldn't be in so much pain, so quickly.

"You did well enough, Jeni. Now, I want you to run for your Aunt Mae, who I reckon is on her way back from doing washing by the stream, and then to the neighbors, for Lilane and Kari to come help." She names the owner of the adjacent farm and her adult daughter. "We're going to need more hands, I think, and Lilane is the closest we've got to a midwife since..."

She doesn't have to remind me what we lost when we lost Kariana. Now more than ever, I am painfully aware of the fact that, without someone wise in such matters who can help guide mother and babe alike through the ordeal, birth and death are much too close together.

Obedient to her commands, and grateful that I need

no longer be the one to decide happens next, I run off. I find Aunt Mae in the woods, trooping back home with a heavy basket of wet clothes, and gasp the basic details at her. She drops the laundry and takes off running as fast as she can.

It's a good half a league's travel to the next farm, so I need the better part of an hour to run it, even with desperation spurring me on, and I know I must be red-faced and scant of breath by the time I knock on Lilane's door.

She answers at once. "Little Jeni? Whatever is the matter?"

"My cousin Merri is having her baby. Aunt Sarie sent me for help." Though Aunt Sarie hadn't said anything to confirm it, I saw her terror on her face, so I add, "I think something is wrong."

Lilane spits on the ground. "Aye, sure enough something is wrong. Nothing can go *right*, not with the Goddess angry with the whole Quarter. With all the Earth, for all I know."

I want to ask what she means, but I know there's no time to indulge my curiosity, not when Merri's life might be in danger.

"Well, I'll do what I can, though I'm no Kariana—and neither is my daughter, for all she's named for her." She bellows for Kari, who comes running. "Saddle up the mule. We need to ride for Prinnsfarm, and fast. Jeni, you'll walk back?"

"Aye. I don't think I'll be much good in the birthing

52

chamber, and the mule'll go a bit faster with only two on its back."

Lilane lays a hand on my shoulder. "You're a good lass, Jeni. Your cousin is lucky to have you in her hour of need. Rest here if need be, have a cool drink of cider before you start back. My man Taric is out in the field, if you need anything. You look like you've run yourself half to death."

With those words, she and Kari are off. I'm not inclined to rest, seeing as how there's an emergency going on back home and I may be of some use there, but I recognize wisdom when I hear it. I help myself to a cup of cider from the clay jug over Lilane's hearth and force myself to draw in a dozen deep, careful breaths, waiting for my racing heart to go back to normal, before I set off once again toward home.

I didn't even notice the rain on my way here, such a panic was I in. Now I feel it, soaking through my dress and into the thin soles of my shoes as I trudge my way home. I half expect that I'll have missed the excitement and be greeted with a red-faced new baby cousin as soon as I arrive. Another smaller part of me dreads that Merri will slip away from life before I return.

What did Lilane mean, though, about the Goddess being angry with the whole Quarter?

My father isn't a particularly religiously inclined man, and the rest of the family tends to follow his lead. Sure, my aunts leave out little pahyat-shrines and so on, but since Kariana's death, there's been nothing to mark the great festivals for the change of seasons. We haven't much time nor inclination, if I'm to be honest—we're too busy trying to grow enough food to keep body and soul together.

If I were an all-powerful Goddess, might I not be angry if it seemed my children had forgotten about me? I imagine I wouldn't like it too much. Then again, I wouldn't think I'd feel the need to take it out on them. Especially not on an innocent babe who didn't even ask to be born, nor her frightened mother.

These thoughts consume my half-hour walk home in the steady downpour. When I make it back, Jorj, my father, and Uncle Willem are all gathered in the main room of the farmhouse. Jorj is sitting at the table, his fingers white-knuckled around the handle of a tankard of ale. My father is sitting across from him, looking grim, and Uncle Willem is pacing so intently I'm afraid he might wear holes in the floor.

"Jeni," Jorj says, his voice hollow, "What's amiss with my Merri? What's happening in there?"

"The girl knows no more than we do, son," Uncle Willem points out. "She's just returned from fetching help and looks half-chilled to her own death. Dry out by the fire a moment," he suggests to me.

I shake my head. "I'll go see how Merri and the rest are getting along, if it's all right with you."

"Bring word back out to us men if there's time," Uncle Willem says, just a note of pleading in his voice. It would be forbidden, of course, for any of the men to set so much as one toe in the same room as a laboring woman.

The Goddess intended such things to be the work of Her daughters only.

I knock on Merri's bedroom door. "It's Jeni. Can I come in?"

"Aye."

The scene inside the bedroom is nothing like the relatively peaceful one I'd left. Merri is lying flat on her back, her knees in the air and her legs spread wide. Her shift is hiked up around her waist, stained with sweat and, to my horror, no small amount of blood. Her mother and Lilane are on either side of her, each holding one of her hands. Sisi is back too, helping Kari use wet cloths to dab at Merri's forehead. The whole room is a flurry of activity, with Aunt Mae barking commands and Merri's rapid, rough breathing filling the air.

"Something is wrong," Aunt Sarie is saying. "The babe should've come by now."

"It's going to be okay," Merri says. "Jeni is back." Then she leans her head against the pillow and, apparently, faints.

This is Aunt Mae's cue to begin issuing orders anew. "Kari, Sisi, more cold water. We need to keep her going, and that means waking her up. Jeni, I don't know what she's talking about, but if you can bring her any comfort, you'd better do it."

I don't know what she means either, unless the fact that I was here when her labor began brings Merri some measure of peace since I've returned. Nonetheless, I do as my aunt has indicated and switch spots with Lilane, who settles between Merri's spread legs. Whatever she does there must not be too comfortable, as it provokes a sharp cry from Merri, who is suddenly entirely awake.

"What's the matter?" I ask her, and then feel immediately stupid. Clearly, the problem is that she's trying to push a human baby out of her body.

"The pains stopped just after you left. The big ones, the cramps that help bear the child out. I'm trying to push anyway, but I don't...I don't know what to do."

Neither do I, but it seems I can't tell her that, not her wide eyes on me. "It's going to be okay. We're all here with you."

It strikes me suddenly that this is not so different from what I remember of the dances Kariana used to lead us in at the turning of the seasons. True, things are not exactly celebratory now, but this—all the women of the household gathered together, working together, in the hopes of bringing new life to the Earth—this is familiar.

And with that, I remember the song that Kariana used to lead us all in, back in those days. Almost subconsciously, I begin to hum it, thinking that maybe a little music might bring Merri some comfort.

Lilane freezes and turns her head slowly toward me. "What are you doing, Jeni?"

"Just...it's just a song I remember, from..." I fall silent, embarrassed.

"Don't stop," Merri says, or really, pleads. "I like it."

"You would," Lilane adds, matter-of-factly. "It's a song for spring. Growth, and new beginnings—and birth, of course."

"How do you know that song?" Aunt Mae asks, and I shrug.

"I just remember it, is all. Not the words or anything, but the tune."

It seems to be enough. The other women start to hum too, as we go about our tasks. I stay by Merri's side, holding her hand. She strains and cries out, but she smiles through her tears. "The—ah—the pain—"

It's started again, as it should.

She struggles for hours more, but the fear in the room has started to ease. The child is taking its time about things, but it is surely coming. And, so, in the early hours of that morning, after a day and a night's hard labor, it's done. Lilane clips the cord and places the scrawny, squalling newborn in Merri's arms.

Wan and worn, Merri looks up at me. "Look how beautiful she is."

The baby isn't beautiful at all. She's actually rather hideous, red-faced and doughy and bald. But she's also fiercely, vigorously *alive*.

Kari and Aunt Sarie help Merri settle her clothes in place so she's presentable, and Sisi runs to get Jorj.

Merri's smile as she sees her husband is blinding. He almost knocks me out of the way as he rushes to her side, but I don't mind. I don't think I could feel anything but joyful as he presses a kiss to Merri's forehead and stares down at the baby in awe.

"This is your daughter," Merri says, her voice still a little faint.

"She's the most beautiful thing I've ever seen."

Everyone keeps saying that about the baby.

"What are you going to name her?" Jorj asks. It's a mother's right to choose her child's name, but as the father, he must be curious.

"Maliara. Mali for a by-name, I think."

"Perfect. Just like the baby is. Just like her mother is," Jorj says.

Maliara. I remember enough of the Old Tongue to recognize that word from the blessings Kariana used to say. *Fullness. Completion.* A fitting hope for a child born now, in our time of need and want.

And for short, *Mali.* Ill luck.

A perfect name indeed.

CHAPTER FIVE

*O*ur goodbyes are brief. After all our planning and preparation, there is little left to do, and far too much to say, for us to even begin to find the words. How do you say goodbye to the only place you've ever lived, the only people you've ever known?

There's no way to do it right, so we just hoist our bags up over our shoulders and begin the journey. We start with a farewell to Merri, which must take place in her and Jorj's bedchamber. Only days after the birth, she is still too weak to stand.

Merri seems in good spirits, though, smiling at us all. "Just think, Sisi. Mali will like enough be crawling by the time you return."

"If we return," Sisi replies dourly, and Merri gently takes her hand.

"I know we shall see you again soon."

Sisi doesn't answer, her expression cold. I know she

must be thinking about the journey ahead, and what she is afraid may be waiting at the end of it.

Undaunted by her silence, Merri continues. "Please stay safe, Sisi. Thank you so much for what you are risking. I will never forget this."

Sisi's face softens at that, and she bends to give her sister-in-law a tender kiss on the forehead. "Be well, Merri. Goddess guide you and your little one."

"And you on your journey." She turns to me. "And thank you, Jeni. For what you did in my time of need. Whatever it was. I don't understand, and I expect you don't either—but I don't think Mali and I would be here without you."

I don't know what to say to that, so I don't address it, saying only, "I'll miss you both." I kiss the baby, who is starting to look a little bit more like a person and a little bit less like a blob. Her skin, red-purple at birth, is settling into a rich brown, like her father's and Sisi's, and she's looking plumper by the hour. I'll be sorry to miss her sweet baby days, as I know Aunt Mae and Sisi will be, but I'd be sorrier still to let Sisi go off without me.

We leave Merri and the baby behind, Sisi sparing a final tender glance for her baby niece, and take our last steps out of the farmhouse.

The rest of the family is waiting for us by the fully loaded cart. They are uncharacteristically solemn and silent, as though they are attending our funerals. I try to push that thought out of my mind. Unlike Sisi, I'm trying to look at this as the beginning of an adventure, not the start of an ordeal.

Slowly, we make our way down the line of relatives.

Uncle Willem and Aunt Sarie embrace us all, one after another. At their urging, their boys, Merri's three little brothers, do the same, each as briefly as possible. They'd much rather be out playing dice or chasing each other around the yard than have the tedious task of saying farewell to a pack of women as we go off to do something they don't even understand, but they do as their parents urge them.

Aunt Sarie is fond of us all, though, particularly Sisi. When Sisi was small, she used to climb into Aunt Sarie's lap to have her thickly curled hair carefully braided into dozens of long, thin plaits. Now the two women pull away from each other, and both pairs of deep brown eyes are wet with tears.

Uncle Willem is as stoic as my father, clapping Aunt Mae on the back and nodding sternly at each of us. His care shows through in a different way: in the long list of warnings he gives us about how to travel safely. In the past, I would have laughed at his rambles about how to recognize a thief on the road, how to tell a good inn from a bad one, or where to find clean water in an unfamiliar wood. In times like these, though, it's strangely touching to know that, however far we go, he'll be with us in his mind.

Jorj practically follows us onto the cart itself. He ruffles my hair and calls me a sweet little bird and then very solemnly instructs me to take the best care I can of his sister. "You are going along with her to a nest of serpents, and you must be a very careful bird and keep your sharp eye out, for she has no friend at all there but you."

"I'm quite used to being her only friend," I say, a little teasing, but he shakes his head.

"'Tisn't like here, where you may have no other play-mates but are at least in your home, surrounded by your family. Sisi is my only kin left, the only memory of my parents, and the only other descendent of our House—and though I doubt you can understand what it means, having lived here in this lovely edge of nowhere all your life, it is no small thing to be the last descendant of a Numbered House. I am trusting you to take care of her, now, when I cannot."

"I will," I promise, now matching the gravity of his tone. For once, I don't feel offended by his condescension; the moment feels too serious for that, as irritating as I usually find it when he talks down to me in this way.

He makes Aunt Mae swear to the same promise, and then turns to his sister.

Sisi already has tears flowing down her cheeks as she throws her arms around her brother's neck. "Jorj."

"Sigranna. My dearest sister."

They don't say anything else at first; they just embrace one another for a long, long time. Eventually, they exchange a few more words. It seems empty, as though what they really have to say to one another can't be spoken.

"You'll be safe, won't you?"

"Of course. And you'll look after Merri, and the little

one? And teach the babe how much I love her, and tell her stories of me."

"I will. Of course I will. And I have advice for you, if you'll take it."

"Only from you," Sisi says with a smile, but there's nothing light about Jorj's manner as he replies.

"Don't let Lord Ricard bully you. He might be famous for his charm, but he's also said to have a notorious temper. I know how stubborn you are, so use that to your own advantage, all right?"

"And likewise, you must be careful not to run yourself into the ground. I know how much pressure you put on yourself, dear brother." Sisi smiles at him, her cheeks dimpling as they always do when she smiles. "You needn't worry about me failing to speak my mind, Jorj. I should think you know me well enough to know that."

"But don't be too outspoken. There could be trouble if you anger him."

"As you've told me more than once," she retorts.

"I don't mean to nag. It's only that—"

"There's danger in the Capital. You've told me that all my life, Jorj."

"It's more than that. I...I don't know what the Second in the Kingdom could want with you, but I have my suspicions. I don't know what I would do if you were to ever—"

"I know," Sisi says soothingly. I look away, feeling I should give them their moment of privacy to say farewell, but Sisi is already pulling away from her brother's embrace. "I'll be careful. I'll be safe."

Jorj says nothing in return, only nods. I suspect it would hurt his dignity, as a man of the Numbered, to let himself weep in front of all of us. Which is foolish, since neither Sisi nor I hesitate to do so.

I feel a touch from behind me and turn around. My father's hand, big and warm, has landed tentatively on my shoulder. As I face him, he gives me a small smile, lifting only one corner of his mouth.

When he finally speaks, all he says is, "Goodbye, Jena."

I look at him for a long time, expecting him to say something else—some words of fatherly advice perhaps, or a tender farewell. Something about how much he'll miss me. How much he loves me, his only child. Instead, he smiles that half smile, and turns away.

"Come along, girls," Aunt Mae says, and Sisi and Jorj break apart with obvious reluctance. I, however, almost flee the site of my farewell with my father. Sisi and I climb into the back of the carriage, as Aunt Mae sits up front, taking the donkey's halter in both hands. My aunt can't look back as we drive away, since she has to focus on the road ahead, but Sisi and I can, and we do.

Looking behind us, we see the whole family, except for sickly Merri and tiny Mali, assembled in their lines to see us off. Sisi and I stare back at them. Sisi is waving and waving and waving at her brother. He waves back as the wind whips through the carriage, chilling the tears on her face, but she doesn't stop to wipe them away, not while Jorj is still in view. I can just see my father at the back of the crowd, his shoulders slumping, his face as unreadable as ever as the cart shudders into motion.

Two words. That's all he could manage to say to me, not knowing when or if we would return, if we would ever meet again. I had longer goodbyes with every other member of the family, even the boy cousins, who normally think of me as nothing more than an annoyance, and even Merri, who has a babe only a few weeks old and is still too weak to stand. But my father, my closest relative, my only parent, could not even find the words to properly wish me a safe journey. And those two words were more than he usually says to me in a day, a week, some months. He has not exactly been a tender father.

It's not as though he's cruel. I know I shouldn't feel so resentful of him, not when so many girls have fathers who marry them off when they're even younger than I am, or scream at them, or beat them. It's not so bad to be ignored. After all, I have Sisi's constant companionship, and I have work to do that's worth doing, and I'm headed off to the Capital to a royal ball with a purse of golden shekin, which ought to be a dream come true for any country girl like me. Yet, I can't fight the feeling that something is missing. That, as I leave home, maybe forever, there ought to be something for me to regret leaving behind.

CHAPTER SIX

"Oh, honestly, girls, you can't possibly want to hear an old story like that again," Aunt Mae says, though all three of us know she's just dying for the chance to tell it.

"Auntie, please," I whine, playing along.

"We've been stuck in this cart for days," Sisi points out. Two of them, to be exact, but we're already tired of the journey, and there's so much farther to go. We're all desperate for anything to disrupt the incessant boredom. This is less of an adventure than I expected it to be. All there is to see is an unchanging backdrop of flat and unbroken terrain, with the occasional tree to liven things up.

"And we'll be here for days and days more," I echo. Our best guess is that it's going to take us three weeks' journey to make it to the City, but that's based off one map that the soldiers had left with us and Jorj's best surmising, not on fact.

"We're bored senseless, and my leg has fallen asleep siting on this cart. The wood's as hard as any rock." Sisi pouts prettily and rubs the offending limb.

"And there's nothing better than one of your tales to pass the time," I add.

Aunt Mae smiles a little at the blatant flattery. "All right, all right. You've worn me down. I'll tell you both a tale."

"Thank you, Auntie."

"Sisi, you take a turn driving. You know I cannot do two things at once."

"Of course!" Sisi volunteers eagerly. She's happy as long as we're about to get a distraction.

Aunt Mae pulls the reins up sharply, stopping the donkey in his tracks. Maher—the name means speed, for the sake of irony—is thrilled at the opportunity to stop moving, even for the mere moment it takes for Aunt Mae and Sisi to trade spots. I remain in my seat, pulling my blanket up over my legs, as Aunt Mae settles in next to me. She leans back, getting comfortable, while Sisi nudges the reluctant Maher back into a slow trot with a few careful prods of a stick we keep for this purpose.

"What was it that you girls wanted to hear?"

I look to Sisi, who glances back over her shoulder, to decide.

We both consider for a moment. I know what I want to hear—a story of magic. It's always been my favorite of Aunt Mae's many types of stories. I especially like the few tales of the adirim that Aunt Mae knows, whether about the great kingdom they had here before the establishment of our own Kingdom of All the Earth, or their ruak, or their secret and mysterious ways.

Sisi prefers stories of intrigue. She likes tales of politics and court gossip.

We used to squabble over it regularly as children. But now I don't mind letting Sisi choose, and she's kind enough to select a compromise.

"Tell us about the First King?" Sisi asks.

"If you insist." Aunt Mae clears her throat. As I wait for her to begin speaking, I notice that there is no sound at all. I can't even hear the wind in the trees, and the cart is gliding silently down the road. I'm even holding my breath.

It's as though all the Earth is waiting to hear the story. Our town is too small and rural to attract the peddlers and players Jorj remembers from his youth in the castle of Eastsea, but we've never lacked entertainment, not as long as we have Aunt Mae to tell us tales of every wonder our Kingdom has ever held.

"Well. Our Earth is an old Earth," she begins, the traditional opening to any story. "And its histories are lost to time, which will consume us all in the end. The circle of time opens here, with the oldest story that has been handed down to us."

Sisi prods Maher forward again, and the cart slowly jolts back into motion. Aunt Mae's voice is just loud enough to be heard over the clattering wheels as we resume our journey.

"For a long time, there was nothing but the Earth. Gaia, the Goddess of the Earth, the Goddess who is the

Earth itself, governed all Her creatures, and no one could contest Her rule. Many beings lived in harmony back then. There were terrible and mystical beasts, like the ziz, a bird so immense its wings could block out the sun. The pahyat, Gaia's many children, lived quiet, simple lives, not marking the change of years. The adirim, for all their fierce ruak, were no greater, not then. Even their legends do not describe this time, for they lived in wildness, as the beasts do now. For days, for years, for centuries stretching onward, such was the only way of life on Earth."

Aunt Mae pauses a moment, as if struggling to remember. It's been a long time since we've heard this particular story. It's one for children, after all. And yet it is wonderful to imagine, this Earth she paints for us. Most of the creatures she describes haven't been seen in generations, except for those who can blend in with humans, like some of the pahyat. They say the rest have disappeared from the face of the Earth.

Maybe it isn't a faulty memory that makes Aunt Mae pause. Maybe it's grief, the same that is swelling in my heart—grief for the beautiful Earth of the old stories, and for those of us who have to live without it.

"But then everything changed. It began like every other day: the fair bright sun rising over Gaia, the light of Her love shining down on Her children, but something different was destined to come. A great storm began. For the first time, rain fell on the surface of the Earth, and thunder and lightning roared. In the wake of such a storm, all the beings of the Earth cowered and stared for they had never seen such destruction.

"But something even stranger than the Earth's first rain was to fall. A great golden cloud rolled in from the Eastern edge of the Earth. No one had ever seen such a wondrous thing. All the go'im that dwelt in the Earth in those days came to see what had happened. They all emerged from their homes and waited and watched the golden cloud for what seemed like months. Suddenly, two shining figures emerged from the cloud. They were dark of skin and dark of hair, and yet their flesh shimmered with the golden light of power, as though they were composed of the cloud of ruak that had brought them, and not born from the Earth our Mother. These were Gaia's chosen children, and they were to be the First King and Queen of this land."

"But where did they come from?" Sisi asks.

"Don't interrupt me," Aunt Mae retorts. "We're getting to that part."

"Sorry, Auntie."

In a portentous voice, full of deep seriousness, she continues. "No one could ever figure from whence they came. One day they weren't there, the next they were. That is all that can be said with any certainty. Still, there are many rumors of how such beings came to be, when all the other creatures living were born from the body of Gaia Herself, the Earth. The adirim say that Gaia Herself gave birth to them, not from Her physical body, the Earth, but from Her godly body above. And the pahyat say there were other Gods, not just our gentle Mother Gaia, but others that are fearsome and unknown, and that they created humans in defiance of the power of the Goddess to be the destruction of Her other creatures. No one can be certain which of these peoples is right, if indeed either of them are."

"Fascinating, to say the least," Sisi interrupts again. At a single, sharp stare from Aunt Mae, Sisi silences herself once more, allowing Aunt Mae to continue. Sisi even looks slightly ashamed of herself.

"All we know is that when the first man and the first woman stepped out of that shining cloud, they were as naked as newborn babes, though their shapes proclaimed them to be adults. They descended hand in hand, looking up toward the sky as their bare feet touched on the Earth for the first time. All the beings of the Earth trembled before them, for they knew they were facing those greater than themselves. The First King and his Queen had descended onto the Earth for the first time."

"Didn't they have names?" Sisi asks, sensibly.

"Why would they need to have names? They were the only beings of their kind and needed no further distinguishing. But they had many things that the others didn't. They had language and art. The King taught the peoples of the Earth how to govern themselves, living not wildly as beasts do, but in towns and cities and tribes. In turn, the Queen also taught them to use their ruak to create magic, for though many of the creatures, those we now call the adirim, were powerful in ruak, they knew not how to use their power until the new beings arrived. Adirish magic, under the supervision of the Queen, built the City at the center of the realm, and forged the High Road we travel on, even now."

I've heard this story before, of course, but that part of it is new to me. Or, rather, I've never heard the tale while on that very road, so it's never struck me with such intensity how much our whole Kingdom is shaped by the figures in this story, and by the shadowy forces of magic that we know so little about.

My whole life, I've been told to fear magic. Or, never told, exactly, because no one wants to talk about it except in old tales. But Kariana, who only wanted to bring us peace and prosperity, was burnt. And we never spoke of her or her magic again, once she was gone.

I see the reason for that fear, if this great road that stretches across the entire Earth could have been built by that power. I fear it too. Not as much, though, as I wonder at it. And long for it. Long for the knowledge of what was, and perhaps also—though even the thought seems absurd —for the power to reshape the Kingdom to my will.

"The First King and his Queen had four children, the First Four Men. It was they who brought balance and order to the land, founding the Kingdom where we live today. Their father taught them how to rule as he had done, and their mother taught them to use their ruak so that they might preserve these mysteries for generations to come. In his wisdom, the First King realized that all of his children were intelligent, noble, and good enough to govern. Nonetheless, he also feared that these great princes would one day pit themselves against one another over who would inherit and rule when he was gone, back to Gaia. In order to stop this conflict of brother against brother, the King divided the Kingdom into Four Corners. Each of his sons was given absolute rule over their respective Corners."

"But who were they ruling over?" Sisi asks. "If the First King and his Queen were the only people, whom did they rule? And for that matter, when they married and set up households of their own, whom were they marrying in the first place? Weren't there any girls? Did they intermarry with the adirim or pahyat? Or their own sisters?"

"No, but I suppose they did rule over them. Their sisters and children *and* the go'im, I mean. Everyone. Perhaps Gaia gave them wives, or perhaps they did not need wives. That's not the point of this story, though."

"I thought the point was what we can learn from it. The history of the Kingdom," Sisi interjects. I wish she weren't up at the front of the cart, so I could give her a good kick because she's about to ruin everything for both of us if she doesn't stop bothering our storyteller.

"I think the point is to keep ourselves occupied on this ride, one way or another," I interrupt, and Aunt Mae nods approvingly, pacified, for which I am grateful. I want to hear the story, not my cousin and aunt squabbling with each other. It's not like anyone knows the truth of how humans came to dwell on Earth, or why. It's just a story, which might help us pass the time without fighting with one another.

It probably isn't even true. This road was probably made by hard-working men, not by some force we can't understand. And there were probably never any such things as zizit and magic schools and such. I remind myself of that before I get too enamored with the story.

"The little bird is right. As I was saying, they divided the Kingdom into four pieces, from each Corner of the known Earth to the center, where the King and the great City were, and each of the sons ruled over his section. Later, when each of the First Four Men had sons of his own, with *whomever* it was that they chose, they divided the land again, each Corner into Quarters, and that's how we get the division that separates us today. It is how we know who will protect us in a time of war, and who we are obligated to pay our tribute to. All our Numbered lords and ladies are descended directly from the First King and Queen—and before you ask, Sisi, I don't know who everyone else is descended from."

"So that includes me, then?" Sisi interrupts again. "You're saying, what, if I went back far enough, the first Queen is my many-times great-grandmother?"

"If you believe the stories are true, then I suppose so."

"But do you believe it?" Sisi presses. "Is it just a story, or is it the truth?"

"I don't know. All I know is a story my mother told me, which her mother told her, and so on and so forth. If you want to research actual history, you should look in the Royal Library. All I have are stories," Aunt Mae says plainly, without even a hint of her usual sharpness.

Sisi answers with a note in her voice that sounds very much like shame. "I'm sorry, Aunt Mae. The stories are wonderful, real or not, and I do want to hear them. I apologize if I insulted you. I was being foolish."

"Well, that's all right then," Aunt Mae responds, entirely mollified. "Where was I? Right. The King became sickly at the end of his life. He was so wise, so close to the great power of Gaia, that he knew when death was about to reach him. They say the Goddess Herself whispered it in his ear, calling him back home to Her loving breast. He knew he had to make a plan for the Kingdom. He had divided it so that his sons would not fight for power during his lifetime, but he did not want the Kingdom to splinter forever into four parts at his death, nor for the children he had nurtured to kill one another to unite it under one of them.

"He begged Gaia to intervene, and so one of the great magics of the land was created, binding the crown only to the worthiest member of the royal family, forever. With Her own hand, Gaia chose among his Four Sons and their Four Sons, and still, She so chooses among the First Sixteen in the Kingdom, naming the worthiest of them to rule over all Her children.

"So, the Kingdom was established, and so it would continue until the seventh generation with the Great War of Succession. But that's another story for another day."

"What's so great about a war?" Sisi asks. "They all seem to have such fancy names, and all that ever happens is that a lot of good, innocent people die tragically early deaths."

"They're great because they're an enormous and important part of our history. And because people made sacrifices, from the First King and Queen down to your own family, so that you could be here today and have what you have."

That silences Sisi, but I can tell there's still something on her mind. I wish I could pry, though I know she won't say anything else in front of Aunt Mae. And probably not at all. She's been intermittently silent and snappish throughout the journey, as she is today. No doubt the end of our travels, and the meeting with Lord Ricard, are weighing heavily on her. But she doesn't speak of that, of course. She says only, "Thank you for the story."

For the rest of the day, little else is said. I watch the land roll on beyond us, the orchards of our Quarter beginning to grow patchy and the landscape becoming hillier as we approach the border. I wonder if there's any truth to the tale. Not so much the history, but everything else. Did the adirim once walk these roads? Did zizit fly through the skies? Did strange creatures hunt through the forests we're leaving behind us?

More likely than not, I'll never know. Even if I could try to track these stories down in the royal library, that would do me little good—I couldn't even read them. Besides, what do I need to know history for? I'm an ignorant farm girl from the middle of nowhere. Going to the palace for a party doesn't change who I am. It doesn't make me special. The only thing that's special about me is my friendship with Sisi, which certainly won't help me learn the secrets of our Earth.

Still, as the landscape rolls past us, I wonder what it might once have looked like. I can almost see it, golden and perfect. No, I *can* see it. It's hazy and faint, and I know it's only in my imagination, but I see what this place once was.

These thin, patchy trees, now full and rich with green leaves, stretching up toward the sky. These barren woods, now filled with strange beasts, eagles with cats' heads and flying six-winged worms and tiny elephants all watching from the woods. And this empty Earth, now occupied by a man and woman standing together, tall and dark and lovely, not unlike Sisi, dressed in simple garments of pure white, raising their hands to the sky as the Earth split for them, leaving this scar across Her surface, this road that we journey down now.

I blink, and the vision fades away, leaving me feeling cold and exhausted. I'm grateful when the sun goes down and Aunt Mae suggests making camp for the night.

We haven't passed an inhabited town since we left our own behind, so we end up simply sleeping on the side of the road, as we have been doing on our journey so far. Aunt Mae turns the cart over onto its side, and we pull the blankets over the top to hide that we're there. We tie the donkey up to a tree a little ways away, in the hopes that he won't run off or be stolen. He's mean and lazy enough that he probably makes a poor prospect for any thief with half a brain.

The sun wakes us unpleasantly early the next morning, the unexpected brightness making me greet the day with a glower and squinted eyes. At least no unfriendly strangers have disturbed us in our sleep. We make a sad little breakfast out of the last of our now very stale bread and a morsel of cheese each, washed down with a single still-juicy apple and a few swigs of the precious skin of water Aunt Mae is rationing out with dedicated care, unsure if we're ever going to see a river or a well again.

Having quenched our fatigue, our thirst, and our hunger as much as we can amidst the perils of the road, we set the cart aright, and begin our journey once again.

CHAPTER SEVEN

e've been traveling for two weeks before we even lay eyes on another person. By now, my cousin, my aunt, and I are all violently sick of one another's company. Aunt Mae must have told us every story she's ever heard. We've played every foolish game any of us can think of. And for meals, we're down to dried apples, stale crackers, and slightly dingy river water, which isn't improving anyone's temper in the slightest.

The High Road itself is still as deserted as it's been since we left the farm, which means we've had no trouble from any passing strangers—but also no one to trade with. Our rations are running low enough that, after yet another meal of molding and damp crackers, Aunt Mae agrees we need to pull off the road and follow the signs that Sisi tells me say "Town Center."

Sisi guesses that we're somewhere in the Fourteenth Quarter, in the middle of the eastern portion of the Kingdom, though we haven't yet left the Fourth Corner where our home is. We still have to travel through the rest of the Fourteenth Quarter and then cut across part of the Second Corner before we'll arrive at the City.

Or so we *think*. Sisi is merely cobbling this knowledge together from Jorj's maps, but her guesses are the best we have to work with.

On our way toward the center of this unfamiliar town, we pass a young woman hauling a bucket of water. I'm downright shocked by the sight of her. Not by her appearance—she's an ordinary girl, small and slim with reddish hair cropped short around her ears, though she's paler-skinned than most folk in our Quarter. No, what surprises me is seeing her at all. I'd almost forgotten there were other people on the Earth.

She's clearly struggling to haul the heavy pail down the road. Sisi calls out to her. "Can we give you a ride?"

"Thank you, 'd be most kind of you." Her accent is unfamiliar to me. Her vowels are much slower and more rounded. But, though she looks and sounds unlike anyone I've ever known, I recognize her as a farming girl, not so different from us. She climbs into the back of the cart with her full bucket and points down the road. "Center o'town is that way, and that's where I'm headed. I'm guessing you're looking for the inn?"

"How'd you know?" Sisi jokes, smiling as she looks down at our travel-worn clothes. "I'm Sisi. This is my Aunt Mae, and my cousin Jeni." For once, she uses our by-names and not our True Names, Sigranna and Jena, which she usually insists on even when it could get us into trouble. Even Sisi knows better than to start speaking the Old Tongue in front of a total stranger.

"Lajie. It's nice to meet you. What brings you to Bartston, especially with how things are going?"

Sisi also has at least enough sense not to tell the whole story. "On our way to, uh, to celebrate the Midwinter holiday. We're hoping to pick up some supplies before we head back out on the High Road."

"To the City, I assume?"

"Aye."

Sisi doesn't elaborate, and the girl—Lajie—looks her over for a long moment, as if searching for more information. But Sisi is stony-faced, and eventually the girl shrugs. "All right, then. If you want to keep it to yourselves, I won't push you. With the soldiers here, it's best not to share too much, anyways."

"The soldiers?"

"Aye." She doesn't elaborate, and we return her courtesy, not pressing her for any more details, just as she had done for us.

We wind our way slowly through the darkening streets, following Lajie's directions at the crossroads. The sun is setting, casting a glow over the dirt road. Maher's hooves slowly pat the street, sending up small clouds of dust each time. I look out at the town, at the several dozen small houses within eyesight of each other. It's so different from our Quarter, where families live on their own farms, spread out for leagues around, and the center of town is just a green we use as a marketplace, usually empty except for holidays. People here seem to keep to their homes for the most part; other than Lajie, we don't pass anyone on the street. However, unlike the burnt-out wreckage I saw on our way here, I do spot a few pale faces peeking out of windows, looking out at us. There seem to be far more people here than there are in Leasane.

Lajie hops out with her bucket, headed back toward her home. Before she disappears, though, she points toward the center of the small town. "You can find the inn in that direction. It's the only building with three stories—can't miss it."

"Thank you so much, miss."

"Thank you for the ride into town, and good luck on your journey. May the Goddess guide you, wherever it is that you're going."

It's a kind wish, and we thank her for it. Following Lajie's directions, we have no trouble at all finding the inn. Its three stories mean it towers over the small single-floor cottages in the center of town, and it's made of solid wooden slats.

Weary and covered in dust from the road, we pull up in front of it and practically fall out of the carriage. Our feet have barely touched the ground when a stout young man comes rushing out the front door, holding his hands out in front of himself as if to ward us off. "There's no room, madam, mistresses. I'm sorry."

"Every room is taken?" Aunt Mae asks, surprised.

"It's the Golden Soldiers, madam. They're cleansing the region."

"Cleansing?"

"You haven't heard?" he says. "Well."

"Can we come in and have a cup of ale at least?" Aunt Mae asks. "Maybe you can see if there isn't something you can do? There must be someone in the town who has a spare room, and we can pay—"

"You wouldn't want to stay here," he says flatly. "Not when the soldiers are in town. And it'd probably be best to keep the young mistresses out of their view. My poor sister's been hiding away since they got into town. They're—"

Before he can say anything else, another man stumbles out the door. He's broad-shouldered, ruddy-skinned, and blond, with a gleaming smile and dressed in the familiar purple-and-gold livery of the messengers who'd gone back and forth between Sisi and Lord Ricard. He slaps the innkeeper on the shoulder. "Henric, man, we need more beer."

"I'll be with you in just a moment, sir."

The soldier turns his head, seeing the three of us for the first time. When he catches view of Sisi, a slow grin spreads over his features. He lazily reaches out for her arm, and I watch helplessly as she freezes, rigid and terrified. "Who is this pretty little thing?" he asks.

"I am Lady Sisi of Eastsea, Four Hundred and Fifty-Third in the Kingdom. You will unhand me at once." It's the first time I've ever heard Sisi use her own title, although sometimes Jorj will call her that in jest, or when she's in trouble. But there's nothing playful at all about Sisi's tone as she tries to step away from the soldier.

The man lets go of her, holding his hands up with a

nasty, mocking smile. "I'm sorry, *milady*." Despite his sneer, it seems like her bluff has worked, at least enough so that he takes his hands off of her. "Do come in for a drink, pretty *lady*. Some of my men in there are lonely, out here in the middle of nowhere. They'd appreciate some much-welcomed company, especially from such a fine young *lady* as yourself."

Every time he says Sisi's title, he does it with a vicious sneer. At the last usage, he takes her hands in both of his, using his grasp on her wrists to pull her body flush against his.

Sisi doesn't react this time. She doesn't even move. She seems to be frozen with terror.

I look over at the innkeeper, Henric, who shakes his head at me slightly, like a warning. Aunt Mae's hands are trembling. None of them are going to do anything, I realize, suddenly and shockingly. None of them know what to do.

Neither do I, but I can't do *nothing*.

"Leave her alone!" I shout, uselessly, I know.

The man just laughs. "Jealous? You're not as pretty as the other one, but I figure we can find some use even for a fat little thing like you."

I hear men's voices booming from within the inn, and laughter too, that same sick laughter this soldier turned on me when I tried to speak. I see at once that there is no point in me raising my voice, though. He's no longer even looking at me, just trying to force Sisi past us, through the open doorway and into the inn, to the laughing crowd of soldiers.

He stumbles close to me, and I smell the stale ale and foul meat on his breath. I can see Sisi, shaking slightly, and the wide-open terror of her beautiful brown eyes.

Something moves through me. I don't know what, exactly. But I feel a strange surge of energy through my body, and I know I have to act.

On instinct, I push at the closest part of him I can reach, right at the center of his chest. I'm only hoping it will be enough to get his attention off of Sisi and on to me. It works better than I had expected—drunk and clumsy, he swings his fist back at me, still laughing. He has to let go of Sisi to do so, though, and she stumbles backward, rubbing her wrist where he'd grabbed her.

Sisi screams out my name as the soldier's meaty fist moves toward me, but there's no need. He's slow enough that I can duck right underneath his blow, making him stumble off-balance. He lunges to grab me, but I dance one step backward. A lifetime of working in the treetops has given me grace, at least, surprising as it may be in *a fat little thing* like me. Clearly, he isn't expecting it.

Grasping into the thin air where I was only a moment ago, he overbalances, trips, and falls face-first into the muddy ground by the inn's entrance. It's enough of a distraction that Sisi is able to get clear of him.

We have to move fast, but we're back in the cart before he's found his footing again. I gasp for air as Aunt Mae grabs the reins and drives us away. Even Maher seems to understand this is an emergency and moves with a speed I did not know he was capable of as we leave the inn behind.

A cloud of dust rises in our wake. I can't stop myself from looking back, where I can see the soldier stumbling after us, still calling out, "Lady! Hey, lady! Pretty lady!"

None of us say anything. Sisi won't look at either of us. We drive on into the night; by silent agreement, none of us stop, except to change out drivers long after the moon has risen, when Aunt Mae can't stay awake even another second.

I volunteer to take the next turn driving. I'm tired too, but I don't want to leave Sisi alone to drive while the rest of us sleep, not after what she's been through today. I sit forward on the hard bench of the cart and shrug off my cloak so the chilly night air will keep me awake as I take my turn at the reins.

It doesn't surprise me that Sisi can't sleep. She sits beside me at the front of the cart, starring out into the darkness of the night. I don't want to make her talk about it, so I just listen to the rhythm of Maher's hoofbeats steady on the ground.

"Jena," she says, suddenly, her voice barely above a whisper, "Thank you."

"You'd do the same for me." Although she'd never have to. I've never had to deal with what Sisi endures, men calling out to her on market day or even grabbing at her on the street. Although I envy her beauty in some ways, I've never been jealous of that.

"I was so scared. I couldn't seem to do anything at all. It was very brave of you to stand up for me."

There was nothing brave about it. I just didn't want to see her hurt. But I don't argue with her. I can only sit next to her, be here with her. We don't look at each other or speak, but in the silence, I feel as though I finally understand her fear of what she's facing, of what awaits us in the unknown City. I only hope that I can find some way to stand between her and danger once again. Though I probably shouldn't push the Crown Prince into the mud.

But I probably will, if I have to.

We drive on into the darkness of the night. Aunt Mae sleeps soundly behind us. And I wonder how I can keep Sisi, the person I love most, safe from those who will never see her as anything more than a prize to be won, a delicacy to be devoured.

CHAPTER EIGHT

*B*y the next morning, Sisi has four perfectly round bruises blooming on her wrist, red fingermarks standing out against her dark brown skin. Aunt Mae fusses over them, of course, but there's nothing to be done. All she can really do for Sisi is have me take over her turn driving and let her rest.

Sisi tries to insist that she doesn't need it, that she couldn't possibly sleep, that she'd rather take her turn. And yet within five minutes, she's snoring loudly in the back. I sit up front, near Aunt Mae.

As I suspected, she had her reasons for sending Sisi to rest. She wanted to talk to me alone.

"You were right brave yesterday. Not to mention cursed foolish."

"Sorry, Auntie," I parrot, though she must know I don't mean it at all, any more than she means her scolding.

"Well, then," she says, and I know I'm not in trouble after all.

The road goes by our cart for a while, neither of us speaking. We drive by another abandoned house, this one graced with two large glass windows like the one of which my father is so proud—both shattered and the space covered back over by lattice cobwebs and bird's nests.

"Sad to see what the Kingdom is coming to. Used to be safe for a woman to walk this road alone, they say."

"Do you know of anyone who has?" I ask tentatively. I always wonder where my aunt gets her stories from, especially those about the Kingdom beyond Prinnsfarm. She's told me herself that she's never traveled, but she still acts so wise. On the other hand, I'm afraid to ask—too much prying can shut her down entirely.

"Well, your cousin, for one, though Sisi wouldn't remember it. Merri, may the Goddess soon restore her to the fullest of health, would have walked back and forth along much of it to come to where Sisi and Jorj lived, and then to return with them—though soon the trail she took branches off, I think not far from here, leading easterly toward the sea. But those days were long after the great era when the road was built, and when there were cities at all the crossroads, fed by trade from all the Four Corners of the Kingdom. Or so they say. The only person I can think of who might have seen it before the decline, or at least in the early years of its descent, would be your mother, Jeni."

I don't know if it's because of the new circumstances,

because I feel oddly adult in this unfamiliar place, or just because I know that for once in my life my father won't swoop in from behind and in his quiet, firm way, silence any suggestion that such a person might have ever existed, let alone that she might merit discussion, but I find myself with the courage to ask about my mother for the first time. My heart races in my chest as I repeat, "My mother?"

"Aye."

That's not an answer. It's barely even a word. However, it's also more than I usually hear on this subject, so I decided to take the risk of prodding just a little. "When would my mother have walked along the High Road?" I venture.

"Why, when she came to live with your father, from wherever it is she came from. And I assume when she left again, although of that I can't be sure. It's hard to be sure of anything, where Ia is concerned."

It's the first time I can remember ever hearing my mother's name spoken aloud.

I must have already known it—I know I must have. It's not the first time I've heard it, because I recognize the word, I remember it somehow. Such an unusual name, too, not like triple-syllabled True Names or the simple by-names most girls go by.

Yet, I know I've never heard my father speak her name aloud, and I wonder who dared to. In our house, Aunt Mae orders everyone around cheerfully, but it is my father who is always silently at the center, and who all my life, without ever quite having to command it, has always forbidden any mention of her.

Aunt Mae is looking at me with a curious expression. I don't say anything while I wait, wordlessly praying that she'll continue. I can hear my heart hammering in my chest as she answers, benevolent as the Goddess Herself, "I suppose you've never heard the story, then, have you?"

"Never, Auntie," I answer briefly, hoping that if I keep my answers short, she won't remember that she's not supposed to be telling me this. I also send up a little prayer that Sisi will manage to sleep peacefully through this conversation. If she wakes up, she'll surely interrupt with a million questions, and then Aunt Mae will fall silent, and I'll never find out what I need to know. I wordlessly promise the Goddess that I'll tell Sisi everything as soon as we're alone, as long as she stays quiet through this.

"Hmm. You mustn't think too badly of my poor brother. It was very hard on him. Prinn as a boy, well, he was the same as Prinn now, just as you might imagine him. He was always quiet, always serious, always kept himself to himself. He opened up to Ia, though." She shakes her head. "I'm going about this all wrong. Besides, this is too serious for a journeying tale. The old stories are better for a time like this, to keep our minds off the road. I ought not tell you at all. Or perhaps I ought to have told you long ago."

"Why do you say that?" I ask. I'm worried that pushing too hard on this, that saying anything at all, will close the brief and precious window of opportunity I have right now to get this secret out of my aunt. Yet I am equally sure that if I fall silent too easily, I'll never forgive myself for letting the story go untold, for losing what might be my one chance to learn my own history. "Why not tell me?"

"Your father wouldn't wish it." Then she laughs and snaps the reins. "Well, then again, he's not here. It won't hurt him if I tell a bit of the tale—though, mind you, not a word of this to him when we get back home."

It's an easy promise to make, since I don't know if we'll ever return home, and if we do, I don't expect to be suddenly having a lot of heart-to-heart chats with my father. "You have my word, Auntie."

"All right. This was—how old are you now, Jeni? Four and ten, is it?"

"Aye." I'll turn fifteen just after Midwinter, though I don't expect anyone to mark it.

"So, it must have been just a little more than fifteen years ago, at Midwinter. That's just when we'll be arriving at the palace, come to think of it. Fifteen years exactly from the day that your mother walked off the High Road and into our lives. I wasn't there when she and Prinn first met, but I wrestled the story out of my brother later on. Wasn't easy, as I imagine *you* can imagine, knowing Prinn and how he is."

My aunt is a fond elder sister. She always acts as if my father's unbreakably sullen silences are nothing more than a rather endearing quirk.

"I do remember the weather the night she arrived. I couldn't sleep that night, the wind and the snow were whipping by the house so. It felt like the very roof was near to being blown to bits. Our little window, of which my brother is so proud, was quite whited out in the storm. He had just had it put in that spring, and I was worried it would shatter before the next one. I wonder why that sticks in my head so, the way that window looked. I went off to bed soon after, but I couldn't sleep. I could hear Prinn up, pacing about. I think he couldn't sleep either, although when I asked later, he said something woke him in the night. He said he'd had a strange dream, but not a nightmare.

"Well, what he meant by that bit of nonsense I couldn't ever say. The point is, he was awake, smoking his pipe, and carving a piece of wood for another one, minding his own business as he tends to do, when suddenly there was a knock at the door. Prinn was nervous, of course, as anyone would be—someone being at the door in the middle of the night in a storm when he wasn't expecting any visitors, and his nerves already on edge what with that dream and being up so late.

"He told me later that he tucked his carving knife into his pocket before he went to answer the door. Just to be safe. He let the door creak open, and in the dark doorway, framed against the sky, saw the shape of a stranger. He was surprised to see neither a beggar nor a burglar, but a beautiful young woman. Despite the cold and the storm, she was wearing nothing except a thin white shift, yet she wasn't shivering. She was barefoot, and yet she held herself as upright as any Numbered lady. Her skin was as golden as the firelight. She had midnight-dark hair, pitch black, that fell past her waist, and green eyes, just like yours. He'd never seen a green-eyed woman before—surely you've noticed, Jeni, there's no one in our village with the same eyes you have, that unusual color you inherited from your mother."

Of course I've noticed that. I'm the only green-eyed member of the family. Out of my passel of cousins, out of all the girls that live in the village, no one looks like me. Dark eyes, like my father's, are the most common, but there are a few fair people with blue eyes. No one like me, though, fat and tawny-skinned and green-eyed. All my father's kin have light brown skin, while Sisi and her brother are a gorgeous dark brown, almost black. I resemble neither part of the family, neither in my coloring nor in my body. Most folks in the town are slenderly built, like my family is, with Sisi's voluptuous figure making her stand out as much as my heavy frame earns me scorn. I've always been odd because of my looks. It isn't enough that I'm quiet and shy, or that I have no mother, but I also have to be visibly, obviously different.

Beautiful, Aunt Mae says my mother was. But no one has ever said that about me.

"He was captivated by those eyes at once, before she even began to speak. When she did, he was struck by her accent, one she never lost in the time she was with us—a strange one, I've never heard it anywhere else. It sounded like music when she spoke. I never quite figured out where she was from. If you asked, she'd dodge the question so you didn't even realize she'd done it. You could always understand her perfectly, though—sometimes even before she said anything, you'd know what she meant. She had a way of looking at a person...Anyway, I'm getting ahead of myself. All she said to him that night was, 'My name is Ia, and I come to ask shelter from the storm.' He invited her in straightaway. I always suspected it was because, even at first glance, he'd taken a liking to her.

"Still, even if she wasn't such a very beautiful woman —and she was—anyone with a heart would have taken her in out of that storm. The poor thing was hardly dressed and so frail-looking, and that storm was so terrible. So Prinn let her into the house, gave up his bed for the night and slept in his chair by the fireplace. In the morning, when he woke, he thought she'd be gone, disappeared back into the dream she seemed to have come from. Instead, she was standing over the stove, toasting bread and preparing tea from her special recipe. It was sweet and floral, like nothing he'd ever tasted before, and he says it's the first thing that made him fall in love with her.

"She asked him what she could do to thank him for his hospitality in her hour of need, and he assured her there was nothing, except perhaps to take a walk around the farm with him and tell him a bit about how such a fine lady could have found herself knocking at his humble door in such a storm in the middle of the night. So she did. She said she'd leave that day and not trouble his generosity any further, but he asked her to stay for supper, and one thing led to another. She never did end up leaving, as she'd said she would—one more night turned into three, and then ten, and then a whole moon had waxed and waned, and before two more had done so, they were man and wife."

"Where did she come from?" I blurt. "Did he ever find out from her?"

"If he did, he never told me. No, Prinn has always been too private for my liking." Aunt Mae grins. "I'd rather know the gossip."

Those words fill me with hope. If I am lucky, she means that she is enamored enough of being the story-teller, and with the thrill of sharing a secret, that she won't remember her promises to my father in time to stop her tale before the end.

"They were married on the first day of springtime. The sky was bright blue, and all the snows had melted away at last—although oddly, there were more to follow that year, late snowfalls into the spring months. But on that day, there was not a drop of either snow or rain, and some of the little flowers had started to bloom. I can remember how they looked, shoots of bright green and yellow crocuses in the brown earth. Lovely, and Ia was the loveliest thing of all."

She pauses as if lost in thought, and I take the opportunity to slide in one shy, tentative question. "You keep saying that, Auntie. That she was beautiful. But you also said she looked like me."

Aunt Mae nods. "It's true, you haven't the special grace she had, although you share all of her features. Well, maybe you'll grow into it, as she had by the time I knew her. For she *was* a great beauty, in spite of that big nose and sallow skin you've both got. Beauty shone out of her always, and most of all, on that day."

She goes on to describe how my mother embroidered the shift she'd arrived in to shimmer like the water under the sun, and so on, while I give in to brooding. I hate being thought of as homely, even though I know I am. It's not like I've ever thought otherwise, like I imagined my aunt was so fond of me that she couldn't see the fact that my many physical flaws are linked together by a total and profound lack of unifying prettiness. I suppose it doesn't matter much. It's not like a farmer's daughter needs to be comely. Sisi does get a lot of praise for her looks, but it's not the kind of attention I'd want. She certainly doesn't enjoy it, and after what happened yesterday, it's hard for me to hold on to any jealousy. I'd rather be mocked, as I was, than grabbed at and assaulted like Sisi. Besides, none of the women in my family are great beauties—though my aunts and cousins are more likely to be described as plain, being skinny and soft-featured, than outright ugly as I am. It really shouldn't matter.

I wish it didn't. I wish I were like Sisi, who is brave and clever and doesn't care about petty things like looks.

Then again, maybe she'd care a lot more if she had to be the ugly one, I think, though I know it's unkind.

"Ia was already pregnant with you on her wedding day. And your father was as doting a husband as anyone has ever seen. It was as if a part of him always knew how little time they were to have together, as if he felt he must fit a lifetime's worth of love into barely a year. His love for her shone like a candle in the dead of a winter's night.

"I've never seen him so happy as he was with her. When she arrived, he was already nearly five and thirty, old to be single even for a man, and I'd begun to assume that he was like me, that he was going to spend the rest of his life alone. It gave me such joy to realize I was wrong, that he was going to be able to settle down and find real happiness, that there would be something in his life other than the farm his father left him. The day you were born... I've never seen him so happy."

"Really?" I ask. It's hard for me to imagine my father holding me as an infant and looking down on my baby self with the kind of tenderness Jorj shows for his infant daughter. He pays so little mind to me now, has barely noticed me for as long as I can remember. I suppose that Aunt Mae might be wrong—or letting her prejudice toward her baby brother shift her recollections away from the truth.

"It was a very hard birth. Ia wouldn't let any of the rest of us in the room with her, just Kariana. It was days they were in there, and we were all afraid she wouldn't make it. Or that she was gone already, for it was silent as the grave in the birthing room. When Kariana came to speak to your father, though, she didn't seem worried at all. And we didn't hear any screaming, not like with an ordinary birth. Still, it must have been very hard, for Ia seemed so young, and you were a big baby—chubby, like your mother, like you are now—but she didn't make any noise for all that time she was in the birthing room. Well, when she handed you to Prinn, his eyes just lit up. I thought I noticed Ia looking at the two of you peculiarly, something... I don't know, almost like relief, in her expression. But she must have been exhausted from the birth, and anyway, I always found her a hard woman to read. What's that word...?

"Inscrutable, she was. It made her a good match for your father, except that it always seems to me—and I've known him longer than anyone—like he's just quiet by nature. Ia wasn't, I don't think. She always had this air about her, not like she was naturally keeping to herself the way Prinn does, more like she was hiding something. I dismissed it at the time, though. I came to regret that, later. When she left."

I've never dared to outright ask my father where my mother went. All the other children I know who are missing a parent, usually a mother, lost them to death. Childbed losses, of children too, but especially of mothers, are very common in the town and the surrounding farms, particularly since we no longer have Kariana. I always knew that wasn't what happened to my mother, though. She's out there somewhere, just gone. She's just chosen not to be with her family, with her child...with me.

I have always imagined that everything would be different if only my mother were around. Whenever I was particularly lonely or felt sorry for myself, I indulged in thoughts about how she would love me the way my father couldn't. She would think of me as being more than just one more mouth to feed, another face in a pack of cousins, a girl less useful to the farm than boys, a disappointingly homely and chubby and sullen child. She would know me for who I am.

It's always been an easy fantasy because she is such a mystery to me. I have never known why she's been gone for the last fourteen years, don't know whether it was her to blame, or my father, or myself.

Maybe, I think in breathless excitement, *I'm about to find out.*

"You were still a baby. It was Midwinter again, so you were nearly a year old. Even your father hasn't heard this part of the story. He never wanted to—I'd have told him, but he bade me never speak of her again. I was the only one awake that night, and he could never bear to hear tell of anything Ia had done, not after she'd left. Wouldn't even let me speak her name. Perhaps you've noticed," she says, almost jokingly.

"I may have," I admit.

"So, he doesn't know what I saw. That night See, I'd been sleeping poorly again. I was troubled by strange dreams, and by your crying in the night, every night. You weren't fussy at all when you were first born—indeed, you were as quiet and good-tempered a babe as anyone could wish for. But that week before Midwinter, you cried every single night, from dusk till dawn. Not shrieking, as babes do, but almost sobbing. It wasn't a natural sound. Ia was up with you every night; she wouldn't let even Prinn hush you, so of course I couldn't go near, but all the same, the noise kept me from sleeping.

"That's why I was up, sitting at the kitchen table, as usual, doing a spot of sewing. Looking back, it seems almost too normal. Fixing those holes my brother Willem always gets in the toes of his socks, I think I was. Is there anything less interesting than that...Ia must not have heard me, for even though I'd never seen her surprised by anything, she jumped when she walked into the room and saw me there, darning those socks. She was wearing only the lovely shift she'd been married in, no shoes or anything.

"I asked her where you were and she said, 'With her father, asleep,' and then I asked where she was going. I almost didn't. Somehow, the words felt forbidden, like I ought not ask, like it was a great secret. I've never been one who had much to do with great secrets, but I've also never been one to mind my own business, so I did go ahead and ask.

"She just looked at me, so sad. I'd never seen an expression like that on her pretty face before. I'll always be able to picture just how she looked when she answered, her face shadowed in the darkness, her eyes glowing. 'Jena'—she always called you that, never by an ordinary by-name—'Jena is going to grow up without a mother. Prinn is a good man, a kind man, but he cannot play both roles to her. And I won't be here. Promise me you'll keep an eye on my little one.'

"I promised because she seemed so strange, so fierce, but when I tried to question her further—ask where she was going, and why—she held up her hands. 'Maera'—she always called me, and all the women, by our True Names, for some reason. It was more common in those days, but I always preferred my by-name, since I was a girl— 'I can't tell you, can't tell anyone. Although I wish more than anything I could stay here and be a sister to you, and a wife to Prinn, and a mother to my little Jena, I cannot. You may not believe me, but that cannot change the way things are. Just... make sure they know I love them, and that I carry them with me in my heart, no matter how far away I go.' And before I could stop her, or ask anything else of her, she had disappeared out into the night, and none of us have seen her since."

By the time my aunt finishes speaking, my mouth is hanging open. "She just left?"

"Aye. She disappeared without so much as a word to your father, in the middle of the night. And oh, he was in a rage at first. I've never seen him so furious before—he's not usually a man hot in anger. Cold, maybe, and withdrawn, but no one can charge him with having too much of a temper."

"That's true enough," I admit.

"Well, that day was different. He was shouting and hollering, knocking things down in the kitchen, and anytime anyone tried to speak to him about it, he would just scream louder. He was in such a fury. Offended, I think. It hurt his pride. He always believed he and Ia had a special sort of love—I still think they did—and that it couldn't be broken apart.

"And of course, it broke his heart. It was hard enough for him to open himself up and let her in, to begin with. Doing so made him very vulnerable. And once he'd done it, and suffered for it, taken such a difficult chance and been, as he felt, betrayed... well, there was no going back for him. His rage passed, but not into acceptance or contentment or even a normal sadness that faded over time. When the anger left, it turned him into a shadow of himself. No matter how I urged him, he never took the kind of interest in you he should have—that I know Ia would have wanted him to. I think he was just too heart-broken over losing her."

I don't know what to say to that, so I just stare off into the distance, watching the dust of the High Road disappear behind our cart's wheels. I don't know how to say what's on my mind: that I don't think heartbreak is a fair excuse for following in my mother's footsteps and abandoning me to a lonely childhood; that I think Aunt Mae ought to have paid a bit more attention to me herself if she wants to congratulate herself so heartily on how she handled everything; that whatever sent my mother running couldn't have been worth it. There's no kind way to say any of it, and I don't want to say it cruelly, so I stay silent and just watch the road go by.

After a few moments, Aunt Mae clears her throat, like she means to say something else— but it's clear she doesn't know quite what that is, and the silence goes on and on, carrying us away from the painful secrets of our home and toward our unknown future.

CHAPTER NINE

There are no further disasters—or revelations—for the rest of our journey. The lack of excitement, though, doesn't prevent the mood from growing steadily more and more tense for the remaining two weeks as we continue to travel to the Capital.

I would not have thought it possible any of us could be even *less* pleasant to be around, but we discover new depths of crankiness as the days stretch into weeks.

I'm short-tempered myself, rocked by the truth about my mother, grateful to my aunt for finally telling me what became of her, and furious that, for fourteen years, no one had. Aunt Mae, in turn, seems to be suffering from mounting guilt over betraying the promise she'd made to my father not to breathe a word of the story to me. And Sisi, never the easiest person to get along with, has been growing steadily more and more irritable as we approach the dreaded meeting with Lord Ricard, especially after her encounter with his drunken soldier.

Spending all day being jostled around in a tiny cart being pulled by an increasingly exhausted donkey, eating stale bread and moldy cheese, and sleeping either on the ground or three to a single bed in cheap, dirty inns hasn't exactly improved anyone's temper.

As is our new habit, we're staunchly ignoring one another, counting the passing seconds and the steady rhythm of the donkey's hooves, when the Capital appears on the horizon. Sisi is the first one to spot it. To me, everything looks at first like more indistinguishable brownish, dusty haze, but Sisi points, and when I follow the line of her finger, I can just see a tiny dot blurring the bluish horizon, directly ahead.

By high noon, when the early winter sun is beating down on us from overhead, we've drawn close enough that I can make out some details. That dot Sisi saw was the outer wall of the City, an enormous structure of dark red-brown brick that barely forms the shape of a curve so vast I can only imagine what it encircles. It's the tallest object I've ever seen, ten times higher than the oldest treetops of our orchard, and from up close, it stretches as far as I can see in any direction. I imagine it could take a full day's ride to get around it.

The High Road leads us directly up to a small gate, which seems to be the only break in the wall. It's a simple set of sturdy iron bars, no taller than I am, and looks most absurd against the splendor of the City's fortifications. This lone entrance is guarded by two men in the royal livery, their hands on the hilts of enormous broadswords they wear at their belts. One is tall and dark-haired, the other short, stocky, and blond.

"Passport," one of them says tersely, and Aunt Mae smiles tentatively. I can tell the men's weapons—not to mention their lack of manners—are making her nervous, but she tries not to react.

"We have an invitation from His Highness, here." She takes out the piece of parchment from the pocket she keeps tied under her skirt. Though crumpled from its long journey, the letter clearly shows the royal seal: the Sign of the Three Powers, with Sword, Crown, and Circle representing Body, Mind, and Spirit.

The men's faces change in unison. At once, they're both scraping low bows. They look like a pair of frightened little boys. "Forgive us, milady. We were not advised of your arrival. I shall call the captain at once to escort you to the palace, unless you have a servant awaiting you."

"We don't. We'd be very glad of the escort."

The blond man speaks again, with another bow. It's as if he can't allow himself to meet our eyes. "Unfortunately, no vehicles except royal ones are permitted within City walls. I am sure when the captain arrives, we will be able to fit you with horses to ride, or perhaps a litter if you are not experienced on horseback."

"We can walk," Aunt Mae says. "Unless it's terribly far?"

"It'll take two hours to get to the center of the City walking. However, pardon me for saying so, in the City, ladies of stature generally don't walk about."

"Pardon *me* for saying so," Sisi interrupts, "but we are no ladies of stature. Perhaps you haven't heard, but His Highness has taken a sudden fancy to summoning farm girls and their aunties to the Capital, and there's no reason I ought to be carried on someone else's back because of it. I've walked on my own two feet every day of my life everywhere I've gone. Today is no different just because I'm walking on new ground."

The first guard falls silent at that. My dear cousin is causing a stir already, and we haven't even set foot in the City yet. I wonder if she's set some kind of record for making a nuisance of herself.

The other guard shoots a look at his companion and takes over. "We meant no offense, miss. I am sure my companion would be all too happy to go and fetch the captain" —the other fellow is at least clever enough to take the hint and scurry off at those words—"so that he may show you the readiest way to the palace, on foot or any other way you prefer."

Sisi looks like she has another clever comment on the tip of her tongue, but Aunt Mae manages to head her off, a sharp tone in her voice. "You are very kind. My niece must be very weary from the road, as *normally she would never speak in such a way*. We will be glad of any assistance you can offer."

The man bows again. Aunt Mae turns and glares at Sisi, who only shrugs.

This should be a fun trip into the City, I think to myself. I wonder how much trouble Aunt Mae will be in if she strangles the Prince's guest of honor before the ball.

Sisi reluctantly agrees to the litter, which, though it may have some faults, is a much nicer way to travel than the back of the market cart. We sit in a small, enclosed space, laden with silk pillows and covered with soft, gauzy curtains, while several more of the uniformed guardsmen carry us down the streets and another follows behind, laden with our bags. Still, I might have preferred traveling on foot. It would be nice to be allowed to see the City, after coming so far, and I can't help but feel a little uneasy that we don't know where we're going and can't leave if we want to. Also, we smell pretty rank from weeks in the carriage, and the enclosed space leaves something to be desired in olfactory terms.

I suppose ladies in the City are used to it. I'd rather like to be a lady, even if I don't know much about what that means.

Sisi is the only Numbered lady I've ever known, and she hardly counts. She's no different from the rest of us, except for her looks, which she tells me have nothing to do with it. She hasn't been wealthy nor lived in a great house since before I ever knew her, a time she cannot remember. Certainly, she's nothing like what I picture when I imagine the characters in Aunt Mae's stories, not like the First Queen ruling over all the peoples of the Earth nor the beautiful Numbered ladies who travel from afar to meet and marry handsome princes.

Though she is a beautiful Numbered lady, and though she has traveled from afar to meet a prince, Sisi just doesn't fit the part. The lady in a story would never spend the whole time we're traveling through the City sitting stock-still with her arms crisscrossed over her chest, glowering vaguely at both her companions. Nor do we suit our roles as Sisi's loyal retainers. Aunt Mae is fidgeting with her fingers like she's desperate for knitting or anything else useful to do with her hands. I just sit there, staring through the thin, pink veil that separates us from the Earth outside and wondering what is out there, what is waiting for us at the palace. I can only see shadows moving on the other side of the fabric, light and dark in turn.

The two hours it takes for us to be carried to the palace seem much longer. Still, it's sudden when the guards stop short, and we're jostled forward a little bit. Then, they slowly set the litter down so we can climb out, which is a disorienting experience, to say the least. It doesn't seem so ladylike a way to travel when I'm trying to clamber out without blinking like an owl in the bright and sudden sunlight, or to avoid showing a crowd of strange men my underthings as I move awkwardly from seated to standing.

Yet, all the fears fly out of my mind when I look up and get my first glimpse of the castle.

I had thought, earlier, that the City's wall was enormous. That word does not even begin to describe what I am looking at now.

The outer wall of the castle is made of gleaming black stone, so smooth and seamless it appears to be carved out of a single piece of rock. I look up, and up, and up, and my neck is straining painfully before I can see a hint of blue sky above the tip of the tallest tower.

The only interruption in the unbroken wall is a golden gate, guarded by more soldiers in their purple-and-gold uniforms. They salute the men who carried us here, and one of the new guards takes our luggage. Another bows low to us in greeting.

"Ladies. Allow me the great honor of welcoming you to the palace of His Royal Majesty, the High King Balion, First in the Kingdom. I am Padrig, lieutenant in His Majesty's royal guard, Number Eighty-Eight Thousand and Thirteenth in the Kingdom, and it would be my particular pleasure to escort you to His Highness."

At a snap of his fingers to the other guards, the gate is lifted for us, the mist disappears, and we follow Padrig into the palace itself.

We are inside the black wall for just a few seconds—it must be enormously thick, because it blocks out all the light. I'm left stumbling to follow Padrig through the pitch-darkness until the second gate creaks open and we are at the end of our journey at last, seeing the sight we have traveled across half the Earth to reach.

On the other side of the blackness is a vast courtyard covered in a pristine lawn of perfectly green grass, stretching for what looks like a league in every direction. At the center of the great lawn is a structure of shining glass, or maybe crystal. It refracts rainbows everywhere, reflecting the sun's light into a million different colors.

A guilty thought sneaks across my mind: my father is so proud of his one little window; Aunt Mae always talks of how hard he scrimped and saved to buy a single square of glass. I wonder what he would think if he could see an entire building made of the precious material. Would he be jealous? Or would he, perhaps sensibly, write this construction off as total folly?

After all, the practicalities are astounding to even consider. What happens if there's a storm? What if some idiot accidentally leans too hard on the outer wall—would it shatter? And where exactly do you go to use the chamber pot in privacy?

I would ask at least some of these questions, but Padrig is so stern-faced and silent that his expression seems to forbid any inquiry. Instead, I follow along behind him.

We cross the rolling lawns swiftly, without time to examine the gardens I can just glimpse out of the corner of my eye. In the castle's main wall, made of perfect crystal, there is no visible entrance at all, but Padrig knocks confidently at a section and it opens immediately. Yet another liveried guard bows to us and holds the door wide open so that Padrig can guide us into the entryway.

So far, all I've seen of the famous Capital is a lot of fancy buildings and some men in uniforms bowing to me. I hope it'll get more exciting soon.

No sooner has that thought crossed my mind than another person rushes over. He's unusually short, barely up to my waist, and has a green tint to his pale skin. Thinning, yellowish-white hair barely covers his large ears, which each rise to a point, and he has small, knobby orange horns on his forehead. He's also wearing the brightly colored royal livery, with a narrow pair of spectacles perched on his nose. The entire effect is so unusual that I find myself staring at him in shock, and only with some effort manage not to actually gape, open-mouthed, at him.

The man smiles, revealing thin, pointed teeth—and rather more of them than belong in a mouth, in my experience. I force down an instinctive shudder. "I take it you ladies have never seen one of the pahyat before?" He has a high-pitched, almost squeaky voice, perhaps due to his small stature, but he speaks the Common Tongue easily, without any trace of an accent. Well, for all I know, he's lived in the palace all his life and is better educated than I am myself. I ought not make assumptions.

I manage to shake my head. Sisi, uncharacteristically polite, has to speak for both of us. "Never, sir."

"We are few in number, indeed. You need not worry that it is rude to stare—I am well aware that it is a discomfiting experience for those who are only used to seeing humans." His smile widens, revealing still more of those sharp teeth.

I blush, ashamed at being so politely called out on my rudeness. Whatever he says, and however surprised I am to see someone of an entirely different species than anyone I've ever met before, there's no excuse for gaping at somebody just because they look different. I may be only an ignorant farm girl, but I know that much, at least.

"I am Elan, of the Ykan Glynbin Tribe of the Third People—those your stories like to call the pahyat. As you have no doubt deduced, my tribe are often called the Goblins—a corruption, our scholars believe, of our ancestral clan name, which is ill-suited for human mouths. I am one of those members of my tribe who continues to live and work among humans: in my case, as the steward to His Royal Highness, Prince Ricard."

I feel Sisi stiffen next to me, but she says nothing.

"You must be Lady Sigranna," he says to her. "Truly, the rumors of your beauty are as nothing compared to the sight of it."

"Thank you," Sisi responds, through what I can clearly hear are gritted teeth. If I could do so without drawing attention to myself, I'd kick her. I know she doesn't like comments on her looks, but this man is just trying to be polite.

"And your companions?"

"My aunt, Maera, and my cousin, Jena."

He bows to each of us in turn. "If it suits you, I shall have the footmen take your bags to your chambers."

"Yes," Aunt Mae says. Then, belatedly, as if she's only just noticed that her response was so curt as to be impolite, "Thank you very much."

Elan snaps his fingers. As he does, I realize he has six long, slightly curved fingers on each hand. I force my eyes away so he won't catch me staring again while the footmen appear, seemingly out of nowhere, take our meagre luggage, and disappear again. "Now, although I would be most happy to stand here exchanging pleasantries with three such enchanting ladies all the night long, I would be remiss in my duties not to instead urge you to make use of the comforts of the palace after so long a journey. Do you require food? Drink? Rest? Name your desire, and it shall be yours."

"Well now that you mention it, a bath would be nice," Aunt Mae answers. I don't disagree with her—we usually bathe once a week on the farm, and I feel the dust and filth of the road all the more acutely because we're in these grand surroundings.

Elan bows again. "Of course. The great baths beneath the palace are heated by hot springs and engraved with mosaics made from the finest gems, telling the story of the creation of the Earth by the hand of Gaia. Some have called them one of the wonders of the Earth. There are also private baths in your rooms."

Aunt Mae purses her lips, presumably at the thought of a public bath where strangers might see her without her clothes. "We'll go to our rooms, if that's all right with you."

"Of course, madam. I shall have the servants begin drawing baths immediately." More of the footmen appear at those words and are dispatched by another snap of Elan's fingers. I wonder where this endless stream of men in their shining uniforms of purple and gold are even coming from. Are they just standing around, lurking somewhere behind a shining pillar, waiting for someone to order them about? Don't they have anything better to do than wait to begin whatever chores they're ordered to at a given moment?

Apparently being a royal footman is rather like being a girl on my father's farm.

"Do you require any refreshments? I imagine you are quite thirsty after such a long journey."

Not wanting to hear anymore of Elan's constant

questions, Sisi, thankfully, intervenes before he can ask again. "I think we should go ahead and retire. Master Elan, I place my confidence in your good sense for any further decisions." She sweeps a graceful curtsy—when Sisi developed the capability to be so ladylike, I've no idea—and the steward is left little choice but to bow in response and show us upstairs.

Unfortunately, the trip up to our rooms feels at least as long as the entire voyage from Prinnsfarm to the Capital. We're led up a long flight of beautifully wrought golden steps, past a hallway of a dozen gilded and lovely doors, through an atrium inset with gorgeous twinkling silver, and everything is perfect and luxurious and rare and I would trade it all for the chance to sit down for even half a minute. Finally, we approach another large, gilded door of reddish-brown wood.

Elan retrieves a large, equally golden key from the pouch at his waist and unlocks it.

"You will find that your suite has many accommodations. I hope they will all be suitable to your needs."

Our weary little trio follows him into the first room. Once again, I am struck by the distinctive feeling that I ought not be here, that my very shabbiness is going to ruin something. The room we're in—the sitting room, I suppose—has a large, roaring fireplace at the center, and around it three couches, each with golden feet and backs, and upholstered in some sort of soft, fuzzy fabric. The floor is more of that burnished marble, so white that it hurts my eyes to look at. I'm nervous to let my dirty feet, stained with the dust of the road, touch it.

"Baths have been drawn for you, as you requested. You will find in the bathing chambers a large ebon basket. If you would like to deposit your garments there, they will be laundered and returned to you. Maids are waiting just across the hall to assist you in dressing, and you may ring at any time for them—that's the small silver bell—or for me, with the larger golden bell, should you need any assistance whatsoever. Is there anything else I might do at the moment?"

"No, thank you. You're dismissed." Sisi says.

He bows again and disappears.

As soon as he's gone, I turn to Sisi and raise an eyebrow. I'm tired, yes, but not too tired to tease her a little. "Dismissed?"

"Hey. I'm supposed to be the Lady Sigranna, heir to the lost house of Eastsea, gracious, Numbered, and beautiful. That entails ordering people around."

I consider this statement briefly. "Technically, isn't Mali the heir now?"

"Oh yeah." Sisi laughs. "Deposed by an infant. Well, so much for all of Jorj's work coaching me on royal etiquette."

"Seems like you have a natural talent for it."

"I mean, it's not that hard. Just pretend you think you're better than other people. They've been taught to act like you are, so it's not difficult to make them think it."

"That's awfully cruel."

"That's life in the Kingdom."

Aunt Mae clears her throat. "And that, girls, is enough. Baths. Now. No more political machinations,

Sisi, and no more tempting her into them, Jeni. Baths, clean clothes, food, bed. In that order. All further nonsense waits until the morning."

"See? It's not hard to pretend you're in charge. You don't have to be one of the Numbered, just imitate Aunt Mae!"

Her last jab delivered, Sisi flounces through the door to the bathing chamber. I follow her in silence, as my aunt ordered.

The room is covered floor to ceiling in mosaic tile. The design depicts a map of the Kingdom in intricate blue, teal, and gold. Thin lines of gilded mortar show the High Road, and a glimmering crown inset with jewels depicts the City. There are three tubs in the room, separated by tall folding curtains of carved white bone for privacy. Each is filled to the brim with water scented with roses and heated to steaming.

At home, we usually bathe only on Sixthday, and only in the winters. In the summertime, we just go jump in the river, which is freezing cold, but is at least fresh and clean and doesn't require quite so much work. For us to bathe indoors, the men have to haul back the water from the river as they come in from work. Aunt Mae heats it in a big, huge kettle, and we all help dump it into the tin bathtub, dinged and dingy from several generations of dirty family members climbing into it. The men go first, in descending order of age, since they're the ones who have to haul the water. Then Aunt Mae, then the other adult women, and finally the children, from oldest to smallest. The water is usually filthy by the time I get my turn near the end, clouded with dust and dirt and all kinds of other things, and lukewarm at best, sometimes uncomfortably chilly for the winter weather.

In short, it's nothing like this. I strip down and clamber into the steaming hot water, leaving my stained dress on the floor.

I remain in the water for a long time, until it grows cold against my skin. My fingers are shriveled all over by the time I decide to get out. When I do, I find a large, fluffy piece of cloth waiting for me. It doesn't look like the rags we use to dry ourselves with back home, and it's warm. Nonetheless, I can guess its purpose, using it to dry off my limbs and tuck around myself as I peek around the corner.

Sisi has already left, but Aunt Mae is still enjoying her bath, her eyes closed and her head tilted back against the edge of the tub.

"D'you know what I'm supposed to do with the tub?" I ask her. "Empty it, or...?"

She doesn't open her eyes as she answers. "I dunno. I'd just leave it for now, I suppose, though it seems a bit rude. Maybe we can ask that steward when he comes back."

She seems disinterested in anything I have to say, so I leave her to relax and make my way to the bedroom, dressing myself in fresh, clean clothes. I brought a simple peach linen dress, the one Merri had been taking in for me, and although it's patched at the knees and one of the elbows, it fits me well enough. It's a hand-me-down from Sisi, and so a little baggy at the chest and hips and a bit tight through the stomach—Merri had not quite finished her alterations when her labor began, thus derailing the entire project—but I look all right in it.

In the sitting room, I find Sisi reading something— some sort of card. I'm interested in what it says, of course, but far more pressing than whatever is written on the scrap of gilt-edged parchment is what's behind it: a three-tiered tray of little pastries, fruits, and tarts, and several steaming pots of tea. I pour myself a nice, hot cup and stir four cubes of pure white sugar into it.

Sisi, looking over at me, wrinkles her nose. "That's disgusting. I don't know how you can drink it like that. Especially if you're going to eat all those sweets too, and I know you are."

"It's good. Don't be silly, you're missing out on one of the great joys of life."

"Pure, unadulterated sugar?"

"Precisely." I load up a small, beautiful pink porcelain plate with one of every kind of sweet from the tray. They make a lovely rainbow. At home, most of the food we eat is some shade of brown. Brown bread, brown stew, apples canned or jellied or baked till they're brown. Of course, in harvest time there's the red of the fresh fruits, and the green and gold and orange of what grows in the garden, but none of it approaches the bounty on offer here.

"So," Sisi says, as I shove an entire tartlet with some sort of sour pink fruit on top into my mouth, "our treats came with a little note from His Lordship."

"What does it say?" I try to ask around my mouthful

of cream. Unfortunately, some of the pastry crumbs leak out the corners of my mouth. Sisi sighs and leans in, wiping them away, and I blink at the sudden pressure of her hand cupping my face.

I'm struck by a strange urge to lean close to her and put my lips to hers.

Before I can question that thought, though, she pulls me into an embrace and buries her face in my shoulder, feeling her chest heave up and down as if with sobs. Tentatively, I reach out one hand to rub her back, feeling her unsteady breathing. "Sisi? Sisi, you have to tell me what's the matter. I can't read minds. I'm right here. I just want to know if you're all right."

"I'll never be all right again."

Well, at least that's dramatic enough to be typical for Sisi. Slightly relieved, I rephrase. "What in Gaia's name does it say?"

She hands it to me, and I sigh.

"Sisi, you know I can't read this. Tell me what it says, please."

"Nothing. That's just it. It says nothing at all. It's all… formality. Perfectly courteous. Perfectly ordinary. He's pleased to welcome me and to know that I made a safe arrival. His steward let him know that I am as beautiful as promised and he's looking forward to my company at dinner before the end of the week, et cetera, et cetera. That's all. It's nothing to be upset about, right?"

"Right. Although obviously you are."

She sits back against the velvety couch, wiping her

eyes. "Yes. Obviously, I am. Because this is going to be my life now."

"It doesn't have to be. You don't have to go through with this. We're already here. We can just nab whatever expensive gifts we can get, go home, and everything will go back to the way it used to be."

"Is that what am I supposed to do? Go to dinner with one of the wealthiest and most powerful men in the Kingdom, hear his request to become his mistress, and then politely decline? Thank him for the trip to the palace and then head peaceably home again and say no more about it?"

The word *mistress* rings in my ears. It's the first time she's actually put into words what she's afraid Ricard might be after, and all at once it makes sense what she's been so afraid of all this time. "You think he wants *that* from you?"

"Jorj is the Lord. Like you said, now I'm not even the heir. What else could he possibly want?"

I know all about sex, obviously. I live in a house with a few very happily married couples, and the walls around our loft aren't particularly thick. Besides, Sisi told me all Jorj has taught her about the subject. Even desire, though I've yet to feel it myself (perhaps because I don't exactly spend a lot of time with young men), is not a mystery to me. No one could be Sisi's best friend without recognizing the power of her beauty. But knowing isn't understanding. "But why would he have you come all the way here for *that?*"

"They say I'm the most beautiful woman in the King-dom, you know."

Out of anyone else's mouth, it would sound intoler-ably vain. From Sisi, though, it comes out as a resigned sigh of barely restrained misery. I can't even be annoyed with her. "So I've heard."

"The Prince, no doubt, is used to having the best of everything. Why not have me too?"

"But you're not...I mean, you're not an object, you're a person."

"Try telling him that," Sisi sighs, looking down at her own perfect body, clothed only in a white slip that stands out starkly against her smooth, dark skin, with something close to disgust.

I don't know what to say to that, so I curl up next to her as we sip our tea in silence. She picks up the tiny gilded card with one hand and reads it over and over again, worrying at it with her hand until the edges are ragged and worn.

CHAPTER TEN

*T*he first day of my new life as Mistress Jeni, attendant to the beautiful Lady Sisi, in the royal palace at the center of the Earth's Four Corners, begins with Aunt Mae shaking me awake. Which means that thus far, my glamorous new life is not so different from my previous existence as Jeni the farmer's daughter.

"Get up, get up, Elan needs us in the parlor in five minutes!"

I fight the urge to roll over and go back to sleep. Last night, I couldn't get any rest without the warm, familiar weight of Sisi in bed next to me. Sleeping under the over-turned cart in the dirt by the roadside was easier. At least then I had Sisi next to me, like always.

Still half-asleep, I stumble through the tasks of getting up, idly combing my long hair with my fingers before pulling my one good dress over my head. I look like a mess, but a hundred hours of dolling myself up wouldn't do much to improve my looks, as my cousin Merik used to say when he was feeling particularly nasty. And no one cares what *I* look like, anyway.

Elan is sitting in the parlor. I, however, am more interested on what is on the table beside him: a breakfast of pastries and sliced breads, cheeses and fresh-churned yellow butter, fruit fresh and dried and preserved in jams. He must notice my hungry look at the treats, because he nods at me.

"Please, Lady Jeni, help yourself. I took the liberty of having breakfast brought up because time, I fear, is short. We have much to do, and we cannot keep His Highness waiting *too* long."

I'm not sure what exactly the crisis is, but on the subject of breakfast, I don't need to be told twice. I am polishing off my third plate by the time Aunt Mae and Sisi have both emerged from their rooms. Aunt Mae gives me a sharp look, no doubt a reprimand for either the shabbiness of my dress, the way the pastry is crumbling down my front, or both. She always scolds me for eating too much, even when our stores allow for it, though I don't see why. Sisi eats like a bird and she's bigger than me, while the boys, and especially Merik, can eat to bursting and stay as skinny as sapling trees in their first season of sprouting. My body is the way it is, whether or not I like it (I don't), whether or not I go in for another one of those small pastries with the bittersweet paste on top (I do).

Perhaps she simply finds my habit of taking whatever treats I can get my hands on impolite, for Aunt Mae and Sisi both seem to have no appetite, or they're too courteous, or too overwhelmed, to eat much. While they sip politely on their tea, Elan opens a sheaf of papers and begins to explain our schedule for the day. "I have arranged for several of the palace's seamstresses to call on you this morning, immediately after you finish your repast, if that is acceptable to you. Ladies usually wear gowns to the ball, and we shall have them made to your measure and to your taste, for both the Midwinter Ball and other court functions that may arise. Do you know how to dance?"

I say "Yes," at the same time as Sisi says "No."

She shoots me a look, like I'm being unbearably stupid again, and explains, though I'm not sure whether it's for Elan's benefit or mine, "We know country dancing, not court dances."

"Then the King's own dancing master will see you in the royal ballroom after luncheon. He instructed the Prince and the King themselves when they were boys, as he is widely regarded as the best teacher in the Kingdom."

I, personally, am rather excited by this news; I love to dance, and it will be fascinating to meet a man who taught the King himself. Sisi just frowns, of course, but I'd expect nothing else from her.

The rest of our schedule includes a luncheon with two Numbered ladies who are apparently Sisi's third cousins twice removed, an afternoon lesson in courtly etiquette, and a consultation with the palace hairdressers.

"And His Highness sent you this." Elan holds out a

small, black velvet pouch. With trembling hands, Sisi takes it.

Inside is a shimmering emerald, hung on a gold chain spun so thin I can barely see it. The green jewel is enormous and beautiful, about half the size of my own fist.

"Give His Highness my thanks. It's beautiful," Sisi manages to make herself say.

It certainly is, but from the way her eyes tighten as she says it, I somehow suspect she does not mean the words with sincerity—though she might indeed be pleased with such a fine gift. If we could just leave now, and sell the necklace, I think we would never have to worry about any of our family going hungry again.

Something tells me that isn't going to be an option.

"I will convey your thanks, of course. Is there any other message for His Highness? I am meeting with him not long after this, and it would be my pleasure—and of course, my duty—to bring him any messages you may have." Elan looks expectantly at all three of us.

I search my suddenly blank brain, looking for any way I can make myself find the words to address the *King's brother,* even if it's indirectly.

"Please thank His Highness for his hospitality," Aunt Mae replies.

That's what I should have said! But I didn't think of it in time, and now Elan is bowing and leaving the room.

Ah, well. It's not like anything I would have had to say would have mattered enough to be noticed—I'm just here to tag along behind Sisi, the way I've always done. In a way, I'm grateful for it. I've been jealous of Sisi and the attention she gets plenty of times in my life, but I wouldn't want to have to be the one taking the lead in this new place.

As soon as the great double doors shut behind Elan, Sisi goes to drop the emerald on the ground as though it's nothing more than trash, but then catches herself. Instead, she hands it to Aunt Mae. "Will you keep this for me, Auntie? Put it somewhere safe."

Aunt Mae looks a little queasy at holding something so precious, but she hesitantly takes it from Sisi and goes into her own sleeping chamber. I suppose that answers my question about Sisi's feelings about the gift of jewelry, then.

It does seem an incredibly intimate sort of present to give someone. Back home, no one can afford *jewels,* of course, but boys give chains of handwoven flowers to girls they're courting, and married couples exchange metal bands that they wear around their wrists to mark their bond to each other. Maybe things are just that different among the Numbered. I wouldn't know, but I have to imagine that there's some symbolism to giving someone jewelry.

Sisi has turned away a lot of presents over the years: bottles of wine, freshly picked flowers, carefully baked sweets—all from admirers whose interest she did not return. I suppose this is simply more of the same to her, in spite of the worth of the gem and the prestige of its giver.

Or maybe even *because* of both of those things. Maybe it's the fact that this is no different than how Sisi has been treated by everyone outside the family since she first began to grow into maidenhood that gives her the courage to treat a royal gift with such nonchalance.

Just another man she doesn't want, giving her things she didn't ask for, as if she'll trade herself away for trinkets.

I don't have time to voice that theory to Sisi, though, as we're soon joined by Mari, who introduces herself as the palace's head seamstress, and number Three Hundred and Seventy-Six Thousand, Eight Hundred and Twelve in the Kingdom. I wonder if everyone around here does that—so far it seems like even the servants are obsessed with knowing and sharing their Numbers. The only person who hasn't done so was Elan, and, as a pahy-ati, he obviously wouldn't be able to trace his descent from the First King and Queen. I wonder if I'm going to stick out too terribly without a Number of my own, or if it's time to start counting out generations on my fingers until I can figure out that I'm number eight million and sixty-four bazillion in line for the throne, or some such thing.

In spite of her Number, Mari seems almost familiar to me—not because I've ever met her before, but because I've spent my life around women like her. Aunt Mae, for one, who takes to her at first sight. Mari is soon ordering both Sisi and I around with the ease of any of our aunts. Arms up, arms back, sit down, now turn, touch your toes, back up again.

"You're both fine, healthy girls," Mari remarks approvingly. "There's been a cursed fad for skinniness in the palace lately. I say a lady with no flesh on her won't look well in any gown, no matter how it's tailored. Now, the two of you will be a pleasure to outfit. Though Mistress Jeni, you've yet to grow into your looks."

Of course. What would a conversation be without an unsolicited insult about my appearance? I'd hardly know what to do with myself.

"Still, you have the right round features and the perfect coloring for a maiden on the verge of flowering. Never fear, we'll make you up to look the part. A little corsetry, a bit of my work, and we'll give you the curves you're still waiting for, suck you in a bit about the middle. You could look as lovely as your cousin here."

Only the certainty of incurring Aunt Mae's fiercest displeasure stops me from rolling my eyes at that. I'll never be as beautiful as Sisi. They can do whatever they want to make my chubby body look as shapely as hers—just because we're both big girls doesn't mean we'll ever look alike—but they can't fix my face.

"Now, Lady Sisi, you're perfect as is. Why, we could send you into the ballroom in your traveling clothes, and you'd still be the talk of the land. But of course, we aren't going to do that! I'm so pleased I get to work on your gown. I think we'll be able to make a *real* impression on all the guests—even on His Highness."

Sisi doesn't answer at all, not even a polite dismissal. Mari seems unfazed by her utter rudeness, filling up the silence with pleasant chatter.

"Well, that's all I need for today to get started on your gowns for the ball itself. I'll be back tomorrow with some sketches, to see if you approve of my plans. And I'll have a few things sent up as soon as I can so that you'll be properly outfitted in the meantime."

No sooner has she departed than more footmen start arriving. They set the table for lunch—fine porcelain plates, real silver cutlery, crystal goblets—and then lead in our guests. Patine and Ransi are apparently both Numbered ladies of the Third Quarter, in town for the winter season. They share a common great-grandmother with Sisi—which appears to be news to her as much as it is to me—and are around our age, which is no doubt why they were selected as our companions.

The meal is eaten in indescribably awkward silence. The two Numbered girls pay no more attention to Aunt Mae or I than they might to a fly. In fact, they treat us with exactly the same aloof condescension they treat all the other servants, whom they are ignoring just as casually while the meal's many courses are brought before us and cleared away in elegant succession.

They *do* try to engage Sisi in conversation, of course, but she's even more stubborn than usual. In fact, she's brought a thick leathern book to the table and is reading it while she absent-mindedly nibbles on her lunch. No doubt if we were at home Aunt Mae would give her the thrashing of her life, but I'm not quite sure that's allowed here, and apparently neither is Aunt Mae, for she just glares daggers at the top of Sisi's bent head as Sisi ignores all of us.

I don't even know where Sisi *got* a book. Certainly, we didn't bring one with us! We've never owned such an expensive object.

At least the lunch is delicious. We're served a soup of poached chicken and finely minced herbs, followed by fresh river fish in a creamy sauce, all with a loaf of the sort of finely milled white bread I'd never tasted before yesterday. Even Patine and Ransi's condescension and Sisi's blatant rudeness can't erase the pleasure of such a fine meal.

When the tables have been cleared, and our reluctant and unwelcome guests have excused themselves from the table, it's time for our dancing lessons.

I'm excited and nervous in equal measure. I love to dance, but Sisi's comment this morning has made me think that a fondness for the simple circle dances we used to do on holidays will be of little help at a royal ball. I hate the idea of making a fool of myself, something I feel I've done more or less constantly since we arrived here.

These worries are slightly eased by my excitement about finally getting to see a little bit more of the palace. Dancing would seem to be the one activity we can't actually do in our chambers, expansive though they may be.

One of the silent footmen leads us down the corridor, around the corner, and through a solid oaken door into a ballroom. The space is lit with the sun refracted through a thousand crystals. It is undecorated except for the open crystalline wall that overlooks the palace's gardens, and empty except for a tall, very thin old man leaning against a cane. He has pale, almost see-through skin, and his hair is pure white. Deep wrinkles carve through his face, nearly obscuring his vision. Yet he still bows to each of us with great courtesy and grace. In spite of his age, it's easy to see how this man must be a dancer.

"I am Balertius. Ninety-Four Thousand Two Hundred and Third in the Kingdom. I taught the King to dance. I taught the King's father how to dance. Many lords, many ladies, their parents, their children. Now I teach you." His voice is heavily accented, though of course I don't know enough about geography to be able to place it with any kind of confidence.

He circles around both of us, watching carefully.

"You are Lady Sisi, no?" he asks my cousin. "The one that was sent for? The famous beauty?"

"I am Sigranna, sir," she answers. I hear Aunt Mae sigh at her insistent use of her True Name, even now, even in the palace.

"Hmm. Reluctant to claim what you are, I see. You do not wish to be called a lady? Nor a great beauty?"

"I don't see how that's relevant to whether or not I can dance," Sisi bites back.

To my surprise, and relief, all that provokes from Balertius in return is a loud laugh. The sound of his laughter echoes in the large, empty room. "You are a clever girl. There is more to you than your looks, I see this. But you do not know very much about how to dance. To dance is to become a great beauty, to *embrace* the beauty within you, even if you are not beautiful in the face or in the body. I will teach you."

At first, we're not permitted music, or partners. Balertius keeps time by pounding his cane rhythmically against the floor.

We must look like fools, wrapping our arms against the empty air. Balertius uses the tip of his cane to nudge our arms into the proper position, to straighten our wrists, and then to delicately arrange our fingers in just the right shape. He kicks my feet closer together and Sisi's wider, and then grabs her hips to pull her upright. It must be a quarter of an hour before he is satisfied with our positions.

"So, we begin."

Begin? I had thought we must be nearly done by now.

He goes back to tapping the floor with his cane, which is marginally preferable to his tapping us with it, I suppose.

My arms are aching and my feet are throbbing by the time he finally relents. We've learned the first two steps of something called the pavaine. It would be more accurately called the *pain*, I think. Nor am I pleased to learn that there are two dozen steps in its simplest variation, and that we are likely to be called upon to know a hundred dances by the time of the ball.

"How is that even possible?" I grumble, shaking out my arms in a vain attempt to get some feeling back into them. "I mean, how can you possibly remember all of that stuff?"

"Most people start practicing when they are still small. The Prince, the King, they were no more than three when they started. You are too old to learn, but still, I teach you," Balertius says, and there's something almost like gentleness in his voice. Then he smacks the cane hard against the smooth stone floor, and Sisi and I both jump at the cracking noise it makes. "Now go! Karili is waiting."

In spite of my complaining about Balertius' harshness and the tedium of the steps, I admit to myself that I've almost enjoyed the dance lesson. It's the closest I've come to actually getting to *do* something since we arrived here. The same cannot be said for our next lesson: etiquette.

Karili, our instructor, is waiting for us in our chambers. At a glance, I can tell that she is as young, as pretty, and twice as haughty as Patine and Ransi were. Sisi shoots me a wicked look.

Don't you dare, I mouth at her. But she only grins at me, and then strides over to Karili, who is sitting on the edge of her chair, legs carefully crossed, hands folded in her lap, gown and hair perfectly arranged. Sisi spits in her hand and sticks it out for Karili to shake.

"I'm Sigranna. Nice to meet you."

Karili rises elegantly to her feet. *She* must have started her dance lessons at an appropriately early age. "You must forgive me for correcting you so early in our acquaintance, Lady Sisi, but I would be neglecting the role for which His most gracious and royal Highness selected me did I not. Ladies of station do not use their True Names, and we curtsy rather than shaking hands."

"Why?" Sisi asks, flopping down onto the chair behind her and kicking her feet up onto the table. Aunt Mae, who took great care to teach us manners as girls, lets out a low groan of despair somewhere behind us.

Karili is too polite to stare at Sisi, but I'm sure she would if she could. Besides, it's not like Sisi doesn't know the reason. Everyone knows girls are given True Names as babies, and everyone knows it's not done to go around using them. "Why, I...I'm sure I can't say."

"Don't know, or can't say?"

"All the ladies use their by-names. Even the Queen Mother, may she rest in Gaia's embrace—"

"Why not the men?" Sisi has actually *interrupted* her mid-word now, which is a level of rudeness I didn't expect, even from her.

"Why, men don't have True Names and by-names, just names! Is it different in the countryside?" Karili puts on a fairly impressive show of keeping her tone limited to polite curiosity, but it's obvious that Sisi is hitting her mark. There's only so long Karili can respond with perfect courtesy to Sisi's outrageous behavior, and I don't know what this well-mannered lady will do when she's run out of polite options.

I take a tactful step away from the brewing conflict and toward the outskirts of the room. If either one of them explodes, I don't want to be caught in the middle of it.

"So, men are allowed to use their True Names all the time, then," Sisi continues.

Karili defers politely. "I suppose you could look at it that way, yes."

"Then why aren't we women afforded the same freedom?"

Karili tries not to let any expression at all show on her bland and pretty face. It's almost working, too. "Women also wear skirts, and men do not. Some things just are the way that they are, for no good reason, or indeed for no reason at all. Even if the meaning of it is not obvious, it is still worth following traditions, in order to get along with others. That is why we have a system of etiquette—so those of us who live in close proximity to one another know how to be most respectful of the thoughts and ideals of others. It is this that I have been instructed to teach you, my lady."

"You may consider me wildly selfish, then, but I prefer to go by the name my mother gave me before she died. Even if it is the *tradition* to do otherwise."

I groan under my breath. Once Sisi has brought her dead parents into an argument, there's no coming back from it, not for anyone. And as I expected, Karili just stammers an apology and takes a step toward the door.

"I'm so sorry to remind you of a painful subject, milady. Perhaps we can reconsider the topic tomorrow."

"That suits me fine."

When Karili has left the room, Sisi turns and grins at me. "That went better than expected."

"You didn't have to chase her off like that."

"I know, but now I've the afternoon free. See you at suppertime—or when the next idiot comes in to drag us out for another pointless lesson."

Before I can protest any more—and before Aunt Mae, whose eyes are gleaming murderously, can intervene—Sisi has disappeared into her room. I hear the sound of a lock hitching shut behind her.

I wonder what she could possibly be doing in there. Other than the luxurious furniture, my room was empty of anything entertaining. Perhaps she's lain down on the feather bed for a nap. After the dreadful sleep I got last night, it's not an unappealing idea.

Still, we have duties, and I want to do well here, even if Sisi seems determined to make an enemy of everyone we meet. I sleepwalk through the meeting with the hairdressers, and barely taste the luxurious dinner that is served to us, but at least I show up.

Aunt Mae suggests a round of cards while we digest, and I accept gratefully. Anything to have a break from more rules, more lessons, more strangers.

I hear one of the maids whisper that card playing, too, is apparently unladylike, but on that subject, I'm arriving at Sisi's level of complete disdain for the word and all that it signifies. I just want to pretend things are a little bit normal, and maybe have some fun along the way. And playing cards with Aunt Mae, who is—tonight as always —wickedly good at it, certainly qualifies.

"Any notion what your cousin is up to?" she asks me, after she's trounced me at the first hand. We're playing with our after-supper chocolates as forfeits, and she pops two in her mouth, grinning as she asks.

"No."

"She didn't even come out for supper tonight."

"I noticed."

"Well." She sets her cards down and looks me in the eye. "You'd tell me, wouldn't you? If you had any idea of what she's been doing in there for all these hours? Or why she's acting so...mysterious?"

Mysterious is one way of describing Sisi's behavior

today. I might call it disgraceful, myself. She might not like the sort of people that her third cousins or Karili are, but they haven't done anything to wrong her either, and she seems to be trying to upset them on purpose. Sisi can be difficult, but cruelty is not like her.

"Of course I'd tell you, Auntie," I promise, although I'm not sure it's the truth. Sisi is obviously trying to keep something secret. If I could—if she were to trust me with it—I would try to protect it for her.

Aunt Mae probably knows me well enough to recognize the deception, but she doesn't say anything. She just wins another half dozen chocolates off me in two more rounds of cards and sends me to bed.

Exhausted from a long day of tripping over my own feet and being shamed for using a napkin incorrectly, I fall into my bed. This time, I'm asleep at once in the unfamiliar room. I don't even miss Sisi's presence beside me as I slide easily into unconsciousness.

It's a deep sleep indeed that I'm awoken from by the touch of a hand on my shoulder. I start to scream, but another hand clamps down over my mouth hard. I have just begun to resign myself to my imminent murder when I recognize Sisi in the near blackness of a room lit only by the embers of a dying fire. "Quiet, you idiot," she hisses, and takes her hand away so I can speak.

I whisper, "What are you doing sneaking in here? I thought you were going to kill me in my bed. There's a door. You could have knocked on it."

"I didn't want anyone to know I was here. Had to

wait until everyone was asleep. And didn't want to risk making any noise. Scoot over."

I do as she tells me, sliding all the way over to one side of the bed so she can climb in next to me. The enormous, feather-soft bed is rather lonely for just one girl. It is draped with silken sheets and damask coverlets stuffed with goose down, and the bed itself is carved from the purest ebony.

Yet as Sisi settles in next to me, I start to feel at peace, even though everything is different now—the luxurious bed has replaced our tattered, old mattress; the delicate glow of the fire illuminates my room; and there's the fear, not of being scolded by family members, but of being overheard by the spying maids. Still, it's a relief to be back together, as Sisi draws the thick damask coverlet over both of us so we can whisper together in the safety of the dark, quiet night.

"I didn't want to tell you where anyone might hear, but I think we're safe in your room."

"I should hope so," I retort. If my bed isn't safe, I don't know what is.

"Don't forget, the maids all work for Lord Ricard. They could be listening in. They're probably required to," Sisi cautions, and then draws in a deep breath. I feel the mattress rise and fall with the pressure of her inhalation, and I shift a little closer to her, so I get the warmth of her skin almost touching mine, too. "I've been reading," she says.

That is *not* the Earth-shattering secret I was expecting. I tell her as much, and she laughs at me.

"Hoping for more excitement than the contents of a book?"

"Aye."

"Things here on Earth are very rarely like a tale, Jena. You would do well to remember that."

I hate when Sisi acts like she's so much smarter than me just because she's a little bit older, so I ignore that comment. I want to find out what on Earth she's up to, not quarrel with her. "Why reading?"

"It's part of why I agreed to come. For Merri's sake, and the family's, yes, but also because the greatest library in the entire Kingdom is here, in the palace. As the Prince's honored guests, we have access to any volume we like. I've been having the maids bring me dozens of different books, all sorts, to disguise my true purpose. Hopefully, they won't be able to find any pattern to what I've asked them for."

"What *is* your purpose, then? I assume you aren't just reading for pleasure." I've never known her to do so. Admittedly, it's not like there were books hanging around on the farm, but, knowing Sisi, if she'd had a passion for reading, she'd have already found a way to make it happen.

"Indeed, I am not." She hesitates, her voice becoming even quieter, so that, even pressed close as we are, I can barely hear her. "What do you know of magic, cousin?"

"Um..." Once again, I feel like I am at my lessons, and *not* as the star pupil. "There are two sorts. Good magic, governed by the konim in the Capital, who use their power to learn about the Earth, never to interfere. And the other kind."

"Surely you know what it is called."

She must be goading me. Any fool can name blood magic, wielded by the villain of every childhood story, playing the central role in every nightmare. It seems too perilous to speak the words aloud here though, in the dark, with listening ears and danger all around. "I do know it," is what I settle for.

"And you know what's become of magic, since Lord Ricard took his place so close to his brother's throne? Jena, do you know what became of my parents?"

I don't see what the one question has to do with the other. "Sisi, you're not making any sense."

"I do wish you wouldn't call me that, you know."

I scowl at her in the darkness. As if she ever respects *my* wish to be called by my by-name so we don't get into trouble. "Sigranna, then. It doesn't exactly trip off the tongue, though."

"It's my name. It doesn't need to be easy to say."

I get the sense that I'm annoying her—it must be her biting sarcasm that clues me in—and I don't want to drive her back to her own room. "Start with the last question. What do your parents have to do with this?"

"Well, it's complicated, and it would take quite a family tree to explain it to you in full, but my mother could claim descent just like the King and his brother can, from the First King and Queen directly, and so she would have been called to Test her right if anything ever happened to His Majesty. You know how everyone here is always saying what Number they are in the Kingdom?"

"Yes."

"That's how closely related they are to the First King and Queen. And so, how close they are to the throne. And it's the order they are Tested in."

"I thought the throne went to the next person in line, the King's brother or son or what have you."

"They have to pass the Test first. That's one of the things I've been reading to try to find out about—what exactly this Test is. All I can find is that it's some sort of magic, just like in Aunt Mae's story, and that it was put in place back in the days of the First King and Queen to determine who is worthy to have the throne. And of course, that Ricard *failed* it."

"What?" I exclaim.

"Keep your voice down!" she reminds me in a harsh whisper, and I bite my lip as she continues. "Ricard is King Balion's *older* brother. So, when his father was King, he was Second in the Kingdom. He would have been the very first to take the Test, to get the chance to become First in the Kingdom, and so the King of All the Earth. He failed, and his brother took the throne."

"But what's this got to do with you and your family?"

"My mother was only Twelfth in the Kingdom at the time. Eastsea was never wealthy or politically important, but with the way the marriages and everything worked out, that was her number. It means that, if anything happened to King Balion, she'd be tested. Strong ruak apparently ran in the Eastsea line. Maybe Ricard thought it would give my mother an advantage in the Test. Maybe he was just afraid of magic, or that he'd fail again and be humiliated. So, he had our mages accused of doing blood magic, and put to death. Then when my mother and father got sick, there was no one to heal them. The people were afraid, and someone—maybe one of the Golden Soldiers, maybe Ricard himself—spread a rumor that fire could stop the spread of the pox, so they set the manor ablaze. There was no one to protect Jorj and I, and neither of us had my mother's ruak. The smartest thing to do was run."

"That's terrible. Sisi, I never knew." Sisi has never spoken much of the days before she came to live with our family, though I know she and Jorj talk of it from time to time in private. She must not remember much, and the story is so very sad. I've never wanted to push her to discuss it.

"I didn't either. Jorj told me, warned me really, when I agreed to come here. He wanted me to know what I'd be facing. What Ricard really is."

"And that's why you're here. You want revenge?" I ask. Finally, it starts to make sense, why Sisi is here, why she's acting so strangely, why she has such a hatred for Lord Ricard, a man she's never even met. If she blames him for the death of her parents, of course she would hate him.

"Not revenge. Answers. It's not just my parents. He's done so much harm, Jena. You remember." From the hard tone in her voice, I can perfectly picture the very scene she's speaking of, the burned and ruined cabin, the overrun fields.

"I know about what happened to Kariana, but he didn't do that, did he? It was the soldiers—"

"*His* soldiers, acting on *his* orders." She moves even closer to me, her breath tickling warmth against the shell of my ear. "And Kariana can't be the only one. My parents, and how many other nobles that stood in his way? Kariana, and how many other mages whose power was a threat to him?"

"What are you going to do about it?"

"Watch. Learn. Plan." Her teeth glint white in the dark as she grins. "I'm going to find out what that Test is if I have to read every Goddess-cursed book in the entire royal library. I'm going to find out why he failed. I'm going to find out what he wants, and I'm going to make sure he never, ever gets it."

The thing no one ever remembers about Sisi is that she is markedly terrifying when she gets an idea in her head. She is beautiful, which people tend to use as a shorthand for *empty-headed,* often to their own misfortune. No one ever looks at me, which is why I slip right beneath people's notice, but no one ever stops looking at her for long enough to think about her. I know she hates this state of affairs with every fiber of her being. I also know that she intends to make every use of it that she can.

"Let me help," I blurt.

"There's nothing you can do."

Those words, delivered so calmly, spark something in

me. I'm rarely angry, but suddenly a hot fury bubbles up to my throat. "You don't know that. You don't know everything."

Sisi hesitates. When she speaks again, her voice is gentle. "I need to go through these books without being noticed. You can't help me with that."

She's not wrong. I can't even read my own name. "But maybe I can learn."

I can barely see her face in the near darkness, so maybe I imagine that she looks impressed. "Maybe you can," she says, and kisses the top of my head, her lips as light as a feather. My heart pounds in my chest at the gentle touch.

It's nice that for once she's not telling me I'm too stupid to help or that I don't know enough or can't understand things. It's nice for us to be back on the same side.

"We'll start tomorrow, okay?"

"Okay."

She shuffles a little closer, curling an arm around me. "Is it all right if..."

"What?"

"If I stay here, just for tonight?"

"Of course."

I think about asking why, but I decide it's better not to. Soon, her breathing evens into the steady rhythm of sleep. I try to mirror her—tomorrow will be a long day, and I should try to rest too.

The audacity of it, her absolute confidence in herself, shakes me and impresses me. I'm not like that. I never have been. Having heard Sisi's plan, I'm not sure if I should wish I were a hero like her or be glad that I am the way I am. A little bird, quick and always unseen—but I may be able to fly out of danger, and Sisi never will. She shines too brightly, not only with her remarkable beauty, but also because of her brilliant mind and her unrestrained anger. She'll never be able to turn herself off, turn herself down, fit in, be safe.

And I certainly can't change her; unlike Sisi, I'm not mad enough to imagine I can reshape the Earth to my will simply because it doesn't suit me as it is.

Yet, if there's anything I can do, if there's some way I can help Sisi on her quest for answers or revenge or a better Earth, mad though it may be, I'll do it.

I'll always be at her side. Though I might rather she wanted to stay out of trouble, I've never been able to change her mind on that, and I'll never leave her to face her battles alone, even if she willingly gets herself into them.

No, unlike Sisi, I don't believe that one foolish girl can change the fate of the Kingdom.

But for her sake, at her side—believing it is possible or not—I will try to make sure one can.

CHAPTER ELEVEN

In the light of morning, my cousin and aunt go about their routines. It feels as though I'm watching them from behind a heavy pane of glass. I can see, but I cannot touch. I have been doing this all my life, I realize, watching and listening and perhaps even learning, but doing nothing with that knowledge.

No longer.

I'm going to be a part of things now. Even if that means I have to change everything. At lunchtime, Sisi makes the announcement. "I have made arrangements for Jena to receive one additional set of lessons."

"And what is that to be?" Aunt Mae replies, sounding a bit incredulous.

"As a lady, Jena ought to know how to read and write. I have spoken to Elan, and he knows the perfect young man for the task."

"A young man?" Now her skepticism is outright distaste, although I should think she knows better than to fear for my virtue, especially with Sisi around to keep any admirers' attention firmly away from me. At least she isn't harping on the idea that I have no need to be messing with books when there's important work to be done. Maybe now that we're in the palace, all of that has changed. It's not like there are apples to be picked, after all, or dishes to be scrubbed, or mending to be done.

"He was studying to be one of the konim, before the Prince, apparently...well, he is a very knowledgeable young man. Not to mention a member of the Kingdom's highest religious order. Jehan is his name. Eight hundred and somethingth in the Kingdom, I can't remember. He'll be here after we survive our etiquette class—with your permission, Auntie, of course."

"A priest?"

"Aye," Sisi explains, "One of the last. He was chosen as a boy by Garem, the Chief of the Konim, to replace him one day. Jehan has never set foot outside palace grounds. Elan tells me he is a most scholarly and respectful young man."

"Well." Aunt Mae frowns. "Are you sure this is needful, Sisi? Jeni has done all right without reading before now."

I disagree, but don't object. When it comes to persuading Aunt Mae of things, Sisi is definitely more equipped for success than I am.

Sisi explains, with a casual wave of her hand, "I'm already getting so many letters and things, I need someone to help me keep my calendar. If Jena is my lady companion, she must be able to serve the role fully."

"And this has nothing to do with all those books in your room?" Aunt Mae asks shrewdly.

"Of course not."

"Hmph. I'll allow it—provided you attend *all* your other lessons today, Sisi, Jeni."

I haven't left any of our lessons early, so it's easy to tell who that is directed at.

"Even etiquette, Auntie. I swear it," Sisi says. And she fulfills that promise to the letter, even as the work drags on endlessly.

I wish I could find a moment in the busy roster of our lessons to thank Sisi, but surely she knows how much it means to me without me saying anything—not just that she'd arranged for the lessons, but that she sits quietly through a full two hours of etiquette in order to make it possible for me.

I don't pay any attention to Karili's obnoxious babbling, not with the excitement of a reading lesson to look forward to. Karili doesn't seem to notice my distraction—it's Sisi, and not me, who needs to be trained up into a proper lady.

I'm practically bouncing in my seat by the time the next instructor arrives. Jehan is a skinny, dark-haired man, wearing a shirt that's a little too big for him, pants that have been patched too many times at the knees, and a terrified expression. He can't be older than five and twenty, and he's got freckles all over his golden skin. I like the look of him at once. He reminds me a little bit of myself.

"L-lady Jeni?" he asks.

"Just Jeni, please. The title is my cousin's. Will you sit?"

"Th-th-thank you. Um. Master Elan said—I should—"

"I want to learn to read," I say frankly. Nervous as I am, I can hardly feel at all afraid of this poor, stammering lad. "Can you help?"

"Yes, yes, of course."

We start with the alphabet. He teaches me how to shape each letter and the sound they make. It takes most of the day, but he says I'm a quick learner. I hope he's not just flattering me—I do feel like I'm progressing fairly quickly through the exercises he sets for me. By the time night has fallen and I notice Aunt Mae skulking impatiently around the edges of the room, I am able to read out the four letters of my by-name, *J-E-N-I*, as well as the *A* that would change it to my True Name. This isn't much of an accomplishment: Kariana taught me at least this much before, but it's been years and I couldn't remember any of it prior to the lesson. Still, I feel as though I have a little more insight into one of the great mysteries that surrounds me, and I'm not sure I would have that without Jehan's patient teaching.

"Would you be able to come back tomorrow, or...?" I ask. "I'm sure you might have duties elsewhere, you must be busy..." I don't know exactly what a member of the konim does. Leasane is far too remote to have ever had a priest of its own sent there, so I've no knowledge of the way the whole thing works.

He answers as smoothly as I've heard him speak yet.

"Frankly, milady, there's very little to do. It's just me and Garem there now. The rest are long gone, and... I fear Garem is no longer entirely with us, either. I'm happy to leave the Tower of the Konim whenever I have the chance."

"Then will I see you tomorrow?" I ask, trying to keep the note of hope out of my voice. I don't want to seem too eager.

"Tomorrow, milady." He bows and takes his leave.

It's going to be a long time before I'm ready to help Sisi dig through the thick leather-bound books that fill every inch of spare space in her room, but at least I'm doing *something*.

I also send myself on another errand. I tell Sisi first, which feels like a necessary courtesy—this is, after all, *her* master plan to discover Lord Ricard's evil intentions and destroy him utterly. But I don't accept her offer to come with me.

"You," I whisper—we're in her bedchamber, and it's late, but there's no reason not to take as many precautions as we can to avoid attention—"are rather too noticeable, my dear cousin. People would *know* if you were out wandering the halls. I, on the other hand..."

She sighs loudly. "Curse you, you're right. I wish you weren't."

"Sorry. But I figure you need the information, even if you can't gather it yourself. We shouldn't wander around the palace blind, and it might be good to get a sense of where things are. I don't know if you've noticed, but they've basically either kept us locked in this splendidly gilded prison or sent servants to lead us where we're going like dogs on a leash."

"A very elegant leash."

"Indeed," I agree, for we've been waited on hand and foot, wanting for nothing, as long as we've been here. And we have not been allowed out of the servants' sight except for when we've been safely ensconced in our chambers. "I don't think I even know how we could get outside from here."

That makes her frown, as she realizes that I'm right. We're effectively imprisoned here—and she far more than me, for I at least can hope to slip beneath the notice of the servants. "When are you going?"

"Tomorrow, while you're having your luncheon." Sisi has been invited to dine with Patine and some of her other cousins, more Numbered girls distantly descended from a neighboring line that none of us knew existed until she got the invitation. "I figure Aunt Mae will be distracted worrying about whether or not you'll disgrace yourself and our entire family by using the wrong fork or something, and I'm not expected to be in any lessons, so everyone will probably forget I exist." As usual.

"That's a great idea."

"Thanks," I say, a little surprised. I know Sisi loves me, but she's never particularly free with praise. It simply isn't her way.

"I might just make a manageable spy out of you yet."

I stick my tongue out at that remark, and Sisi laughs. It's almost like old times.

The next day's morning appointments go by quickly.

We've progressed to learning actual dance steps, not just having our posture corrected, and Aunt Mae handles everything with the dressmaker. Sisi winks at me as Mari departs—and it's time for my adventure.

Sisi makes a big enough production out of dressing for her luncheon that I am able to creep out of our rooms while Aunt Mae is distracted by fussing over her hemline. Sisi catches my eye and smiles at me as I push the door to our rooms soundlessly open, and a warm spark of joy travels through me. It's nice to be back on the same side as Sisi, and against someone else, even if our mutual enemy this time is far more terrifying than an annoyed relative, and the possible consequences much more dire than some extra chores.

I draw in a deep breath, for the first time since I arrived in the chamber where I've been a pampered prisoner for the last weeks. Now, a little less exhausted than I was after our long journey, and a little more capable of curiosity, I can take the time to look down the long, shimmering hall. I notice closed doors every few feet of its length, crafted of the same gilded wood as the one that leads into our assigned rooms. I tiptoe down the hallway, cautiously moving away from our chambers.

I'm too nervous to open any of the doors, unsure what I would do if I actually saw someone. I could get in trouble, and even if I didn't, it would be awkward. No one actually *forbade* us from leaving the rooms we were assigned to, but I don't exactly think they want me sneaking through the halls either.

So, for today, I keep my exploration to pacing the

length of the hallway. I take in every detail I can see: the gentle curve of its shape, the polished golden shine of its walls and floors, the oppressive quiet, broken only by the patter of my feet against the ground.

On my second lap back down to the base of the hall, I notice little hidden panels in the walls. They're barely visible, only thin lines against the gold, but when I press on one lightly, it swings open to reveal a long, unlit staircase. I'm not sure what these secret doors are for, but it must mean something. I carefully close the panel again.

I try to store every little observation away in my mind, so when the time comes that I need them—if indeed it ever does—I'll be able to recall each detail I've encountered. Perhaps it will do Sisi some good, as she tries to learn her way around the palace. Unlikely though that seems to me, I still feel better doing this than I did waiting around in our rooms. Even if all I ever do with the information is spin it into a story to tell the children of the family one day, after I return to my home in the middle of nowhere, at least I'll have done something.

My walk, though I only go as far as up and down the hallway twice, takes almost an hour. I place one foot in front of the other to measure out my paces, trying to get a scope of the size of the place besides my stunned sense of its immensity. At the far end of the hall, I find only a closed door, made of heavy oak. I vaguely remember walking through it in the rush of our arrival, and I conclude that I'm not ready to venture out past the seemingly empty hallway where our rooms are. I need to get a little more familiar with the layout of the palace first. The possibility of getting lost in its many hallways is far too real, and too frightening to risk.

Though I'm unwilling to continue out into the other parts of the palace, I retrace my steps back past the entry to our rooms. I follow that path all the way in the opposite direction, to find that at the other end, the hall spills out into the open, to the crystal wall that marks the very edge of the palace itself. We're on the ground floor, so there's just a single step down, leading into the garden, clearly visible through the translucent walls. I'm too nervous to leave, but just glimpsing the bright flash of greenery does something to me that I'm not quite sure how to describe. I've been cooped up inside our suite of rooms for nearly a week. Spacious though they are— much bigger than the entire farmhouse in size—I haven't so much as seen the sun while I've been here.

I stand there for a long time, leaning against one of the gently gleaming golden interior walls, staring out through the crystal at the garden. I don't know how to describe the feeling that comes over me. It's as if there's an ancient, wordless song rising up in my heart. I even let myself hum along. I can just barely feel the touch of sunlight on my face through the thick crystal of the palace wall.

Like almost everyone in the Kingdom, my family worships Gaia, the Goddess that is the Earth itself. She is the Mother of all of us, from whom we came, and to whom we one day return. I've known those words, and the many small rituals of country worship, all my life. From the yearly dances Kariana once led through our fields, to my aunt's habit of leaving the best bit of a special meal aside "for the Goddess," to my uncle Willem's fondness for swearing in Her name, I have rarely gone a day without passing mention of Her. And I've rarely thought about Her any more deeply than that.

Yet, as I stand there, feeling the heat of the sun, seeing the perfect beauty of the unbroken green growth in front of me, something rises in my heart. I don't know what it is—worship, or gratitude, or something else I don't know how to name. I don't look for the words, just let myself feel that nameless and perfect warmth, the presence of the Goddess in the green.

CHAPTER TWELVE

*S*isi can't put off her face-to-face meeting with Lord Ricard forever. He summoned us here so that he could see the girl rumored to be the most beautiful creature in all Four Corners of the Earth, and he won't wait until the night of the ball to do so.

Of course, the order comes in the form of an invitation, hand-delivered by Elan, along with another elaborate gift, this one a pair of white pearl earrings. "His Royal Highness, Prince Ricard, Second in the Kingdom, begs the honor of Lady Sisi's presence at dinner tonight."

"Tell His Highness I will come," Sisi responds, and she doesn't even visibly grit her teeth. She's become a more accomplished liar over the course of our stay here.

Elan bows and departs, leaving the three of us alone to make our preparations. Aunt Mae and Sisi are expected at the Prince's quarters at sundown tonight— Sisi as the guest of honor, and Aunt Mae as the chaperone who will protect her reputation. The whole thing seems foolish to me, since the whole *point* of Sisi having been brought all this way to the palace in the first place is that Lord Ricard wanted to lay claim to the most beautiful woman on Earth, an activity which would seem to contradict the presence of a chaperone. But I didn't design Numbered etiquette, that much is for sure, and I won't pretend to understand it.

In fact, I am so irrelevant to this whole venture that I'm not even invited to dinner. Sisi sulks when she realizes that. But I'm not qualified to chaperone because of my youth, and that means that I would only be intruding on the dinner.

"It's okay, Sisi," I try to tell her. "I can keep myself occupied for a few hours." There is plenty of palace left for me to explore, after all.

"But I want you with me, Jena. How am I supposed to stand up to him without you there? I'm stronger with you at my side." She says all that quietly, so Aunt Mae can at least pretend not to overhear.

"It'll be okay. We'll plan before you go, while I'm helping you dress. And as soon as you get back, you can tell me everything."

Sisi favors me with a small smile. "Thank you, Jena. You always know what to say."

I'm not sure how much my words actually helped— she seems only a little less tense—but I'm still pleased she at least wants me to feel I'm useful, in spite of the fact that I can't come along to the dinner with her.

Instead, I focus on the preparations. She needs her ears pierced, for one thing—farm girls don't generally have a lot of need for jewelry, so neither of us have pierced ears, but it would be the height of rudeness not to wear Lord Ricard's gift to the dinner, according to the etiquette lessons we're still struggling through daily. That, at least, makes some small measure of sense to me, unlike much of what we've learned here—but I can see how, if someone gave you a gift, they might want you to be sure and wear it.

I've never done this before, but I understand the theory. I wipe down a sewing needle and meet Sisi's eyes.

"You ready?"

"Just get it over with," she says, gritting her teeth. I push the needle through her ear, surprised to find it no harder than breaking through tough cloth for a stitch. A single drop of blood wells up. "Huh."

"Was it bad?" I ask.

"Not at all. I'll do yours next, if you want." Sisi has enough jewelry now, sent by the prince, that she can afford to give some of hers to me.

"I'd like that," I agree. I'll never look as pretty as Sisi does with the white pearl earring against her dark brown skin, but it would be nice to have something elegant. I'm jealous of her pretty things, even though I know she doesn't want them.

I do. I don't think I'd take what goes along with them to get them, though. Sisi seems in turns enraged by and terrified of Lord Ricard's attentions, whether it comes in the form of gifts or notes or, as with tonight, an actual face-to-face encounter. And I have to admit that I don't quite understand why.

Oh, Sisi is always to some degree unimpressed with the men who fawn over her beauty. No doubt it's worse with Lord Ricard, since he hasn't even *seen* her, just heard rumors about the most beautiful girl on Earth and decided he had to have her. But, little though she likes any of the boys or men who have expressed interest in her over the years, I've never seen her like this, except maybe right after the Golden Soldier tried to grab her arm on our way here.

Sullen and quiet by turns, always with her mind on something else, Sisi doesn't even seem like herself—and I know her better than anyone. What I don't know, not really, is *why*.

I know she blames Lord Ricard for Kariana's death, and possibly even for the loss of her own parents. I know she despises the idea of being kept like a trophy.

I *don't* understand why she doesn't simply walk away. Surely no one would actually dare try to stop us from leaving the palace—and since Sisi is now the owner of a small fortune in jewels, it's not like we'd have to worry about things back home the way we did before we came. She could just sell a few of Lord Ricard's presents and we'd be the richest family in the Quarter.

I'm hesitant to ask, knowing that Sisi's temper has been a fearsome thing of late, but she seems to be in a talkative mood, especially as far as Sisi's moods go, so I dare to ask, "What are you so upset about tonight?" as I pierce her second ear.

"I'm worried I'll lose my temper and bite clean through Ricard's head," she says, turning to admire her new earrings in the mirror. "These look well, Jena, thank you."

"Everything looks well on you. It's hardly an achievement on my part to make you look good, cousin."

"Nonsense. You could have made them uneven, or any number of other things. Now switch with me, it's your turn."

She offers to let me choose from a wide variety of earrings in her collection. I don't want to lay claim to anything studded with diamonds or made of gold—two materials so rich even I, ignorant as I am, can recognize as extraordinarily valuable—so instead I tell her to pick for me. She chooses simple golden studs with a brilliant green stone in each.

"Emeralds," Sisi explains. "A good choice. They'll match your eyes, I think. They'll suit you far better than they do me."

With her rich coloring and exquisite features, *everything* suits Sisi, but I wager it would annoy her if I said as much, so I just say, "Thank you. You don't have to go giving me your precious jewels just to make me feel better, you know. It's very nice of you."

"Please. It's nothing. I've only got the one set of ears." With that, she slides the needle through my earlobe. It burns, exactly one second's duration of fiery and ferocious agony, and then she's putting the earring itself in. "Lovely," she pronounces me.

I turn toward the mirror just as she had. In spite of a thin trickle of blood where the needle had punctured my skin, I can see in myself some of what I usually only see looking at Sisi. I look like a young lady. Maybe even like a beautiful one. "They're lovely."

"I've still got to do the second side. Turn around."

I pivot obediently. While Sisi is fussing over me, trying to find the perfect angle for the needle to pierce my skin, I try again. "I mean, you did agree to come here, but it seems like you hate the idea of having anything to do with Lord Ricard—why is that?"

The needle rips through my skin. "You know, you have the most peculiar ears," Sisi muses, completely ignoring my question. "I don't know how I never noticed, in more than ten years of sharing a bed with you. You've got this extra little bend here, and it almost looks like your ears are pointed at the tops."

I scowl at Sisi. I've actually noticed the exact thing she's commenting on before—it's a small fold of skin within the shell of my ear, where most people's are smooth. And my ears have a funny shape—coming to a point at the end, not rounded as most folks' are. She's not telling me anything I don't know. And I still hate having any of the ways I'm physically different emphasized to me. Which Sisi, better than anyone else, has reason to know. She must be bringing it up on purpose to distract me, which isn't very nice but *is* very typical. "You're not answering my question."

"I know." She sighs and throws herself across the bed. "The truth is, Jena, I don't *know* what I'm so scared of. Because I don't know what Ricard wants from me."

"That makes sense." It's more than a little absurd that one of the most powerful and important men in the whole Kingdom would drag an orphaned girl across the Earth to attend a ball, showering her with gifts before he'd even met her. I'm as confused as she is. And I can see why that would make her all the more uncomfortable, knowing he expects something from her but not knowing what it is.

"There's only one thing I can think of that he might want."

I pause. I have some idea of what she means, from our earlier conversations about it, but I know how little Sisi likes to discuss the topic of desire, especially the desire that men tend to feel for her. I don't want to make her more uncomfortable than she already is, with her meeting with Lord Ricard looming. "You mean...sex?"

"Not just that. I don't even know if he'll want me that way—and neither does he, for he's never so much as seen my face. I imagine what he wants is status."

"But he's Second in the Kingdom. You're only Four Hundred and Whatever."

"Fifty-Third," she corrects, and then laughs a little bit at herself. "Goddess, here I go, acting like any of this *matters*. When the Earth is dying. When farmers and their families are going hungry because there's not enough food to eat. When the other peoples who have walked the Earth with us for as long as anyone can remember are all dead or disappearing. And here I am, playing a game in which I suspect I am nothing but a prize. That's what I mean, cousin, when I say I fear Ricard wants me for the status. He sends me these trinkets of his affection because he means to keep me as a far richer symbol. A beautiful thing, to be admired and envied by all."

I can see how that would be Sisi's worst fear. All she wants is to be treated like she is more than her looks, and to be *useful* to our suffering Earth. I can't imagine anything she would hate more than to be admired, and envied, and useless. "So tell him that's not what you want," I suggest.

"Jena," she sighs. "I can't just tell him no."

"Why not?"

"Because he's the *Crown Prince,* and I'm just the last of an unimportant country house. No one will stand up to him for me."

"Aunt Mae would never make you do anything you don't want," I argue. "We could just leave and ride for home."

"Do you think he would let us go so easily? Do you think, even if our stubborn old donkey managed to outrun Ricard's fine horses, he wouldn't be able to follow us to Prinnsfarm? To the ends of the Earth, if he so chose?"

The thought shakes me to my core. "You're saying you're afraid you won't have a choice?"

"I'm saying I expect that I won't. That, whatever it is Ricard decides he wants from me, I'll have no choice but to give it to him. And since I don't know what that will be, or why he might want it..."

"I understand." And I do, far more than I ever have before. She's dealing with something almost beyond the scope of my imagination, but now I at least know enough to be able to think how it must be affecting her. No wonder she's been so different from her usual self since we arrived at the palace. She must be constantly on edge, waiting for the next gift to arrive, wondering what the price for all these favors she never asked for will be, when it comes due.

Sisi's eyes dart toward the door—still firmly closed and locked—and then she whispers fiercely, "I hate him, Jena. I hate what he did to Kariana, and to women like her. I hate him for the role he may have played in my parents' deaths. I hate him for the other things he's done to this Kingdom, things I can't yet prove. But more than any of that, I hate him for making me feel this way. Like I'm just some *thing*, powerless to stop him from whatever game he's playing. Alone against a threat I can't hope to prevent."

"But you're not alone," I tell her. "I know I'm not much, Sisi, but you've got me. You'll always have me."

That wins a small smile from her. "You're a better friend than I deserve, little bird."

"Don't call me that. I'm not little." I indicate my girth with a grin.

"You are short, though."

I stick my tongue out at her and she laughs.

"What did I ever do to deserve a friend like you, Jena? A friend that would follow me to the ends of the Earth like this, and still make me laugh?"

"You didn't have to do anything," I say simply, truthfully. "Just be you."

Sisi rises from her bed then and crosses the room back

over to me. She drops a gentle kiss on top of my dark hair. "I love you, Jena. I hope you know that."

"I love you too. More than anybody." We don't say it a lot, but it's true, and it always has been. I hope it always will be too, no matter what dangers we have to face.

The moment of tenderness doesn't last long. With Sisi, it never does. "Well, my loyal lady companion, can I trouble you to help me dress?"

I arrange Sisi's skirts and do her hair so that she's ready to go in plenty of time. She's still looking a bit fretful, not at all like her usual confident and composed self, but she doesn't seem to be quite so much on the edge of a breakdown anymore, and I decide to take that victory where I can find it.

My evening, spent in the rooms waiting for them to return, is not so much peaceful as boring. I'm too shy to try to engage any of the maids in conversation, so I end up eating my (admittedly very fine) supper of roast hare in silence.

It's nearly midnight, and I, still used to going to bed with the sun and rising before it comes up in the morning, am yawning fiercely by the time Sisi and Aunt Mae troop back through the doors.

Aunt Mae gives me a sharp look. "You ought to be abed, Jeni." She glances from me to Sisi, and back to me. "Well, I suppose I'll only catch you creeping through the corridors in the middle of the night. You might as well go tell your cousin everything, Sisi."

Sisi, subdued, leans over and kisses Aunt Mae's cheek. For the first time, I notice Sisi has grown so tall that she actually stands a few inches over our aunt. "Thank you, Auntie. I won't keep Jena up too late, I promise. We've lessons in the morning, after all."

That uncharacteristic conscientiousness earns Sisi a suspicious glance, but Aunt Mae lets us go, back into Sisi's room with the door closed and locked behind us.

Sisi immediately begins undoing the back laces of her gown, and I rush over to help her. "Damned thing is cursed uncomfortable, and Ricard wouldn't rest until he'd stuffed me full of delicacies from all Four Corners of the Earth."

I remind myself that she has good reason to be upset, and that it's not fair to be resentful just because she's complaining about having been fed fancies from all over the Kingdom by a handsome prince, something any ordinary woman ought to be thrilled about and which I, personally, rather imagine I would enjoy. Well, at least the first bit, with the pastries—I'm not sure what I would do with a man's attentions.

Now stripped down to her corset and shift, Sisi steps out of the abandoned gown, leaving it pooled on the floor. I help her unlace her corset and tentatively ask, "So, was it horrible?"

"Not as much as I feared," she admits. "Ricard didn't do or say anything inappropriate...though that leaves me with the same trouble as before, simply not having any way to know the nature of his intentions."

"What *did* he say?"

She draws in a deep breath, now free from all her restrictive garments and clad only in a white linen shift.

To me, she looks more beautiful like this than she had in her jewel-encrusted new gown. I start helping her unpin her hair, so it can rise back into its natural puff of curls, as she explains. "He was nothing but courteous."

"Wait, wait," I interrupt. "I can't picture this story. Start from the beginning. What does he look like?"

She laughs at that, as I'd intended her to—although my curiosity about the King's own brother is no jest. "He's tall, taller than me even. Very slender. I'll grant him that he has a handsome face. Pale, with strong features. He has chestnut-brown hair that he wears cropped very short. Are you appeased, or shall I also describe the details of his wardrobe, and each of the sixteen courses that were served at supper?"

Honestly, I wouldn't mind if she did—I like to be able to picture a thing in my mind's eye—but I get the sense that she's hoping to draw to some sort of a point, so I don't push her for any more unimportant details. Maybe one day she'll regale me with them while we ride back toward home. For now, I'm happy to listen to whatever she needs to say. "No, no. Tell me whatever you wish."

She lies across the bed, resting her head on her crossed arms. "So, handsome and charming, that's the Prince. Cold, too, as you'd expect. He was clearly always thinking of something else. We made conversation—you might not see how I'm capable of it, but in fact I did manage to keep things civil."

"I know you *can* get along with folks when you want to. You just choose not to."

"Exactly," she says triumphantly, as though she

doesn't notice—or doesn't care—that I'm teasing her. "I always say you understand me as no one else does."

"And... you wished to get along with Lord Ricard?" I'm glad that Sisi hasn't gotten herself clapped in a dungeon for impertinence or something like that, but I can't say I quite understand how she has changed course so quickly, when just a few hours ago, she was convinced the man was responsible for every evil that had ever been done in the Earth and probably a few more that were still in the making.

"Not exactly. But no more did I wish to fight with him." She isn't meeting my eyes. "I think... I think he's cleverer than I expected. Cleverer even than I am."

It's not like Sisi to admit herself bested at anything.

"I'm afraid," she continues. "Afraid to move against him. Afraid to keep meeting with him. Afraid even to go on gathering information as we've been doing. All the night long, he kept making these little comments—nothing explicit, nothing that I could have said was beyond the boundaries of courtesy—but just enough, so that I got the sense that he knows what you and I have been up to, that he knows we're trying to figure out what's going wrong in the Kingdom and that we suspect he's behind it."

"What sorts of comments?" I ask, trying to hide the way my voice trembles in the middle of the question. The thought of Sisi being afraid of anything, anything at all, is enough to send a shivering chill down my spine.

"Oh, it's hard to describe, really. It was just...just the tone of voice, I guess. He'd pass me the wine, and then say something about how it had been a particularly good year for grapes in the Third Corner, and I could tell that what he was really saying was, *I know you've been snooping around, I know you've been looking at farm records and weather patterns and seeing all the changes since I sent my soldiers after the witches.* And I honestly can't say *how* I knew what he meant, because, like I said, every word out of his mouth was perfectly courteous the entire time I was there. It was almost surreal, talking to someone who spoke so much like he was reading from a script rather than actually speaking *to* me."

That does sound unpleasant. "And do you feel like he threatened you at all?"

She sighs. "That's a hard question to answer. If his jibes about the state of the Kingdom were subtle, anything he said about me personally was a thousand times more so. He didn't leer at me, not really, not in front of Aunt Mae. But of course, he said a great deal about how well I looked in the gown, and in the earrings, and there was one..."

"What?" I prompt gently. Not just because I want to hear—although I very much do—but also because I get the sense that Sisi badly needs to speak the words. After something like what she's been through tonight, an ordeal that filled her with fears and doubts without being *clearly* threatening in some obvious way she could point to, she no doubt could use some reassurance that she was not to blame, from someone she trusts. And obviously, I have nominated myself for the task.

"There was one thing. That he said. When he saw

the gown, he said... 'I knew that color would look well on you. I had Mari send up the sketches, and I've thought about it every night since.'"

I shiver. "Sisi, are you *joking*?"

"I wish I were," she responds, not meeting my eyes.

"I thought you said it was *subtle*! That's not subtle at all, it's... well, it's disgusting!" The thought of this man whom she fears and despises thinking about Sisi at night, taking the opportunity to remind her that he fantasizes about her beauty and her body, fills me with anger. If Lord Ricard were here, I'd shove him into the dirt, just like I did with that soldier of his at the inn.

"I just..." She hesitates, and I remain carefully quiet. I don't want to push her to share anything she'd rather not, especially not about such an ordeal, but I also want her to know that I'm here for her, here to listen. "I just—there was so much in that. Like, it was such a reminder that he has total control over our lives here, and we're completely in his power. Everyone works for him. The people who make our food, who make our clothes, who dress us, they all answer to Ricard, and if he told them to do something, they'd have to do it. And... and more than that, he's thinking about me, *like that,* like... like, basically, an object. It's the very thing I've been so afraid of. And, I know this sounds paranoid, but...how does he know what I look like, to picture me in the gown?"

That's a really good point. I wish it weren't. "You think he's been spying on us?"

"I don't know. But I have to wonder. Did he hide somewhere to get a glimpse of me? Does he have a way to see into these rooms? There's so much we don't know, and it just felt like... It felt like he *wanted* to remind me of that. Like he was enjoying the fact that he had all this power over me, and... I don't know, Jena. It just... it made me so angry."

That's a lie, and I know it. Sisi isn't angry. She's terrified.

But I love her much too well to call her out on it. Let her be angry, if she can.

Sisi shares my bed that night, by wordless agreement. I can't bear the thought of sending her off to sleep in her own room, where she'd no doubt be tormented by the memories of Ricard's carefully chosen barbs and the anticipation of what more lay in her future meetings with him.

She falls asleep easily, as she often does. I can't sleep, though. I'm consumed by the thoughts of what she'd told me of this night.

I just don't *understand*. I know what it is to look at Sisi and feel something like admiration, even desire. All my life, I've longed to be as beautiful as she is. Recently, sometimes, I find myself with other longings, too—to press my lips to hers, to take her hand in mine, to catch another glimpse of her as she leaves a room. I don't know what that means, but I know it's what men feel when they look at her, too.

And yet, I can't imagine caring about that more than I care about her. About her righteous anger, and her hope for a better Earth. Her brilliant mind, and her love for learning all she can about the Earth and its Kingdom. Her love for me, and the small ways she shows it.

I would love Sisi the same if she were as ugly as I am. I just wish the men, like Lord Ricard, who want to lay claim to her could feel the same. Or, better still, that she and I could go back home together, and stay safely out of their reach forever.

CHAPTER THIRTEEN

*W*ithin a week, my exploration becomes much bolder. Each day, I wait until Sisi is out and then start to journey further into the secrets the castle holds.

My first stop is the hidden stair I discovered on my very first expedition. It's pitch dark in the stairway, and my heart pounds, imagining what sorts of horrors could be lurking here, so carefully hidden away.

Step by step, I continue downward, my hand sliding along the smooth, blank surface of the wall. I wish for a handhold, but find none. The only means I can think of to comfort myself is to count each pace, to keep track of how long I've been descending, to remind myself that, whatever it feels like, it has not actually been forever. I can always return to the well-lit safety of my rooms.

At the count of fifty, I stop, having run face-first into another door. With a little pressure, I am able to push it open, which is a relief, since the alternative would be to die trapped inside this wall. I take a deep breath, preparing myself for whatever might be on the other side, and step through.

Suddenly, everything is brightness and noise. I have discovered not the horrible dungeon I was imagining, but a servant's passageway down into what I can clearly recognize as the palace's kitchen. The frightening dark silence of the secret stair is entirely gone, replaced by a busy hive of activity. There are dozens of cooks and maids and messengers bustling around—a few of the maids in livery, but most of the people dressed in the same sort of simple homespun clothes I wear at home when helping with the chores.

Well, that explains how the servants seem to appear and disappear out of thin air. They're traveling by these well-hidden stairs, set into the wall so that no one notices their comings and goings.

I remain half-hidden in the doorway, looking around at everything: at the great central table where half a dozen cooks are engaged in chopping various fruits and vegetables I don't recognize; at the two roaring, wood-burning ovens, each large enough that a full-grown person could easily fit inside. I shake off that disturbing image and turn to head back up the stairs.

Before I can, someone, a short, sharp-faced woman, catches sight of me. "You, girl!"

My heart stops in my chest for a moment. I've been caught skulking around here, where I don't belong, and I'm surely about to be in trouble. What will I say? How will I explain my presence here? Curiosity—the truth—

seems a suddenly weak excuse for creeping about the palace like a thief. I hope I don't get Sisi into trouble, at least. Her own studies with the books, her plan against the Prince himself, as little as I understand all that, is certainly more dangerous, and if I cast suspicion on her...

But my whirlwind of anxious thoughts is interrupted when all the woman says is, "Take this!"

She thrusts a heavy platter toward me, with a roast chicken on it. I follow where she points, carrying it from the central table to a side station where a stout young man slices it with a carving knife. When that's done, I'm ordered on to the next station to help drizzle a golden sauce over the whole plate.

It takes me most of the afternoon to find a tidy opening for my escape. Finally, I carefully place the last elegantly carved piece of fruit I've been dipping in a mixture of sugar and cinnamon onto its heavily laden silver tray, and flee back up the same staircase I'd arrived by. Once again, I manage to become unnoticed.

I am not as lucky back in our own rooms. Aunt Mae is waiting for me when I arrive, wearing a heavy scowl. "Where have you been?"

"I'm sorry, Auntie. Just, well, I was just walking around." It's not quite a lie.

She smacks me hard on the ear. I wince, though I'm grateful my punishment isn't worse. "Stay in the rooms from now on! I don't want you getting lost or into trouble."

"Yes, Auntie."

After that, I confine my excursions to the nighttime,

after Aunt Mae has gone to bed, and I don't stay gone as long as I had that day in the kitchen. I leave at midnight or later, and stay out for an hour or two at most, and I'm always nervous every second that I'm outside of the safe area of acceptability marked by that heavy gilded door. But I can't bring myself to stop.

Soon enough, I have a mental map of the entire palace. It's laid out just like the Kingdom itself: four sections, sprawling out from the inner center, like a wheel. In the middle section, which I realize is where we've been taken for our dance lessons, are the useful rooms: the throne room, the banquet halls, the offices, the infirmaries, the kitchens down below, and the high tower where the priests live up above. Radiating out are the four long, thin sections, one for each type of Gaia's children: for the beasts of the field, the adirim, the pahyat, and of course for the humans.

Only the latter two are inhabited by people. The Quarter of the Pahyat houses those few, like Elan, who are still in royal service. I leave them their privacy, not wanting to snoop around peoples' homes. The Quarter of the Humans is, of course, always bustling with Numbered and servants alike, and I leave it as quickly as possible.

Instead, I limit myself to the entirely unoccupied wings of the palace. The animals don't care if I peek in their stables or coops, and the adirim haven't been seen in years. So there's little risk I'll be caught as I walk where they once walked.

I start with the Quarter of the Beasts. Some of the

rooms are so big, I can't see the ceiling when I tilt my head back all the way; others are so small, I can't crawl inside. In one abandoned chamber, I find scorch marks on the wall and wonder, almost laughing at the absurd idea, if dragons might once have slept here. But most of the rooms are ordinary, holding the kinds of typical animals that a palace of this size needs to keep itself running: horses, poultry fowl, pigs, cows and bison.

Finally, my midnight walks grow bolder, taking me to the furthest wing of the palace, across the well-populated central hub—I cut through the kitchens, managing, this time, not to be taken for a scullery maid. This is the Quarter of the Adirim, the legendary go'im of great magical power. The most mysterious, and mightiest, of all of Gaia's children. My heart thrums in excitement as I enter the main corridor.

This wing, though, is locked away. I can't get the door open, even when I push with all my force, pressing my shoulder against the unyielding oak. Whatever secrets are in there, they are kept from me.

Well, then. If I cannot find the secrets of the palace on foot, I will need other ways of learning them. I certainly can't go back to my ignorance now, not when Sisi needs me, not when I've just begun to glimpse how much there is to know.

But my duties to my Numbered cousin do not begin and end with her schemes to unseat Lord Ricard. I also need to ready her for the evenings when—more and more frequently—she is called to dine with him.

I am the one who has to help her into the best of her

new gowns, one of a pearly blue shade that sets off the richness of her complexion. Her hair, as dark as a raven's wing, puffs out in a perfect halo around her head, ending just above her finely sloped shoulders. One of Lord Ricard's many expensive gifts, a glimmering golden necklace, encircles her throat and hangs down to the low neckline of the dress, emphasizing her full bosom. Despite the sour expression on her face, her skin is practically glowing from a range of ointments and lotions I have applied.

"How do I look?" she grumbles.

I sigh. "Stunning, as always. Of course."

"There's no 'of course.' I'm having dinner with the Second in the Kingdom, Jena. I have to look the part."

"I thought you would want to look as hideous as possible. Drive him off, and all that." I'm half-joking, and of course I don't think Sisi could ever quite manage looking hideous, but nonetheless she sighs at me.

"You don't understand," Sisi says, smoothing her skirts.

I barely manage to stop myself from rolling my eyes.

Sisi finishes fussing with her dress just as Elan arrives to show her and Aunt Mae to the dining room. My aunt, as official chaperone, must be at all of their meetings.

Instead of joining the supper, I'm to spend the evening sitting here in our rooms, dining from a plate the maids will bring me, waiting for them to come back. Apparently, this supper is a private affair, so I'm not invited, but Aunt Mae also has to be there, to stop things from being *inappropriately* private.

All these rules give me a bit of a headache. As much as I hate being excluded from all the excitement, at least I don't have to worry about applying the etiquette lessons I've only half paid attention to. Especially when they seem to contradict themselves as often as not.

I consider going out to wander the palace, but I suppose I ought to be back in this room at the moment my aunt and cousin return, lest they begin to worry. The night will have been stressful enough for them both without returning to find me missing. More than that, Sisi often comes back from these evenings with Lord Ricard in a quiet rage, and Aunt Mae can't calm her half so well as I can.

I need to be there for her, as soon as I can. Still, that doesn't mean my evening has to be entirely wasted. I can at least practice the skill I know I need most if I am to be of real help to my cousin: reading.

I tiptoe into Sisi's room, where the books are, and look at them. I can't read any of the words, but I try to make out some of the letters. I recognize the "J" that begins my own name. My lessons have taken me that far, at least.

When I stumble on the golden book that Sisi had been reading earlier, one about the homes and civilizations of the adirim, I flip it open, just to take in the unfamiliar sight of black text on white parchment. We don't have a single real book in our house—we have no need for one. My father keeps the household accounts in a worn old journal, made of clothes worn down to rags and stitched back together by Aunt Mae. He writes in it with a lump of charcoal that wears away quickly. It's functional and simple and I've never paid any attention to it, unlike this book. This is a different kind of object entirely; though it's of no more use to me than my father's ledger, it exerts a strange pull on me. It's beautiful, like everything in the palace, and as I look at the dark lines against the white pages, I can't stop myself from wondering what secrets are hidden in this strange sea of symbols.

As I flip through the pages, I see a map of the Earth. I recognize what it must be instinctively: blue for the waters of the sea and the rivers that run through the land of Gaia, small triangles that depict mountain heights, tiny drawings of trees to represent forest and grove. I even see a picture of a crown and wonder if that means the Capital, where I am now.

There's little else I can even try to identify, as small handwritten labels distinguish all the other places in the map. I try to deduce the words, but it's like every other time I've tried to read outside my lessons with Jehan— without the context, I am entirely lost. Still, I make what meaning I can out of it.

I look in the southern and western part of the map, away from the City, and know that must be where I came from. These thin, scrawled lines show the outline of the second Corner of the Earth, where Leasane is. I can follow the great road part of the way—the meaning of the long black line seems obvious, and at least there, I can muddle out the capitalized H and R for High Road to confirm my guess—but I'm not sure which of the many small black dots represents my own hometown, if any of them do. Maybe Leasane is so small a place it doesn't deserve to be named on this map, though it was once the entire universe to me.

I push away my sudden, surprising sadness and make myself focus on the possibilities that lie before me. I trace my finger toward the East, along the road away from the City, farther than I've ever gone. Aunt Mae said that my mother went east when she left. I wonder how far. I wonder if she went all the way toward the great blue expanse of sea on the far side of this map.

One town in particular catches my attention. It has a silver dot, where most of the places on the map are represented in plain black, and a word—a name—is scrawled above it. I wonder what it says. I squint, which of course does nothing to improve my literacy. Still, I find myself imagining what it would be like if that tiny dot were where my mother came from, and trying to picture what it might be like there.

I imagine all sorts of things. A place of comforts, of rich fabrics and woods as this palace is, but without the sparkling and sterile exterior. Maybe there's always enough food to eat—not the odd delicacies of the palace, but good, rich, solid food. Comforting, as Aunt Mae makes it, but prepared by my mother's hands.

I wonder if it's a place filled to the brim with friends and family. Perhaps my mother has married again and maybe I have another father there, one who isn't so quiet or stubborn, one who wouldn't hold himself so far away from me. Maybe I have a brother or sister, the way all the other children I know do. Maybe even several.

I can see myself as part of a band of laughing, playing children, included not out of kindness or pity, the way Sisi tolerates me, but simply because I belonged. I would have something to do, something useful. Good work, like I do on the farm, but more fulfilling. I know I must be good for more than climbing branches. Maybe I could find what that is.

Maybe she looks just like me. That's what my aunt says. Maybe we would stand next to each other like reflections in a mirror, knowing each other, seeing each other, and maybe we would both know at that moment that we had found what has always been missing from both of our lives.

Maybe she'd hold me close and tell me how sorry she was to have left me. That it was a mistake, it always had been a mistake, and that all she wanted now was to be a true mother to me.

Maybe all these wonders, or more that I cannot even begin to imagine, lie in that town, any one of these towns, these little dots on Sisi's borrowed map, each one an unknown and wonderful Kingdom of its own. Maybe I will see all of it with my own eyes, someday.

Before I can lose myself any further in this foolish line of thinking, though, I hear the door open and look up. As I've become used to in the wake of these dinners, Sisi looks a mess.

Well, all right, she looks as lovely as she did before she left, but with her lips bitten red as if she's been trying to stop herself from saying something that was just on the tip of her tongue. I can even see the wetness of a tear welling in her eye.

I look up at her, biting back my urge to babble apologies for being in her room, searching instead for the right words to comfort her. Finally, giving up on being able to actually bring her any peace, I simply ask, "Sisi, what's wrong?"

I'm braced for a storm of wrath, shouting, screaming, anything. It's what I expect. Instead, Sisi goes to sit at the corner of the bed, slowly, slowly, moving as though each of her limbs is intolerably, unbearably heavy. "I can't, Jena."

"Talk to me."

"Please, don't ask me to."

I stand there for several long, long moments, frozen by my fear for her and my own uncertainty. Finally, I close the distance between us, lean in almost close enough to kiss her, and rest my hand gently against her cheek. "I love you, Sisi. Whatever you're facing, whatever this is, I'm at your side. Even if you can't tell me."

She reaches up and laces her fingers through mine, pulling our joined hands down to rest in her lap. "Make me a promise, Jena?"

"Of course."

"After the ball, when I have to... I'll have to stay. Promise me you'll leave this place. I don't want you spending your life trapped here."

"I'm not leaving you," I say at once, instinctively.

"You're meant for more than this. More than what lies ahead for me."

"I'm meant to be with you."

She squeezes my fingers gently in hers. "You are so young."

This is the Sisi I can barely stand, who thinks she's *so* much cleverer than everyone else. One of my favorite things about her is that she doesn't have a sense of pride about her looks, for all everyone else is always praising her for them, but she can be painfully condescending in other ways. I start to snap back at her, but something about the trembling in her hands stops me. She lets go and turns away, and I realize with a terrified jolt that Sisi, strong, unshakeable, all-knowing Sisi, is trying to hide her tears. "I promise," I say, my own voice thick with an emotion I do not recognize.

CHAPTER FOURTEEN

J'm trying to get better at reading, but it's hard. I still get bogged down in the words quickly if I work at it too long. I practice every day until, at times, my head is throbbing with the effort of making sense of all of the words and I'm so weary I can hardly make my eyes stay focused on the page, the letters fogging into nonsense.

Still, I try. Now that I've explored every part of the palace I can that isn't locked up tight or flooded with people, and with the Midwinter's Eve Ball still a few weeks away, there's little else I can do to help Sisi, or to feel close to her. I have to unlock this secret, the mystery of how the words give up their meanings through the page, if I am to make myself of any use in her quest to find out Lord Ricard's secrets and discover why magic has abandoned the Kingdom.

Jehan warns me sternly that it will be a long time before I can make it through anything like the thick volumes of history that Sisi keeps on her shelf. But he brings me simpler books. Among the volumes in the royal library are myths for children and narratives written in everyday language. Reading them helps me understand something of the great books my cousin always has her perfectly shaped nose buried in. While she's digging through those dense volumes, I start to look over her shoulder. Sometimes I can even keep up with Sisi's reasoning as she debates the issue she's currently considering.

That's something, at least. I may not quite be earning my keep as an aide to her search yet, but we can have a real discussion. I don't offer too many opinions of my own, but I'll ask the odd question, hoping I'm not annoying her too terribly.

"It seems the adirim really did once walk the land of Gaia," Sisi comments. We are reading—or more accurately, she is reading, and I am watching her read—an unbearably dry book titled *One Year Amongst the Fair Folk: A Few Thoughts on the Adirish Personages of Gaia* by Elidino Karrson. It is somehow even less exciting than it sounds.

"You think so?" I ask.

"Can you imagine this Elidino having the necessary imagination to make such things up? He just wrote about watching an adirit use their magic to fly from treetop to treetop with all the excitement I might use to describe doing the laundry."

"All right, I'll give you that he doesn't seem the creative type. But do you think it's true that the adirim could really fly? Maybe he was impressionable, and he heard someone say something, and wrote it down—"

"It's a decent thought, I'll give you that, but...you remember the game we used to play back on the farm, Heard-You-Say?"

"Aye." It's a simple game, popular among farm children, given that it requires nothing whatsoever in terms of materials to play, and can be done even between chores if one is quick about it. The players sit in a circle, and one begins with a phrase, whispering it into another's ear. That player then passes what she heard onto the next, and so on, until the last player gets the message and recites, 'I heard you say...' with whatever message he has heard. It's usually hopelessly garbled nonsense, much to everyone's delight.

"I think when someone passes a made-up idea along, it becomes like a game of Heard-You-Say. If none of these people had ever really seen an adirit, the story would change. One would hear the adirim called the Fair Folk and think it meant they were blond of hair. This story of them flying would make them winged like bats in some versions, and birds in others, and butterflies in a third."

I have to concede that she's made a fair argument.

"Yet when you look at what's been written about them, even in books by different writers written hundreds of years apart, it's entirely consistent from one writer to the next. they look like humans, but taller, with long dark hair and golden-bronze skin. Their beauty is unmatched. They are able to use magic with a force we can neither understand nor duplicate. They even use it to fly. They speak only the Old Tongue to each other as a means to keep themselves distant from us, and they are unlikely to approach us at all. They generally live in small groups, living among their sisters and mothers. I don't even see any male adirim mentioned in this book, or the others I've read."

"So you're saying—"

"I'm saying that if there were really no such thing as adirim, there would be some variation. We wouldn't get the same exact story again and again. The fact that we do means that all of these writers are writing about something. Something real."

"You think so?"

"I do."

"You think there are really adirim out there?"

"I don't think there still are, no."

"Well, what happened to them then?"

"I think Ricard killed them. Like he did Kariana. Like he essentially did to my parents. Like he does to anyone who disagrees with him or threatens his power," Sisi says, and there is a silence. It goes on for a long moment while I draw in a shaky breath, trying to wrap my flailing mind around what she's just said.

"You must be joking."

"No. I believe it. I think that there were adirim in the Kingdom until very recently. They used to walk among us, in times within living memory. How else would people have written it down? But when the Royal School for magic was finally closed down, and after trade with the pahyat stopped, I suspect that the adirim began to withdraw from the Kingdom. Not completely, not as they have now, but they were no longer living with people, no longer having children with them, no longer a part of society, no longer ruled by our King. Instead, they went back to their own lands, somewhere in the Eastern part of the Earth. After all, it's where the First Queen came from, and she's the one who brought magic into the Kingdom in the first place. I think that makes the most sense. And it's very rare, but I've seen some letters from hedge witches or farmers in that part of the Earth saying that they'd seen an adirit, or even spoken to one. And then, within our lifetime, even that stopped. And no one I know has even heard a rumor of one, though everyone is as sure as can be that they did once exist. So, I imagine that we need to look within very recent years to see what has changed. And *who* do we know who runs a violent and very efficient army and has an extreme hatred for magic in all its forms?"

"Now you're just making things up," I say through my dry throat. The very idea is horrifying—not least because it is extremely easy to believe. I console myself with the fact that Sisi doesn't have a bit of evidence for what she's saying.

"Oh, yes," she admits readily, "But I might still have the right of it."

"It's not like you could do anything about it," I say. Even if she isn't, as she probably is, making things up wholesale, what power could she possibly have over the Prince?

"I intend to wring a confession from his lips sooner or

later. Either he killed them, or he drove them away and made sure they would never return, and we need them. We need magic in this land. You think it's your father's fault that the trees aren't bearing fruit? You think there's any way he could work harder, or care more?"

"Of course not," I answer, almost offended by her suggestion. My father, for all his faults—and I am quick enough to name them all—would rather die than allow the farm, the pride and sustenance of our family for generations, to begin to wither and fail as it has done.

"Right. Uncle Prinn does all he can. We all do. The fact is that in our great-grandparents' time, when your grandfather's father laid his claim to that land and started the farm, no farmer could imagine working without magic. Every part of the Earth had magic! Real magic. Not just the magic of everyday hedge witches like Kariana, who are limited in their ruak, but also a deeper, *truer* kind of magic. I mean the ruak of the adirim, which I believe tied the Kingdom together in a way that was necessary, and which is gone now."

I'm staggered by the vastness of what Sisi is talking about, the beautiful tale she's spinning for me. When I speak, I focus in on the practical, since it seems to be the only thing I can do. "How do you intend to make His Royal Highness confess to this crime that you don't even know he committed?"

Sisi smiles. "Oh, Ricard will tell me everything. Sooner or later."

"That's what you're trying to do," I realize as I say it aloud. "You're hoping you can make him admit to it..."

191

"Thinking he might turn my head with tales of his power, yes. Or perhaps he really believes he did the right thing, wiping out the 'wicked' witches and the unnatural adirim with their so-called blood magic. Who knows? But I do believe that, sooner or later, he won't be able to resist the urge to boast of it to me. He knows I am clever as well as beautiful, and he knows I am *not* impressed with his name, or his wealth, or his station. He'll have to find some way to keep me interested in him."

"Couldn't he just...I don't know, earlier you seemed worried he might...order you to stay." *Force* you to stay, I think, but I don't want to raise the specter of that fear to Sisi unless I absolutely must.

"He could," she admits, "But I don't think he will. I think he wants more from me now than he could get by force."

"Love?" I ask, shocked. "You think he's in love with you?"

She shrugs. "Maybe. I think he wants my attention, which is near enough as makes no difference."

That's wrong. Love isn't wanting to possess and control another person as Lord Ricard wants to do to Sisi. Nor is it simply wanting them around. It's something else, something *more*.

When I look at Sisi, I see how beautiful she is. Of course I do—everyone does. But I see, and feel, so much more. There's fondness, and frustration, and admiration, and adoration, and a thousand other feelings I am too ignorant to have words for. What I feel for Sisi... *that's* what love is.

I want to say as much to her, but I'm afraid. Afraid she'll just smile and call me a dear little bird or something else equally tender and patronizing. I'm afraid that she won't understand that when I tell her I love her, I mean I love her as much as I believe anyone can love. As fiercely as she hates Lord Ricard, that's how much I love Sisi.

Enough that *I* want things that two girls could never share.

These thoughts have been coming to me more and more often in recent days, and as always, I push them aside. I know that Sisi wouldn't understand. Maybe she'd even be horrified, if I told her I want more from her than a friendly, sisterly love.

So, I say nothing about it. Instead, I ask, "What will you do, then? Once you've extracted this confession from Lord Ricard?"

Her smile is gentle, and a little bit sad. It's the most beautiful smile in the Kingdom. Not because of the pore-less perfection of her night-dark skin, or the luscious redness of her lips, or the even, pearly whiteness of her teeth, or the dimples in her round cheeks. But because it's *Sisi's* smile. "Then I'll figure out a way to bring the magic back."

"You don't take things easy on yourself, do you, Sisi?" I ask with a rueful smile of my own.

"I do not. And why should I?"

Why should she, indeed. If you ask me, I think there's nothing on this Earth that Sisi could not do if she set her mind to it.

So she's going to bring down the evil prince and save

the Kingdom, with nothing at her side but a fifteen-year-old girl and a pile of old books. I still believe she can do it.

I love her, I think to myself, and the words hurt. I've said them aloud plenty of times, but I mean something very different by them now. I mean: *I'm in love with her.*

I'll never say as much to her. I wouldn't dare.

But it's a relief, after a lifetime of wondering why I was so different than everyone else, to finally have an answer, in the privacy of my own thoughts, as to why I've always known I'll never marry, never have an ordinary life. I'm in love with my best friend. I'm in love with another girl.

I'm in love with Sisi.

CHAPTER FIFTEEN

*M*idwinter almost sneaks up on us. An evening of dancing and the delights of the City seems so unimportant now. The real purpose of our visit here has nothing to do with any invitation Lord Ricard extended, and it's easy to forget that we—that Sisi —were summoned to be an ornament at a party.

We're deep in study when Karili, our unfortunate etiquette tutor, comes bustling into the parlor. Sisi quickly shoves the book she was reading, *Magicks of Bloode and Earth,* into the couch cushions.

"My lady Sisi, Mistress Jeni, are you not dressing yet? The maidservants should have brought up your gowns half an hour since!"

"Haven't seen 'em," Sisi says, turning to put her feet up on the edge of a chair.

Karili tries valiantly to hide her wince. Part of me wishes that Sisi wouldn't do so much to provoke her—she seems a good enough woman, if somewhat silly. "I'll go inquire at once, by your leave, Lady Sisi."

Sisi gives her an imperious nod. When Karili is gone, she turns to me. "Will you help with my hair? None of the maids here do it quite like you do."

I've been helping Sisi with her curls since I can remember, so I'm no doubt better at it than the palace servants. Most folks here in the City seems to have straight or wavy hair, which goes along with the paler skin of this central region of the Earth. Sisi's hair requires careful shaping to keep it healthy and puffs up into a beautiful cloud around her face when it's not contained.

While servants bring up our gowns from Mari's workshop, I set about my task. I shape her curls into a high bun atop her head, decorating it some with small, jeweled pins—another gift from Ricard.

We whisper while I work.

"I can't believe I'm finally about to meet him," I admit.

"You sound almost excited."

"Of course I am. He's the Second in the Kingdom. One of the most important men alive. And I've spent the last few months helping you obsess about destroying him every waking second."

Sisi laughs at that, but also shushes me. "I'm eager to know what you make of him," she admits. "He is... an interesting man."

She hasn't told me much about what Lord Ricard is like personally. For all that I've learned about his place in the Kingdom, his vendetta against magic and those who use it, his relationship with his brother, his attempts to seduce Sisi, I still don't even know what the man looks like beyond Sisi's description. "I guess I'll tell you later tonight."

"I look forward to it."

The maidservants have returned, making it impossible for our conversation to continue in any productive way, so I take my leave and go to my own chamber to dress.

Two maids I've never seen before help me into my gown. It's the most beautiful garment I've ever laid eyes on, lovelier even than the dresses that Sisi has worn for her dinners with Lord Ricard.

"You look so pretty, Miss Jeni," one of the maids says.

I know that's not true. I've spent enough time around my cousin, the great beauty, to be all too conscious of the fact that I am no such thing.

But when I'm done feeling the tiniest bit bitter about that, and though I'm having a hard time walking in the tight skirt and heeled shoes, I totter over to the large silver-backed mirror and look at myself.

My hair is down my shoulders, dark and straight, only the very front of it pulled back, but there are pearled beads strung into it. The shimmering lightness of the pearls makes my hair look as black as night. Against that, my skin looks, not sallow as I have often been told, but pleasingly golden. The lavender gown I wear, tight and uncomfortable though it is, shows off my plump figure, while its high neckline and narrow skirt do something to disguise the fact that I, as of yet, have no womanly shape to speak of. The bodice—I hadn't noticed before—is carefully embroidered in a pattern of dense triangles, no doubt to further hide my disappointingly rectangular shape. The tightness of it forces me to take small, ladylike steps, so that even when Karili's repeated exhortations to walk carefully and put one foot in front of another are forgotten in the excitement of the evening, I won't be able to do much else. I've been transformed into someone I don't even recognize. The girl in the mirror doesn't look like the quiet little bird I've been all my life, unseen and unnoticed. For once, the words *Miss Jeni* don't seem like a polite fiction: when I look into the mirror, that lady is what I see. A lady of the very court I am working with my cousin to destroy. The irony brings a faint smile to my lips.

Aunt Mae is already sitting in the common room when I go out. "It takes them less time to dress me. There's not much that can be done to fix up an old woman," she says, but I shake my head.

"You look lovely, Auntie."

And so she does. Her thick hair is up, braided in an intricate crown around her head. Unlike me, she has been allowed quite a bit of makeup, outlining her dark brown eyes in blue and dusting her cheeks with blush. Someone's even drawn a beauty mark on her cheek. Her gown leaves her neck bare, showing a lovely choker of beaten gold, inset with a ruby. The fabric swathing her from collarbone to toes is the color of autumn leaves, a rich maroon with hints of gold that show when she moves. It fits more loosely than my gown, especially in the skirt.

"I told them I wasn't wearing a corset," she explains. "Mari didn't like that too much, but there's no other way for me. I'm just too old and set in my ways to go around tying myself up like a leg of lamb ready to be roasted. I teased her into agreeing to it, anyway, saying that if she was any good at her job, she'd find a way to make me look at least presentable even though I'm an old maid with a thick waist. And I think she did it."

"She certainly did. You're beautiful, Auntie." I look around. "Shouldn't we go?"

"We have to wait for Sisi. It could be a while."

"What does one do at a ball anyway?" I ask.

"Dance, I believe. Although neither of us is likely to be asked. I think little girls and old women like us mostly pick delicately at canapés and stand around watching people admire Sisi."

I don't know what a canapé is, but I say, "Luckily I have a great deal of experience in the area of standing around, watching people admire Sisi."

Aunt Mae laughs. "I am sorry for that. You ought not spend so much time in her shadow."

"I don't know where else I would be."

"You may have to figure it out."

Those cryptic words unsettle me. "You think—"

"I think it is very unlikely that your cousin will be returning to the farm with us after the ball. Or ever again."

"Oh." I can't say I'm surprised. A part of me knew, has always known, that this trip meant everything was changing for good. I think of Sisi, trying to make me promise to leave her behind.

Aunt Mae is looking strangely at me. "You'll always have a home with us, though. Both of you," she says.

I'm not sure why she bothers to say that. I'm not like Sisi. I have nowhere else to go. Here in the palace, I am no more a part of life than I was back at my father's farm. I am just as much on the outside, tolerated here because Sisi is used to having me in her shadow, exactly as they put up with me at home because they're used to having me around.

The thought saddens me too much for words, so I say nothing, just close my eyes. It's going to be a long night, full of such loneliness. I shouldn't wear myself out with these thoughts too soon, or I'll weep and ruin my lovely appearance.

The distant, heavy chime of the palace bell breaks through my thoughts. I'm grateful for it, until I count the eight chimes and realize the late hour. "Isn't this when the ball is supposed to begin?" I ask, a hint of panic in my voice. "Where's Sisi? We're late already!"

"Calm down," Aunt Mae says. "I remember when I was a girl, though I know that might seem rather too long ago for you to imagine now. Back in those days, it was quite normal to arrive late. All the most fashionable people did it. It was a means of drawing attention to yourself. No one wants to walk into an empty room."

"But someone has to," I say, confused, and my aunt laughs.

"Yes. Someone has to. But not the most beautiful girl

in all the Four Corners of the Earth. She'll arrive 'stylish and late,' as we used to say, and all eyes will be on her as she makes her entrance."

"Ah." That makes sense, and I feel a bit sheepish over my previous outburst of nerves. Besides, we don't have to wait too much longer. As the clock sounds the quarter-hour, Sisi pokes her head out from the door.

"Are you two ready?"

"Waiting for you."

"All right. We can go soon. Just tell me if I look all right. I'm a little, well..." she trails off nervously, laughing a bit. "This isn't exactly the sort of thing I usually wear."

She lets the door open and steps out so we can see her.

I have looked at Sisi's lovely face every day that I can remember. Even before my earliest memories, I must have seen her, for she has lived at the farm since I was only a year old. For all the years of my life, she has been the first thing I see in the morning when I wake and the last thing I see before I go to bed. I have seen her crying after a bitter fight with her brother, seen her undressed and dirt-stained as she takes her weekly bath, seen her ill enough to puke up her breakfast, seen her hair haloed around her head when she wakes up from sleeping, seen her red-cheeked with rage. In short, I generally consider myself quite immune to the fact that she is the most beautiful woman on Earth, since I have grown up looking at that most lovely face every single day.

Now the sight of her takes my breath away. Literally.

I'm afraid that I might faint. Not that my corset is helping with that.

Her hair is as I dressed it—neatly pulled up into a bun, with a few gilded pins framing her face. Her makeup has been applied so neatly I can barely see it's there, except for a touch of gold in the corner of her eyelids, a dark line of smoky kohl beneath her lashes, and a rich red stain on her lip. Her whole neckline is bare, her gown plunging down between her full breasts. It's made of a simple white toile, smooth and unadorned, the color soft against her dark, gleaming skin. As she spins around to show it to us, I realize that there are thousands of tiny gemstones in all colors embroidered into it, so she flares like a rainbow, like a fire being lit. She's wearing no jewelry at all, none of Ricard's presents, except for the jeweled pins I placed in her hair.

Aunt Mae has tears in her eyes. "Child, you are—you are really lovely. You know that?"

"I feel so naked." She laughs, sounding entirely different from the solemn, suspicious Sisi of only a few hours ago. "It doesn't seem right, going out with my chest uncovered. But apparently it's all the fashion for girls these days, and who am I to argue with the fashion."

"You love to argue. With everything and everyone," I point out.

She gives me a small smile at that. "I suppose you're right. Now come on, I think we're late already."

"You're the one who was late."

"Technically." She sweeps her bare arm out toward the door. "Well. After you?"

I limp down the hallway. It's difficult to keep pace with Aunt Mae and Sisi as I struggle to walk in my skintight skirts and too-small shoes. The ballroom is halfway across the palace, and my feet are throbbing by the time we're halfway there. Nor do I enjoy the long climb up a marble stair to get to the grand entryway to the ballroom, but at least when we reach the summit, I'm greeted kindly by the herald. He's an older man wearing the now-familiar royal livery, and he gives me a wide smile as he asks for my name.

"Jeni," I say, and then hesitate. "Well, my True Name is Jena, I'm not sure which—" Excellent. We're not even in the room yet, and I'm already ruining things. Right on schedule. "From Leasane."

He is gracious enough not to comment on my clumsy manners as he steps through a pair of red velvet curtains and proclaims, "Miss Jeni of Leasane!"

I step in behind him and walk through the curtains. The fabric brushes softly against my skin, and I blink, adjusting to the sudden twinkling light. I'm standing at the top of a set of golden stairs, looking down at a vast white room. Everywhere there are people, all at least as elegantly dressed as I am and most of them more so, and all their eyes are on me. The room is glimmering with candlelight. Since the ceiling is made of the same iridescent material as the outside of the palace, bright rainbows are being thrown everywhere. It's actually rather hard to see anything, the many sparkling lights all but blinding me, and my heart is pounding hard enough that I can hear it inside my head, and loud, swinging music is playing, and *everyone is looking at me.*

I realize I'm supposed to walk down the stairs, not just stand up here and stare back at the crowd. I focus on nothing but putting one foot in front of the other. I try not to look down, since I don't want to seem as nervous as I am. My heart is hammering in my chest as I descend the staircase, down and down and down. I keep my thoughts firmly on not tripping over my tight skirts or my small shoes, and away from panic at the sight of all these people staring up at me, their faces blank with polite curiosity. If I begin taking in the overwhelming scene that surrounds me, I'll absolutely trip and fall. And the shame of that will no doubt send me screaming back to my father's farm, and then how will I help Sisi change the Kingdom?

Finally, I feel flat marble beneath the sole of my shoe. I've done it, and not fallen on my face even a little. I am overwhelmed with gratitude that I have survived the first sixty seconds of His Majesty's celebrated Midwinter Ball.

"Lady Mae of Leasane!"

Aunt Mae walks down with much more ease, descending the flight of stairs like she's going down the ladder from our loft to the garden below. She even manages a bit of a smile at all the people staring at her as she does. As soon as she's made her entrance, she finds me. "This is something, eh?" she asks.

It certainly is something. Something terrifying. Something all the etiquette lessons on Earth, all my sneaking around the palace, could never have prepared me for.

I've never seen so many people in my *life*.

Once again, the voice booms down from above. "Lady Sigranna, Two Hundred and Eighth in the Kingdom, Heiress by Title to His Lordship Jorjianus of Seahame, Mistress of the Fourteenth Quarter and Lady of Carlsbeach."

"I didn't know Sisi was so important," I say to my aunt, who just shushes me. Sisi's Number seems to have been bumped up quite a few places since the last time she showed off her title. I wonder why.

We stare up the stairs together, waiting along with everyone else. Of course, we're the only ones prepared for what we're about to see—most of the people here have never met Sisi, though they must have heard of her.

Then Sisi is making her entrance, into the party and into the Court. And I thought they'd stared at me. No one seems to be able to look away from her for a second as she takes step after lovely, elegant, even step down the long flight of stairs. Even the music has stopped, and the band is staring wide-eyed and wondering at her. All eyes are on my cousin as she makes her way into the ballroom.

CHAPTER SIXTEEN

Sisi's slipper has barely touched the marble floor when a man I have never seen before puts himself in her path. She has to stop short to avoid crashing into him as he smiles at her and bows low. "Milady."

She meets his eyes, giving him a small, tense smile in return. "Your Highness. I should have known I would find you waiting." She extends her hand, and he kisses the back of it delicately. The etiquette Sisi and I tried to learn by rote looks rather better on a man who has practiced it since childhood, although Sisi's natural grace may be what gives her the ability to keep up with him.

I take the opportunity to size up his appearance. He certainly matches Sisi's descriptions, though I'd imagined him looking more sinister, somehow. He's slender, though muscular through the shoulders and arms, and nearly a foot taller than even Sisi, who is big for a woman. He keeps his face clean-shaven, either for the ball or by habit, though he has thick, dark brows and charmingly tousled chestnut hair. He's dressed more simply than I would have imagined a prince would be outfitted for his own ball: a red shirt with gold buttons, neat black pants, and an unadorned gold circlet around his head. It's undeniable that he is a very attractive man, his bright eyes burning intensely as they sweep over Sisi's form.

His voice, though, is calm and steady as he speaks to her. "You look lovely, Lady Sisi, if you'll permit me to belabor the blatantly obvious."

"You know how I feel about comments on my appearance, Your Highness."

I'm a little surprised at the bluntness of her response. For all that Sisi has insisted that she would be only herself—her most abrasive and honest self—around Lord Ricard, I would've thought even she would have to make some allowance for the fact that he is the King's own brother, and Second in the Kingdom. Apparently not. Apparently Sisi is always Sisi, even in the face of royalty. I don't know why I find this even slightly surprising.

She turns to where Aunt Mae and I are standing, quite literally, in her shadow. "May I present my family to Your Highness?"

"It would be a pleasure."

"Aunt Mae, you know His Highness Lord Ricard."

Aunt Mae curtsies.

Lord Ricard returns the gesture with a low bow, kissing her hand with as much grace as he had Sisi's. "It is, as always, a delight to see you, Madam Mae. I hope you will enjoy your evening at the ball, madam."

"A-and you, Your Highness." There's an uncharacteristic stammer in my aunt's voice as she replies to the Prince.

I had forgotten that they'd met before, since Aunt Mae has supervised all of Sisi's previous encounters with Lord Ricard. I'm the only one here encountering royalty for the very first time, and I can feel my heart fluttering in my chest as Sisi continues, "And dear cousin, allow me to present His Highness to you."

"You must be the famous Mistress Jeni." Lord Ricard bows.

I blush, realizing I was supposed to curtsy as soon as he addressed me and have forgotten. If only I'd known in advance how utterly embarrassing this evening was going to be, I could've saved the maids the trouble of pinching me half to death to give me a flush in my cheeks. "Your Highness." I curtsy as low as I can, hoping to make up for the lateness of the gesture. My knees wobble, but—thank the Goddess—I manage to avoid actually tipping over onto my face.

He takes my hand in both of his, his long fingers completely encircling mine. Slowly, he lifts my hand up to his mouth. His lips are dry and warm, the sensation unfamiliar, and his eyes are locked on mine as he presses them to my skin. It sends a shiver down my spine to be so intently considered by this man, with his cold and lovely hazel eyes.

He doesn't say anything more than pleasantries, though those eyes seem to be telling me something much more serious. "It is the greatest honor to make the acquaintance of one so dear to my lady. Lady Sisi always speaks so highly of you and of what a comfort your presence has been to her in this unfamiliar place."

"I do my best," I reply nervously, unsure how else to handle this situation. I wasn't expecting to have to make conversation with the Prince. I just hope I don't say anything wrong, either that will give offense, or, worse, that will give away Sisi's plans.

Lord Ricard only chuckles in response, though, a low and pleasant sound.

The band has struck back up again, the high and warbling note of a violin the most prominent in the tune.

"Your lady kinswoman tells me of your success in that endeavor, Mistress Jeni. Surely, she would never have agreed to my invitation without your companionship, and so I am in your debt. I realize this is the first time I have had the great pleasure of making your acquaintance—a foolish oversight, I am sure."

"I know you must have been very busy," I offer, trying to find something at all to say that won't be offensive or tasteless or just silly.

"Indeed, I am. Sometimes I wonder if I have rather more on my plate than even my dear brother does. Still, it does not excuse my rudeness in allowing such a lovely young girl, and my guest, to go unwelcomed for these many weeks. I am glad that I have had the pleasure now, though I sincerely wish we had met sooner. Lady Sisi says you are her first cousin?"

"Yes, but not by blood."

"Oh?" is all he says, one of those high eyebrows arching.

"Surely you could have assumed," I say, gesturing vaguely at the visual difference between Sisi and myself.

"As my lady is often kind enough to remind me, it is the height of rudeness to assume anything based on a lady's looks—"

"And yet here we are," Sisi murmurs, not quite loud enough for anyone but me to hear. I shoot her a worried glance. Surely, despite the liberties she's apparently used to taking, she can't just go around making snide jests at Lord Ricard's expense under her breath.

"—so, I thought I should risk rudeness by asking, rather than give offense by assuming. If you don't mind telling, the exact nature of the connection—"

At least this is a subject I know something about. Still, I'm not sure how much Sisi would want me to share. I'm grateful when she interrupts his question to tell the tale herself. "My lord, surely you remember the story of my early childhood."

"Ah, yes. A terrible tragedy, I didn't mean to bring it up on a happy occasion—"

"Well, my cousin Jena"—she puts just the slightest emphasis on my True Name, though if Lord Ricard notices, he doesn't comment—"is related to me through my brother's wife. My brother Jorj married a serving girl when he was still in possession of his titles and went to live with her family after we lost our lands. His wife, Merri, is the daughter of Jena's father's brother—if you can follow all that."

"And I thought the royal family tree was dizzyingly complex," he says with a bright smile.

A servant approaches, offering us sparkling wine in slim crystal glasses. Sisi and Lord Ricard each accept one, but Aunt Mae gives me such a glare I dare not reach for a glass of my own even as my aunt takes a long sip out of hers.

"Have you been enjoying your stay here in the Capital, ladies?" Lord Ricard says, addressing all three of us, though his eyes are still very much trained on Sisi.

"Oh, yes. Very much," I say, since it seems like the only polite answer even though it is less than entirely true. "It's been an honor to be here. Everything is so beautiful, and everyone has been so very kind to us."

"I trust Elan has been satisfactory?"

"Yes, he's been wonderful," Aunt Mae says. "He's helped us in so many ways."

"I hoped as much. It's not my preference to have one of the pahyat serving in so exalted a role, but he is simply the best anyone has been able to find. It is an unfortunate truth that, although the lesser people may harbor some resentment to us of higher stature, it is most difficult to do without them. Don't you agree?"

I'm not sure what I'm supposed to say to that. It seems like it would be rude to directly contradict His Royal Highness, Second in the Kingdom, and yet it can't be right to agree with him either, not when he's saying something so nasty about Elan. I think of how the man—or the pahyati, I suppose—had taken the time to reassure me after my request for help learning to read, how he had recognized my loneliness and nervousness and somehow found the right words to soothe them both without upsetting my pride. I can't say that, though, so instead I open my mouth. I *would* argue, I would, but I don't know what words to use. Instead, I only say, "In my village everyone is human, and I never had the pleasure of meeting any of the other go'im before Elan. I must say that I have found him most gracious and kind to us all."

"Ah, for the innocence of a child. You are fortunate to know so little of the true nature of the pahyat—for Elan is, or at least seems, a mere exception to the thieving and greed that exemplifies that people. I hope I shall have the chance to show you my research on the subject, for I consider myself something of an expert. Too few of our great minds, especially since my grandfather closed the last of the Royal Schools, have been turned to this problem, though I think it is the one which plagues us most."

"Forgive me, my lord. I am not sure I understand—what problem?"

"Why, the problem of how the different peoples of the Earth—the adirim, the pahyat, and us poor humans—are to get along with one another." He clears his throat. "But you must forgive me, ladies. I have gotten carried away on one of my favored topics—as a busy man, one with the heavy burden of ruling a Kingdom, I am afraid I think of little but politics. When I have started down the path of discussing it, there is hardly anything that can turn my thoughts from it. It is a most inappropriate subject for three lovely ladies to hear tell of, and particularly at a great ball such as this one."

I don't find it inappropriate. I find it interesting, if perhaps upsetting to hear him insult someone I've come to like and respect in our time here. Still, I realize I'm probably not supposed to say that. So instead I curtsy quickly. "It's no trouble at all, Your Highness."

"It's not often simple countryside girls like ourselves get to hear from such an important man," Sisi demurs, sounding facetious even to my ears—though Lord Ricard seems flattered enough. I suppose she's willing to break her own rules about honesty if it will keep Lord Ricard talking.

"I am glad I can hold your interest, even though I ought not mix work and pleasure so much. How I wish I had my brother's gift! He seems always to be able to forget everything and enjoy himself at balls like this one."

That doesn't sound quite like a compliment. I try to find a polite response. "I hope Your Highness is able to relax. It does seem like a lovely party."

"And I am fortunate enough to have the most beautiful and gracious lady in the Kingdom at my side, as you are too polite to remind me. I ought not forget the extent of my good fortune." He smiles at Sisi, a surprisingly cold expression. It frightens me a little, but Sisi holds his gaze, her own lips tilting upward just a little.

"My lord is, as always, too kind."

"You would be the first to say that of me," he says. "Or at least, the first to mean it. Now, I think the lovely Jeni wisely mentioned I should be enjoying this evening. Perhaps we ought to dance?"

"Your Highness has only to ask, of course." Sisi is still

smiling that strange little smile, the one that sits so unnaturally on her face, at him. She has been wearing it all evening, like a mask.

"I am indeed a lucky man." He turns to Aunt Mae and me, briefly. "Ladies, I hope you will enjoy the ball. Do let me know if there is anything at all I can do to increase your comfort." Lord Ricard bows again. "Now, I was wondering if I could beg your excuses for my company and ask my lady Sisi for the honor of this dance."

Sisi smiles at him, dazzlingly lovely, all artifice. "As I've said, of course."

Lord Ricard offers her his arm, and she places her gloved hand over his forearm, letting him lead her away into the crowd. Aunt Mae and I are left to watch the dancers go by.

There are so many people here, such a blur of motion and activity, that I lose sight of them quickly. The costumes and the jewels eclipse the faces; gentlemen mostly in dark breeches and hose with brilliantly colored shirts, the ladies all in bright or pastel gowns. The couples separate and come together, twirling along with the music as the beat grows faster. I would only stumble over the steps, even if I had someone to dance with, but it's a wonderful thing to watch, and someone has come to offer a cup of chilled punch that Aunt Mae lets me take after an assurance from the liveried maid carrying the tray that it's no stronger than cider or watered wine.

I sip at my drink slowly and watch the people go by. Sisi is the only one wearing white—the other ladies are all in more vibrant colors. Her dress makes her stand out even more as she and Lord Ricard make their way to the center of the crowd. Aunt Mae and I aren't the only ones watching them. The other dancers are slowing, swaying in one another's arms gently so that they can watch the spectacle that the two of them make. Lord Ricard has one hand on Sisi's waist and the other in her own hand, and they are practically galloping across the floor. The pins begin to fall from their careful arrangement in her hair and she laughs as they spin across the floor.

If she's deceiving him, she's a better liar than I thought. I, too, would be fooled into thinking she's having the time of her life, and I know her better than anyone. Or so I think, until they turn the corner so that her face is turned toward mine. Her cheeks are flushed, her smile wide, her barely constrained bust heaving with the effort of the dance and with laughter. She is every inch the picture of joy, but that wide smile still doesn't touch her eyes, and when Lord Ricard turns toward the band to cue them to play again, her smile flags a little at the corners, as if the effort of keeping it up is just too much to maintain.

Still, it would fool anyone but me, who knows her best. It is a clever deception, and all I can do is hope that it will work. I can only imagine what the consequences would be if Lord Ricard knew that she was trying to pry some sort of information out of him that he doesn't want to divulge—when he is such a powerful man and she is only a weak, orphaned girl.

When the dance has ended, they return for their

drinks. Sisi flops into a chair, a little bit of gracelessness that reminds me she really is the same person she's always been, in spite of her carefully performed manners.

She is back to her act, though, a mere moment later, as she looks back up at Lord Ricard. "You've worn me out quite entirely, my lord."

"Oh, how terrible of me. I had rather hoped for another dance tonight. Maybe even a few more."

"How you presume." She runs a finger around the rim of her glass, looking up at him. "But perhaps you may find some means of persuading me."

He looks back at her, with a regard that frightens me a little. He doesn't look at her like he's in love—not, for instance, the way that Jorj looks at Merri. Not even the way that Sisi is pretending to look at him. And certainly not the way I look at Sisi, when I think she's not paying attention.

No, he's looking at her the way Aunt Mae looks at a nice basket at the market. Or a piece of newly woven cloth that she knows we can't afford. He looks at her the way the men look at their dinner when they've come in from long hours of work on the farm and they're weary and starving.

He looks at Sisi like she's something he'd quite like to own, but he can't figure out how he will yet. He looks at her like he's dreaming of tearing her to pieces, and he'll do whatever it takes to devour her.

With an elegant flourish and a small bow, he offers her his hand. "Another dance, my lady?"

She lets her eyes dart over to me for just a moment,

and I see the exhaustion in them, and not from dancing. She's tired of the ruse, and yet she dares do nothing but what he asks. If he sees the mask slip, if he realizes the real goal of all her clever questions and bright ideas, the consequences could be terrible. She has to be perfect and charming every moment or he may realize what she's up to.

So, she takes his hand, and lets him pull her to her feet. She takes a few steps, hurrying toward the dance floor, but she's still looking back at me as they go. I hear, before I see, a soft thump and an exclaimed, "Oh!" as she bumps right into someone. "Forgive me, sir, I didn't see you there."

"No, my lady, you must excuse me," says a deep voice. The voice belongs to someone's gold-clad chest. She has to look up quite a bit to find a face: tan skin and strong features, with a dark brown beard and a soft smile aimed right at Sisi. "I have never been known for my grace. Still, I would have hoped for a better introduction than this."

"Consider it forgotten, then," Sisi says, her voice light. "Perhaps His Royal Highness could make the acquaintance in a more becoming fashion?"

The man turns and nods at Lord Ricard. "Brother."

He does look a great deal like Lord Ricard. But if he's His Highness' brother, then this man must be—

I realize everyone else has already curtsied around us, and even Lord Ricard is bowing. I try to imitate Sisi, who has dropped gracefully into a low curtsy and is holding the position. I manage to get my head as low as she does, though I can't stop my knees from trembling again. Luckily, between the most beautiful woman in the Kingdom and the King of All the Earth, I'm quite sure that no one is looking at my own imperfect posture.

I risk another quick glance upward and see that this man—the King—is wearing the enormous crown that represents his power over all the Kingdom. I don't know how I managed to avoid noticing that. Unlike Lord Ricard's circlet, this is a full crown, triple points made of wrought gold, with the sign of the Three Powers entwined in the front. Just behind him stands a masked figure wearing all black—his bodyguard, I assume, right at his shoulder. I hadn't noticed them at first, so still is their form.

"Your Majesty," Lord Ricard says.

The King extends his hand to his brother, pulling him up and then in for an embrace. "Ricard. So good to see you well."

"I wasn't aware you would be here."

"It is my ball."

"I thought you were consumed with...other matters."

"I have been, but I heard a rumor that the most beautiful woman on Earth was going to be here, and I admit I was most curious to see whether or not that was true. I didn't intend to bump right into her, however."

"And the herald didn't announce you." Ricard's voice belies the slightest bit of irritation.

"Oh, I snuck in through the back. Didn't want anyone getting distracted from their pleasant evening just because I decided to turn up unannounced." He smiles at us. "The lady did ask you to introduce me."

"Of course. Forgive me. Lady Sisi, this is His Majesty, King Balion, First in the Kingdom, Lord of—"

The King waves his hand. "Forget all the titles. My lady, it's nice to meet you." He takes her hand, but unlike Ricard, doesn't bow politely over it, or kiss it, just shakes it for a moment. It's an oddly plain gesture and I find it reassuring.

"Madam Mae, Lady Sisi's aunt and chaperone. And her companion, Mistress Jeni."

"Ladies." The King does kiss Aunt Mae's hand, and she blushes bright red under his regard. Then he turns his eyes to me. He has the same hazel eyes as his brother, but his are shining and kind. He knows, I realize as he looks at me, how uncomfortable I am, that I'm frightened of having someone so important so close to me, and that I don't have Aunt Mae's solidity or Sisi's loveliness to fall back on when I wish to charm people.

"Miss Jeni. Is that for Jeminia or Jelnia?" he asks.

"Jena," I manage in a whisper.

"What a lovely True Name. How unusual. It's so nice to meet you all."

Just as my cousin did, I reach out and shake the King's hand. I can scarcely believe it's happening. His grip is warm and firm, and his smile gentle, and I am trembling a little, but there's something soothing about his presence that makes it hard to fear him as I ought to. He's certainly less intimidating than his stern, suddenly sour-faced brother, whose measured smile has faded into an outright frown in the presence of the King.

"I was wondering, Lady Sisi, if you might like to dance," the King asks.

She looks up from her curtsy, her polite smile fading into a look that I recognize as surprise. "I suppose I might."

"Madam Mae, is that all right with you? My brother is always telling me etiquette is important, so I suppose I ought to ask the lady's chaperone."

"It's fine," Aunt Mae chokes out, seemingly about to have a fit that the King himself has to ask her permission for anything.

"Thank you. Before we go, Lady Sisi, I must warn you, I'm a terrible dancer."

She laughs, surprised. "Then why dance at all?"

He shrugs. "It's the thing to do, isn't it? We're at a ball —technically, my ball—and I suppose I ought to at least pretend to be in the spirit of the thing."

"Very well. I do have one consolation for Your Majesty."

"Which is?"

She grins, showing her even white teeth. "I'm an *excellent* dancer."

He returns the smile, and then they're off.

The King was not being falsely modest—he's terribly clumsy, and only Sisi's care and the attention of everyone else on the floor stops them from whirling into other couples. I wonder what happens to you if you trip into the King while he's dancing. It's probably not very pleasant.

While I'm considering this, Lord Ricard bows to me. "Well, Lady Jeni, it seems you and I have both been left behind by the happy couple. Would you care to console me?"

"You want to dance? With me? I don't know how to dance." I'm so surprised at the offer that I forget I'm supposed to be polite. I've taken the same dance lessons as my cousin, of course, but I never got particularly good at dancing, not in the way Sisi took to it.

The Prince's eyes are still on Sisi, and he seems consumed with watching her dance with his brother. I wonder if it's mere manners spurring this offer, or if he's hoping for something else.

But when he speaks, his voice is perfectly courteous.

"As Lady Sisi is so aptly demonstrating with my brother, an expert partner can help a novice. I would be honored to guide you."

"Of course, then."

I take his gloved hand, and he places the other around the waist of my dress. I can barely feel it through the thick, stiff corset I'm wearing, but his touch is firm enough to help me move to the rhythm. Fortunately, this is a slow song—I'm entirely incapable of the perfectly measured gallop Sisi demonstrated earlier, but I hope to be able to at least move vaguely to this rhythm. I sway along with his guidance. It turns out I just have to focus on not stepping on his shoes, and even I can manage that much.

We've been dancing in total silence for about a minute when he speaks. His quiet voice whispering right in my ear surprises me so much that I jump, and he tightens his grip on my waist so no one will see my movement. "There is something the lovely Sisi ought to know," he says.

"Which is?" My heart is beating fast, and it's not just the exertion of the dance. No, I realize, I'm quite nervous. Afraid, actually. Sisi may be fond of the intrigue that she's created for herself here at court—she seems to even be genuinely enjoying her odd repartee with Lord Ricard —but I'm not equipped to join in. And for all my pleas to Sisi to be included, I would rather not be a part of this particular scheme.

"My brother is the King of this land. He has no understanding at all how the game of the court is played. He doesn't have to, since he's the greatest prize in it. If Sisi wants to play—if she plays it with me—it could work out well for her, and for all of you. I hope she's seen that whatever else I may be, I am certainly generous. I am most prepared to remain so, if she wishes to retain my favor. If she prefers my brother, she may get whatever maidens get out of spending time with a King—a sense of power, I imagine? But I will not take her once Balion has put her aside. Do you understand?"

"I do," I say, meeting his eyes with some difficulty. Now, with the coldness in his voice, the calculated cruelty in his eyes, I can see the Ricard Sisi fears so much, the zealot, the plotter, the killer.

I wonder if Sisi will end up in his bed in spite of it. The thought turns my stomach.

"I trust that you will tell her what I've said," he says flatly. "I am sure you understand the situation you and your family find yourselves in."

"I'll tell her," I say, pulling away a bit, and he smiles.

"And I am sure I need not warn you that this is a conversation that ought otherwise to remain between us." He guides me into a delicate twirl around the dance floor, spinning me out in a circle. I'm dizzy and breathless, and not just from the exertion of dancing. My head spins as I try to make sense of this situation.

"I'll not repeat anything else you've said," I say, though I'm already imagining how I'll recount every word of it to my cousin.

"Especially your aunt. She seems a meddling type. Like my brother. One who wouldn't understand how things work."

"How do things work?"

"In this Kingdom, we all want things from one another. If I have something Sisi wants, and she has something I want, it only makes sense for us to have a fair exchange. And in this case, I have money and wealth, and she has great beauty. We ought to be able to advantage one another."

"I see."

"I don't imagine your aunt would understand that much, do you?"

I've been trying not to reveal anything too much, but

I can't help what comes spilling out. "No. She made a promise."

"A promise? What do you mean?"

"To my father and Sisi's brother. They didn't want to let her come. But they promised that she wouldn't be forced into anything that she didn't want to do. That we'd protect her if we had to. And that's why we're here. Both Aunt Mae and I. We'll take care of her. We're here for her." The words come out as if compelled—I don't know if I should have told him even that much, but I don't seem to be able to stop myself. It's as close as I can come to threatening him. An absurd idea, I know, given all the power he has (and I lack), but I have to stand up for Sisi.

At least I didn't shove him into any mud.

His smile stretches wider. "That's touching," he says, his voice sickly sweet.

I don't like being dismissed that way. He doesn't exactly seem to be quaking at the threat. "She's not something to be traded for or bought," I say, anger showing in my tone despite myself.

"Of course not." He smiles again, just a little too wide.

I can say nothing further. I don't want to be in trouble. And I certainly don't want this terrible man to do anything nasty to my cousin because I said the wrong thing. So, I simply say, "I understand what you mean, my lord. But Sisi will do as she wishes. She always does."

"And do you understand what will happen if she cannot see reason?"

"What will happen?" I dare to ask. Between the

dance, and my tight dress, and the choking fear in my chest, it is growing ever harder to breathe, but I try not to let him see my fear. He has too much power over me as it is.

"I let young Lord Jorj go, all those years ago," he says, his tone carefully casual. At first, I don't understand what he's saying. The dance continues, his strong arms guiding me into the correct movements. "When I had to have the parents removed from Eastsea. I knew there were children—Sisi and Jorj, the heirs—but they were young, a lad of sixteen and a toddling babe, and the boy promised there wouldn't be any more trouble, so I let them flee. You must understand that this was nothing but mercy. They could easily have been burned along with the rest of their house, and then they would be nothing but dust now."

I realize that he's admitting to exactly the crime that Sisi had suspected him of. Here, in this sparkling room, at this elegant party, he is confessing that he had her parents murdered.

"I saved her life then, all those years ago. She might repay me. And if she will not understand that, I will finish the work I started at Eastsea. It is my understanding that young Jorj has gotten himself a child on one of your local women?"

"M-my cousin, Merri. His wife. They have a little daughter."

"How sweet."

He doesn't have to make the threat more explicit than that. It's all too easy to imagine. As I spin around, the bright clothes and shining lights of the ballroom going around me in a blur, the image appears before me like a mirage—tiny Mali, so helpless and small, in the arms, not of her loving mother, but of Ricard's gold-clad and fierce soldiers, a cruel, strong hand closing around her soft throat. "You wouldn't."

And I realize, with a sinking certainty, that he *would*. Maybe once, Jorj and Sisi's noble blood might have given them a measure of protection, might at least have caused something of a scandal if they were killed. But Jorj turned his back on all of that, or escaped it, and now no one would even notice if Ricard came after him and his family. There isn't a person in the Kingdom who would stand up to Ricard, and certainly not for the sake of Mali. Only a girl, only a child, only a farmer's daughter. Just like me.

If Ricard doesn't get what he wants, he's capable of anything. I should have learned that lesson when Kariana was burned. He'll seize what he desires if he can, and if he cannot, he'll destroy it out of spite.

That's true for the Kingdom. And it's true for our family.

"Will you tell your pretty cousin what I said? All of what I told you to pass along?"

"I will."

"Good." He releases me at once, suddenly bored of this, and says, "You can go then, child."

I don't pull away at once. Part of me hopes I can hide how terrified I am, though I know that he must suspect. Lord Ricard is still watching me, smiling that wide, handsome smile that does not quite meet his eyes. The song slides to an end, and he bows. "Thank you for the dance, Mistress Jeni."

"Thank you, my lord," I stammer, and turn away, running as fast as my tight gown will allow me to until I reach Aunt Mae's side.

She takes one look at my pale face and demands, "What on all Four Corners of Gaia is the matter?"

"I—I don't know—I have to tell Sisi. I can't tell you."

"What do you mean, you can't tell me? What on Earth is there that you can't tell me?"

I shake my head. "It's something. It's—I'm not... oh, Auntie." I throw my arms around her waist, grateful to feel the same warm touch that I always have as she wraps her arms around me and hugs me back. For a moment, the brilliance of the ball, the sparkling colors and bright lights and cacophonous noise all fade away and everything is all right.

"Child? What is it? Talk to me, little Jeni. You know you can tell me. You can tell me whatever it is that ails your dear heart. I just need to know—"

"I hate this place," I whisper. "I hate this place. Auntie, I want to go home."

She leans down and kisses my forehead. "Oh, child," she murmurs. Then, more quietly, she asks, "Sweet Gaia, what have we done?"

The music plays on, bright and beautiful. My beloved cousin, the most beautiful woman in the Kingdom, dances with the King of all the Earth. And I begin to weep.

CHAPTER SEVENTEEN

*T*he next morning, I head into the sitting room, still sleepy-eyed and only half-awake after a long night spent tossing and turning with worry. Exhausted and desperate for a cup of tea, I emerge dressed only in the shift I'd slept in, which would be fine were I not immediately greeted with the sight of the King of All the Earth sitting on the couch next to my cousin.

I stumble backward, curtsying. "Your Majesty. Forgive me, I didn't expect—excuse me..."

The *King* is here, and I'm in my *undergarments*. I can't get out of the room fast enough.

Yet he just looks over the back of the couch and smiles warmly at me. "Jena. It's nice to see you again. Sigranna was just telling me about her theory on the time before the First King and Queen reigned over the Earth. It's very interesting. Have you heard about this?"

I notice that he didn't call Sisi by her title, and I wonder if that's because he doesn't have to adhere to such formalities in his position, because he listened when Sisi told him not to, or just because he doesn't have his brother's courtly manners. I suppose either way it comes down to the same thing: the King can do whatever he pleases. I do another small curtsy and say, "Yes, Your Majesty. My cousin has shared it with me at great length—"

"Oh, please." He waves his hand. "I really hope you won't do all of that. It makes me uncomfortable, all the bowing and titling and what have you. My friends call me Lio, and I hope that you and I will come to be very good friends, especially since you and Sigranna are like two peas in a pod."

I laugh, surprised at this homely metaphor. It sounds more like something Uncle Willem would say than the King of All the Earth would. "Lio, then," I say, and it's strange, but no stranger than just standing in front of a King in my shift and nothing else.

"Come, sit with us! And have some breakfast, I'm having a tray brought up and they always bring far more food than any reasonable person could consume." He blinks, seeming to notice my state of undress for the first time. "Of course, if you need a moment—"

"Yes, I'll... well, I'll be right back," I interrupt.

Sisi meets my eyes as I rush out of the room. She raises an eyebrow and grins at me. I stick my tongue out at her.

In my room, with the door safely closed, I ring for the maid. When she arrives, she's pale-faced and shaking a little, and she whispers, "His Majesty the *King* is here."

Well, I can top that. "I know. And I walked out there, dressed like this, before I realized he was."

"He said *good morning* to me." She sounds so horrified at the idea that she doesn't even register what I've said.

"Yes. He's rather odd, for a King," I observe.

"Oh, I wouldn't say that!" she hurries to add, curtailing any further criticism. He is, after all, the King, and thus apparently free to act as strangely as he likes.

Still fretting, she helps me into one of the plainer gowns that has been made for me here, a simple bright blue shift with long sleeves and flowers embroidered around the neckline. It's not quite as simple as my worn homespun, but at least—unlike my gown from last night— I can move around in it.

The maid is still fluttering around nervously. "Are you sure you don't want to have something a little bit, well, nicer? I could do your hair up if you'd like—"

I shake my head. "I'm all right, thank you. I think this will suit."

"But the *King* is out there—"

"I think it'll be all right." I don't want to be dizzy from corsetry while also trying to act normal in front of the King himself, and somehow I imagine he won't care, or indeed notice, what I'm wearing.

The maid curtsies and leaves, leaving me to open the door and join my cousin alongside the King.

Balion has pulled up a chair for me. For the first time, I notice that he's actually not the only stranger sitting in our parlor. To be exact, his bodyguard, whom I assume is a man from his stature, is standing in the corner, silent and unmoving. The eerie sight of his entirely black outfit catches me a bit off guard; even his face is obstructed by a dark cloth. I suppose I'd known about the royal guards, one of the Three Powers of the Kingdom, but to actually see one of the legendary warriors who devote their lives to serving the royal family is something else entirely.

The King seems not to notice, though, and has made himself quite comfortable. "Excellent timing, Jena! Breakfast has just arrived." He offers me a cup of tea and asks how I take it.

"Um, I guess I don't know? I don't drink much tea at home." In the palace I've gotten fond of stirring so much sugar into my cup that I can barely stir it, but I'm rather embarrassed to say as much in front of the King, who presumably has more refined tastes.

"We're poor, you see," Sisi chimes in with a smirk.

"Too poor for tea?" he says, sounding shocked, but he covers for himself quickly. "I'm sorry, that was a stupid question. That's just one of my faults, I suppose. And I have so many. I'll put some milk and sugar in there for you. It makes it easier to get used to the taste."

He hands me the cup and saucer, and a little scone with jam on it. I take it from his hands, feeling charmed. He doesn't seem like an all-powerful ruler, chosen by the hand of Gaia to protect Her children's future. He just seems rather like a nice man.

The kind of man I could imagine making Sisi quite happy. His gentleness could soften her a bit, help her calm herself from the righteous anger that is always boiling in her heart. He could take care of her in the luxury she was born to, and yet would try to understand where she grew up and where she came from.

I shake my head, trying to get rid of the thought. I don't want to waste my time imagining something that, in all likelihood, will never happen. The best I should hope for is that whatever is happening between them is enough to prevent Sisi from getting involved any further with Lord Ricard. Maybe, if we're fortunate, the King will send Sisi safely back home and things can return to normal. Maybe his sudden interest in her will be enough to protect Mali and the rest of our family from Ricard's spite. It wouldn't be the better life I'd hoped for us to find when we first set off on this journey, but it's better than losing everything, than losing Sisi to a man who only wants to use her for his own selfish ends.

I have to remind myself of that several times throughout the morning. It's a *good* thing if Sisi is happy with the King. Something fragile and lovely seems to be growing between them as they sip their tea and talk.

Well, Sisi is talking. The King just listens. Sisi is expounding on her idea that the First King and Queen were only ordinary people, no different than any of us, and that the beings we call the adirim and pahyat were in the Kingdom long before they were, living in peace and harmony with civilizations of their own, not depending on humans to create it as our legends maintain. "We're less important than we think we are," she concludes.

"You mean *I'm* less important than I think I am," he interjects, but he's smiling, and he sounds interested rather than angry. "I'm the one whose authority stems from the understanding, such as it is, that humans are the rightful rulers of the go'im and that *I'm* the rightful ruler of the humans. If my great-whatever grandparents usurped their power, if it came from military might and not from the will of Gaia, then my rule is a false one."

"I don't think we need to go that far. The Kingdom is yours now, and was by right of inheritance as far back as any of us can trace. If we take it back far enough, we honestly don't know where it came from. We tell ourselves that it came from the hand of the Goddess Herself, but we don't have any proof of that—nor do we have any proof that it *shouldn't* be yours," Sisi replies.

"It certainly would be good for those of us who must rule to keep such possibilities in mind. It is too easy to let power go to your head, if you believe you were born to it and that it is yours by divine right."

Sisi looks impressed that he's taking her so seriously. Sisi very rarely looks impressed.

And it isn't just that—the King agrees with most of her points, nodding along as she talks, and occasionally bringing up another book he's read that he thinks she'll find interesting. I can't follow much of the conversation, but it's nice to watch Sisi drawing closer to him with everything he says, smiling at his points, fascinated by his ideas.

It's an enjoyable morning, maybe the first such I've had here in the palace.

And there are many more like it. In fact, I soon tell the maid to please plan on meeting me *inside* my room in the morning in order to avoid any more occasions where I walk out in my underclothes and find the King there.

The poor maid is the only one who isn't enjoying the presence of our new visitor. In fact, she seems to be on the verge of a nervous breakdown from the stress of having to walk past him to begin her morning duties.

Of course, I'm not invited along every time that Sisi and the King—Lio—spend time together. Aunt Mae and I always join them for breakfast in our chambers, but the two of them usually head out for a long walk afterward. The first day, Aunt Mae insists on joining them, but even her considerable resolve cannot stand up in the face of Sisi's most pleading smile and the King's repeated requests. Sisi argues that they won't really be alone, since the King's bodyguard will be at their side the entire time, and Aunt Mae extracts a solemn promise from both of them that they will be on their most polite behavior if they're permitted to go for a walk alone. Apparently, she's quite gotten over any fear she may have had upon first meeting the King, for her threats are dire, creative, and extensive.

King or no King, Balion doesn't seem inclined to risk attracting the considerable wrath of my Aunt Mae, so he makes the required promises. They're gone for the entire morning, missing luncheon entirely and not returning until the sun has started to set in the winter sky. The King walks Sisi back to the door of our suite, both of them giggling over some shared jest. They cling on to each other's hands, and the King even dares to sneak a quick kiss to Sisi's cheek as he takes his leave.

Sisi's eyes are glowing with excitement as she closes the door behind herself.

"Well? Did you have a nice time?" I tease.

"Oh, Jena." She takes both my hands in hers and swings me around in a circle, then pulls me into an embrace.

"Still thinking that nothing can ever come of it?"

She lets herself smile. "I'm thinking that I shall wait and see."

That, at least, is an improvement over her dull certainty that she could do nothing to stand up to Lord Ricard. Her newfound hope gives me some, too.

At first, we hear nothing more of Ricard. I do my best to put him out of my mind, along with the threats he's made against our family, but the worries creep in, especially at night. I don't even know if anyone would tell us, even if something terrible were to happen. We haven't received any letters from home, so there's every possibility that a tragedy has already taken place. Then again, it could just be that Jorj and my father are the only two who can read or write, and that my father doesn't judge the value of a letter to be worth what it will cost to send one to the palace.

Sisi seems to be having far more luck than I am keeping Lord Ricard from her mind. She's usually busy with the King as of late, and when I see her, she's almost glowing with happiness. A week after the ball, we're invited to move our things from Lord Ricard's wing of the palace to the King's. If anything, these rooms are grander, but we hardly spend any time in them. The King is always inviting us to dinners, to walk in the palace's beautiful gardens, and finally, to see the many beauties of the City itself.

The threat of Sisi being forced into anything by Lord Ricard starts to fade away, like a nightmare does in the light of day. Sisi doesn't mention the man at all for nearly a month, as the days begin to grow longer and some of the chill fades from the air. That's why I'm so shocked when she asks Aunt Mae and I to come with her to pay a call on Lord Ricard. Still, of course, I agree. I certainly wouldn't send her there alone, though I don't know what I imagine I can do to protect her.

She sends a maid to his chambers with her invitation, and gets a response at once: yes, he'll meet her in the King's private parlor to take tea with her. We dress formally for the occasion, and the kitchen brings up delicacies of all sorts, though my stomach is too fluttery with nerves for me to touch the food.

Lord Ricard arrives promptly. It's interesting, now that I've gotten to know the King a little better, to consider how much Lord Ricard resembles his brother. They have almost the same attractive features, the same thick brown hair, the same rich hazel eyes, but the King almost always has a peaceful and pleasant expression, and Lord Ricard's malice—especially after the threats he's made against my family—seems to me to shine forth from the very set of his face, before he even speaks.

He bows low in greeting to each of us, as effortlessly polite as his brother is careless about such things. "My lady Sisi. Madam Mae. Mistress Jeni."

"My lord. Won't you sit?"

"I'm not sure that would be advisable."

Sisi just nods. "Very well. I wish to return some items to you." She holds up a bundle of boxes. "I am afraid I cannot keep these gifts you so generously gave me, my lord."

"Do they not please you?" he asks, holding very still.

"Each piece is lovely, and I thank you for your kindness in giving them to me. But I must be blunt with you, Lord Ricard. I fear cannot accept them in the spirit they were meant. I cannot take a present from one man and then be wooed by his brother."

For a second, something flashes in Lord Ricard's eyes, something bright and more than a little frightening. However, when he speaks, he says only, "Is that the way of things, then? Between you and His Majesty?"

"Indeed, my lord."

"I wish you both every happiness. You may keep the jewels, or throw them into the privy, or whatever you will. I have no need of them. I beg your leave, my la— Lady Sisi."

Without another word, and without waiting for Sisi to say farewell, he turns and leaves the room. Sisi is sitting in front of the untouched tea tray. "Well, that went rather better than I'd expected."

"He was so rude!" Aunt Mae exclaims, and then clasps her hands over her mouth. "Oh, I shouldn't have said that. But it's true!"

"But he didn't make any threats, or try to have us killed, or anything, so we're going to call that a win," Sisi says, her tone final. "Besides, I do believe I may have hurt his feelings."

"As if he has any," I scoff.

Sisi gives me a dark look, which silences me, as was no doubt her intention. "Now. Let's call the maids in. I think they may appreciate Lord Ricard's gifts much more than I do."

And that may more than make up for the anxiety the King's frequent visits have caused them, for there are enough jewels for every one of them to leave wearing a small, sparkling fortune and a glowing smile.

I wait until Sisi isn't looking and pocket a handful of the jeweled pins I put in her hair on the night of the ball. It's not like the maids, who all wear their hair cropped sensibly short, have any need for them, and I want insurance that a return home need not mean a return to poverty.

Just in case.

CHAPTER EIGHTEEN

A few weeks later, spring dawns beautiful and bright, the warmer and longer days now gracing the Earth. As the weather warms, King Balion asks us to join him as his guests for the Grand Market.

Since the earliest history of the Kingdom, the King himself has announced the opening of the Grand Market on the first day of spring. In the old days, it was a religious festival, a time to thank the Goddess for the many gifts She brings forth from the Earth. Members of all different peoples would travel from every Corner of the Earth, bearing gems and gold from the far North, spices from the East, and flowers and teas from the South.

Now, of course, all of the attendees are human, not a single member of the other go'im in sight. And because the High Road that leads across the Kingdom is in disrepair, that means few want to actually journey from far away to the Capital. Still, I'm eager to explore what wonders remain. And, much to my delight, the King has invited all three of us as his personal guests, our first expedition outside the palace walls since we arrived.

We have to ride in a litter again to get there, which is hardly my favorite mode of transportation. Still, with the presence of the King, I'm not surprised that security is necessary. He is, as always, accompanied by his silent and masked guard, but we have to remain separate from the crowd, nonetheless. One bodyguard, no matter how intensive his training or ferocious his fighting prowess, can hardly be expected to defend all three of us against a riot or assassins or any of the other dangers that could be lurking in so large a crowd.

When the long ride finally ends and we are at last permitted to dismount, I realize we aren't as far away as I'd thought from where we've spent the last few months. The fair is just outside the palace walls. There are hundreds of tents set up around the City, pressed close to the wall and spanning as far as I can see in every direction. The crowd parts around us, in the wake of the King's guard pressing them to either side, but I am still overwhelmed by the sheer number of people there. I've never seen so many people all at once, not even at the ball. They have every shade of skin from paler than the King's to darker than Sisi's; some have figures imposingly tall and others as short as children; some are dressed in everyday clothing like the simple shifts we wear at home and others in costumes that barely seem to be clothes at all. There are strange flared dresses, some people wearing nothing but cloths tied around their waists, and several people with bright green tattoos across their faces. I try not to stare, knowing how rude it is, but it's difficult not to when the people are so *interesting*.

At the very center, between the tents divided evenly on each side, there is a tall platform. My family and I stand off to one side as the King climbs to the top. He looks small and lonely up there, with no one but his silent shadow accompanying him. I'm sure he must be used to addressing large crowds, since after all he is the King, but I can't help but imagine how nervous I would feel in his place, if I were standing up at the top of that platform with so very many eyes on me.

I can hear him clear his throat, a small, scratchy sound that echoes over the open space, over the suddenly silent crowd. But when he speaks, although the words seem to be memorized by rote, his voice is clear.

"Ladies, gentlemen, all peoples, all go'im from all Corners of this great Kingdom and our Mother Earth, I welcome you to the One Thousand Three Hundred and Twelfth Spring Grand Market. Thank you for making the journey to our Capital, my home city. As always, you honor us with your presence. Our city is enriched not just by the trade that will take place here today, but also by the gathering of so many people from so many wide-spread places. As many of you are too aware, our Kingdom has faced dark times recently. The harmonious union of many peoples has always been our strength, and the will of our Mother Gaia. I hope that today, we will experience this harmony again, and take a step toward again enshrining that value in our Capital city and throughout every Corner of the Earth. Simply by being here—by bringing your trade, and yourselves, to the Grand Market—you are aiding our Kingdom in this most vital work. I will say no more, since I am sure you are eager to do what you came here for, but only to say once again, welcome."

He speaks better than I would have expected, given what a nervous man he is. But then, he has always seemed fiercely intelligent in his breakfast debates with Sisi. The crowd certainly seems impressed, rewarding even this brief speech with uproarious applause. However, no one lingers long—they must be, as the King said, eager to begin their trade.

I wish we had free rein to wander, but Aunt Mae informs us strictly that if we wander off, there's every chance she'll never see us again, and besides, there are parts of the market that are simply unsuitable for two young ladies. That, of course, just makes me want all the more to go explore what on Earth these people could be selling that's improper even to *look* at, but Aunt Mae's expression is forbidding enough that I decide to stick close, even though it would be temptingly easy to duck off into the crowd and spend a few hours unseen, unremarked upon in the anonymity of the crowd. Still, even with the fuss we attract in the King's wake, there's no shortage of interesting things to see.

The first stall we stop at is a jeweler's, a smiling woman who's stockpiled a set of centuries-old treasures made by one of the long-extinct tribes of the pahyat. If I were still in my homespun dress and looking like my normal self, she'd never let me near her precious wares, but accompanied by the King, we're allowed not just to see them, but also to touch and admire them.

We spend nearly an hour under the black velvet of her tent, examining the many treasures of her collection. Many of the items are made of thickset gold and glittering with precious gems. Some of the necklaces are several feet long, with every inch covered in pearls and rubies. Instead of these eye-catching treasures, though, I notice a delicate bracelet lying on a black velvet pillow. It's a very thin circle of silver, inset only with one large, teardrop shaped gem. Despite its small size, it draws my attention, and I can't resist the urge to slip it on my wrist.

"It's so beautiful." I turn my hand slightly, watching the clear stone send sparkling shards of light everywhere. I take it off quickly, not wanting to risk damaging something so beautiful. "Thank you, madam."

"Do you like it, Jena?" King Balion asks me.

"Oh, very much. It's the loveliest thing I've ever seen."

"It is indeed very nice. And it suits you." He turns to the merchant. "Lady, how much for that bracelet?"

"For Your Majesty, it is a gift," she stammers, her eyes widening.

"Nonsense. I won't take profit out of your hands. Tell me how much it is worth." For a moment, his voice sounds commanding, even regal. Then he smiles again. "If it will help, I can go back outside and leave my purse with the ladies, and you can simply pretend I was never here."

Still reluctantly, she says, "It would be eight hundred and fifty shekin, ordinarily."

I wince at that. It's a fortune, hundreds of times what my father's farm had made in even more prosperous years, much more than Lord Ricard sent us for our journey here, and likely more money than I have ever seen in my entire life. "Your Majesty, you mustn't—" I begin.

He sighs heavily, but his good humor still seems intact. "Gaia below, everyone certainly is making this complicated. Jena, your cousin tells me she would never have agreed to come to the Capital without your advice and your company. Consider this a small recompense for that service, if you cannot just accept a gift from me as a friend."

I'm not sure what would be worse: accepting such an exorbitant gift, or arguing with the King himself. I look to Aunt Mae for advice, but, unhelpfully, she only shrugs. I suppose it's up to me, then. And I do so want to keep the bracelet. Feeling guilty nonetheless, I curtsy slightly. "Your Majesty is too kind."

He seems to feel a little awkward about that. Good. I'm happy to pass the awkwardness along. "I'm glad to. Let's get on, then. Lots to see."

He pays the merchant what she asked and a bit more, brushing off her many thanks, and we set off. Though I continue to feel ashamed of the fact that I'm wearing enough value on one arm to feed a Quarter's worth of hungry families, I can't help but sneak glances down at the bracelet on my wrist, admiring the way it catches the sunlight as we walk through the crowd.

We stop next at a merchant of silks and other fine cloths. Aunt Mae exclaims aloud at the workmanship of the textiles, the even, invisible weave, but I'm more interested in the other customer perusing the wares. While Aunt Mae pelts the shopkeeper with questions about her work, I watch this other woman. She's taller and darker than even Sisi, with her lips stained a bright red. Something about the way she moves, a little faster and more graceful than everyone else, her hands almost disappearing as she traces them quickly over the fabric captivates me—and then she turns toward me, and I see her eyes flash. Though her eyes are brown, I see a ring of crimson around her irises, like a pahyati in one of Sisi's illustrated tomes about the Peoples of the Earth.

I realize suddenly how rude I'm being. A small part of me still wants to approach the woman and ask her if it's true, if she's descended from the go'im or if she is one herself, if she knows any magic, but I dare not. Instead, I focus my eyes downward and onto my new bracelet, pretending I've been admiring that rather than staring at this stranger. When Aunt Mae has made her selections, I'm relieved to leave the tent before I can make too much of a fool out of myself.

Our next stop reveals a rich array of teas and spices, out for display in flat-bottomed copper bowls. The merchant is a grinning, grey-bearded man, who happily urges us to smell the rainbow of peppers and salts he has out. I do as he says, taking in the bright and spicy scents.

Sisi leans over a particularly brilliant golden-hued powder and takes in a deep breath—and then sneezes right over it, scattering all the little flakes of spice everywhere.

The man only laughs. "Turmeric, it makes you sneeze. You cannot help it. Do not worry, this is only for smelling, not for selling." He gestures toward the back of his stall, where he has many small boxes stacked on top of each other. "Those, I sell. Here, just to look at. Let me tell you."

He explains the origin of every individual item. Every one of these spices is from a different part of the Kingdom: a bright red one is distilled from peppers grown in the North, the auburn powdered cinnamon from the East, the salts from different regions of the sea. I imagine all the different farms it would take to make such an array of riches—dozens of families just like mine, spread out across the entire Earth, their own crop of these exotic things as familiar to them as the apples we grow back home.

We wander from that stall to another selling rich old wines—the King samples several, as does Aunt Mae, toasting each other and laughing with every cup—to another jeweler, to a fresh flower market, to an old book-seller that fascinates me, though with my still-limited ability to read, I cannot make out the old-fashioned print in any of the books. By midafternoon, we're all weary and overwhelmed, so we purchase our lunches, hot curried chicken in a warm flatbread, and sit in a niche in the city wall, overlooking the action of the market. The tents where merchants have their wares laid out stretch on and on as far as I can see, and everywhere people are moving to and fro.

Lunch leaves a little trail of the spiced sauce around each of our lips. The King doesn't notice his stained face, and so Sisi laughs and leans in to wipe it away. He thanks her with a quick kiss, which Aunt Mae pretends not to see.

I could have spent hours more wandering around the marketplace, but my feet are growing tired and the King's guard leans in close, whispering something to him. "I am reminded," the King says to the three of us, "that I must return home before it begins to get dark. The crowds, you see."

I frown, and Sisi nearly protests, but to my great disappointment, we have to head back to the palace. As soon as we return to our rooms, though, I can to admit to myself that I'm quite weary and content to sit down on the couch, put my feet up on the table, and admire my beautiful bracelet.

Sisi is in another of her quiet moods once the King has left. She doesn't reach for her books, just sits next to me and takes my hand. I don't want to be the one prying into her business—again. Or perhaps I just don't want to be the one she's pushing away—again. So I simply ask, "You all right, cousin?"

She gives me a very small smile. "Yes, Jena. I think I'm happy."

CHAPTER NINETEEN

*B*y now, I can read nearly anything I set my mind to. Several months of weekly lessons with Jehan have me able to keep up even with some of Sisi's denser texts. She still saves the thickest volumes for herself, but at least I can scan an index and read a few passages fast enough to direct her attention where she wants it to go. Her attempts to uncover where the Kingdom's once-rich magic has fled have not slowed since she met the King. Quite the opposite, in fact—her frequent, lively debates with him seem only to spur her into further exploration of the hidden secrets that so fascinate her.

I'd be lying if I tried to pretend like I wasn't interested myself. I don't mind acting as a kind of research assistant, when she invites me to. It's the most time we spend together these days since she spends most waking hours with King Balion. And even without that, I've been drawn into the mystery—I want to know too.

I want to be as clever as Sisi is, and as knowledgeable. More so, even. If she is the beauty, I ought to be the clever one, right? And since I can't change my looks —if ever any magic could do that, it's been long since lost to time—I might as well aim for the improvement within my own control. Namely, I ought to try to *become* clever.

So, I read whatever she puts in front of me, even when it is head-poundingly difficult or eye-wateringly dull. Today's selection is a book on the history of the Grand Market.

At first, I don't see the point of reading something so boring, but Sisi suggests, "It might once have been more than a mere festival. If people came from every Corner of the Earth, could they have been having some kind of political congress?"

"You mean, like the Three Powers?" Now that my cousin and the King are officially courting, I know more about how the Kingdom is ruled—namely, that the King has to get approval from his Guard, the Priests of the School of Magic, and his own Royal Family before he can make serious changes.

"More than that," Sisi explains. "The author seems to be saying that important decisions used to be put to a vote —not of a few different powerful figures here in the Capital, but of anyone who chose to make their voice heard."

"That makes sense. The trade at the festival could encourage a lot of people to come."

"But it's hard to believe that the Kingdom was ever so fair and equitable. It seems like the whole system was set up to put all the power of rule in the hands of one person, always a human, always a man, always from a singular bloodline."

"You haven't seen the palace the way I have," I retort. "There are wings for the adirim and pahyat too, set up for what they need. It was never meant to be just for humans."

"But maybe the throne always was."

"That doesn't mean no one else was ever allowed *any* influence."

So absorbed in debate are we that I don't hear the knock at the window. Instead, a glint of movement catches my eye, and I see a black-clad figure, like a moving shadow, creeping in over the sill.

I start to scream, but fortunately bite it back in time, as I recognize the strange shadowy figure of the King's guard.

"His Majesty sent me for you," says the voice behind the mask. "He wants to show you something."

At once, Sisi is no longer engaged in her argument with me. She's grinning eagerly, and all but throws herself out the window. I look down at the book, blinking away tears. Another time I'll be left behind, I suppose. I really ought to be getting used to it by now. At least I'll get a chance to practice my reading, which I know I should make more of a priority.

But just a second later Sisi's head reappears, popping up in the windowsill. "Are you coming, or what?"

I didn't think I was invited on this expedition, but if she wants me, I'll go. I sigh and follow her.

The King is waiting just beneath the window with a

grin on his face. He takes Sisi's hand in his and shows us the way beyond the palace wall. It's a long walk from the center, through the darkening streets of the City, to wherever he's leading us. If not for the presence of the King and his silent, strong guard, I would be terrified of the dangers that could lurk around any corner. Fortunately, Sisi and I aren't alone.

We duck through walkways and scurry over bridges, turning left and right and every way until I am thoroughly confused. Finally, we turn at the end of a long, thin alleyway and find ourselves in an immense and splendid courtyard. Everything is green and blossoming, and the first flowers of springtime are just visible as the sun sets in the west.

"It's the Dawn of Spring," I say aloud, realizing. I remember these ceremonies from when I was a girl, when Kariana was still alive. Everyone for miles around used to gather for the four ceremonies every year, as one season spun into the next and we celebrated the bounty of our Mother, the Earth.

"The first day of the new season, yes. My brother's asked that we no longer make the old festivals part of court life, and I agreed, but... well. People will still gather," King Balion replies with a shrug. He seems almost apologetic, like he feels guilty for denying his brother's request.

But he's right. People are gathering for the Dawn of Spring, just the way they used to, just as they always have.

And they seem to appear from everywhere, from

hidden corners and the stones surrounding us. We are not many in number—perhaps thirty or so people, mostly women of Aunt Mae's age and older, though there are a few men and some younger folks as well.

This time, the King makes no speech of welcome. Instead, he joins with the rest of the celebrants in a great circle, hand in hand. I take Sisi's left hand and join a stranger on my other side. Someone begins to turn, slowly, and then all at once, movements swelling between our joined hands like a current running through still water. All I have to do is keep up the pace with the other dancers. Even the clumsy King manages to follow along.

We are dancing, turning in perfect, even circles, when someone begins to chant. The words are all in the Old Tongue, and they're carried out in time with the heavy, pounding rhythm of the dance, but I think I recognize in them some of the familiar words of the blessing Kariana once made over our fields. The dance, too, now that I think of it, is not so dissimilar from that simple circle step.

I try to listen to the words of the prayer, but they blend into one another, making an endless flow of sound. Along with the steady step of the dance, I feel myself drifting away from this time, this moment. Around and around we go in the circle, again and again, and I can imagine all the previous generations of worshippers performing the same motions, spiraling endlessly, back and back and back.

In this moment, I'm holding hands with Sisi on one side and with a stranger on the other, standing in this hidden City courtyard. But I can also feel the shadowy touch of thousands of other hands, hear the distant echo of thousands of other voices, see the reflection of thousands of dancers moving in the darkness. I don't know if it is all in my imagination, if it is the hypnosis of the dance itself, or if some other power is working on me, but I suddenly know that what I see is real, the real past collapsing in on the present.

Then I take a deep breath, and the chant stops, and the moment shatters. I don't know how long it has been, whether we danced for a minute or a night. I barely know who I am. My head still spins. When the chill of the night air begins to bring me back to myself, I turn toward Sisi, eager to know if she'd seen what I saw.

"Oh, my feet are throbbing!" she exclaims. "I feel like I've danced for hours. Lio, you'll have to carry me back to the palace!"

And I realize, from that, I'm alone in this strange experience, in whatever wonder I have, however briefly, touched.

"I enjoyed it," I say distantly. "I wish it could have gone on longer."

Suddenly, people are sitting on the ground, opening picnic baskets, laughing and talking, and the mysticism of the evening fades away as though it had never existed. Suddenly, I feel silly, like I must have been imagining something that wasn't really so, even if in my bones I do know that what I saw was—not entirely, but in some vital and important way—real.

I'm so consumed with my thoughts that I don't even

notice as Sisi and Balion wander away. One of the white-clad and pretty maidens in attendance approaches me to try to make conversation: it might be more worthwhile to try to flatter me now that my cousin is so close to the King.

"My name is Jini too." She introduces herself with a smile. "Spelled with a double *I*." I spend a moment trying to picture the spelling before I figure out what she means. My newfound mastery of letters does not extend quite so far as to make it come naturally.

"Oh, that's so much like my name. What's it short for?"

She draws back a little. "Lady Jeni, here we *never* discuss our True Names. What a personal question!"

"I'm sorry. I didn't mean to offend." I eat a chocolate off one of the trays someone offers me. I truly mean it—of course it was not my intention to upset this girl, who seems perfectly nice.

"That's a lovely bracelet," she remarks, clearly strained for something to make conversation about.

"Yes, I like it. It was a gift from His Majesty, from the Grand Market."

"How lovely! Did you enjoy the Market?"

"Very much." I give up and decide to just participate in the conversation. There's no way around talking to this girl, who is nice enough, if a little too persistent. And a little dull. "Have you been?"

"Many times, when I was a child. My parents don't think it's proper for an unmarried lady of my age to go, though. Not that I mean to criticize you and Lady Sisi, of course."

"Of course not. If it helps, we didn't get to see all that much of it either. Aunt Mae kept us pretty close."

"You are fortunate to have such a caring guardian."

"Indeed," I say, wishing for my cousin to return from wherever she and the King have disappeared off to. I feel like I'm failing at this conversation and I'm desperate for Sisi to come back and smooth things over, or, failing that, for Balion to awe her into silence with his royal presence.

It doesn't take long for me to spot Sisi, and I excuse myself from the conversation to approach her. She and the King are hand in hand and smiling, as they so often seem to be these days. Balion doesn't look quite as relaxed as she does though, tension visible in his broad shoulders. Sisi is wearing a red rose in her hair, probably picked from among the flowers that grow so freely here.

Sisi turns to Balion, nudging him with her shoulder. "Go on. Tell her."

He stammers. "Jena, I have something to—something I must say to you. Something I would like to, I mean—"

"Please just do it," I ask.

"Oh, in Gaia's name, you ridiculous man!" Sisi exclaims. She holds her hand forward, showing me a simple, unadorned golden ring around her finger. "Balion and I are going to be married!"

"Oh," I say, taking a small step back. "Oh." I blink slowly, several times. I look at the ring, then at my cousin's beaming face, then at the King. "Of course, I'm happy for you. I'm so happy for you both. Don't you need to ask Jorj though? I thought..."

"Yes, of course," the King replies. "I'll do that. I don't know what I've been thinking. I was just—I seem to have forgotten all protocol. I'm just so—"

"Happy," Sisi finishes. "Isn't that the word you're looking for, my dearest?"

"Happy," he agrees.

"And then I am happy for both of you," I reply, even if it's not quite true.

Aunt Mae, to no one's surprise, is absolutely delighted with the news. It even soothes her rage when we return through the window, well after midnight.

The letter containing Jorj's permission for Sisi to marry the King, and his many fervent wishes for his sister's every happiness, arrives within the week. The King's fastest messenger, riding the best horse in the Kingdom, makes much better time to Prinnsfarm and back than we did in our donkey-drawn cart. The four of us—me, my aunt, my cousin, and the King—sit in our suite together to open the letter, and all of us rejoice when (as I'm sure we must all have expected), the permission for Sisi's marriage is written out in Jorj's strong, even hand.

From that moment on, Sisi's engagement is official—she is the Queen-to-be.

CHAPTER TWENTY

*W*ith the official announcement of the King's engagement to my cousin, the whole Capital seems to erupt into a flurry of sparkling chaos. The preparations for the big day are of the utmost importance. So much must be done in so little time, from formal tests to dress fittings.

The very first hurdle is choosing a date. At the advice of Elan, who has been promoted to the role of King's steward at Sisi's recommendation, they choose the end of Summer as a means to make the festivities look more presentable to the public. Balion and Sisi are eager to be married as soon as possible, but there are some practicalities which it seems even a King must respect. They need time for everything else, for her to be presented to all the right people, and—Elan manages to imply without quite saying—for the scandal of her involvement with Lord Ricard to fall out of people's minds.

There is also a whole list of things that Sisi has to do

to prove her worthiness to be Queen. I didn't know this until she told me, but she has a Test of her very own that she must undergo, just like the choosing of the King himself.

And that's only the finale of a lengthy season of interviews and panels and balls, subtle and explicit ways that Sisi is required to win over any number of people that stand between her and marrying the King. There is much more involved in this than I ever could have imagined. Balion, of course, has lived with these ceremonies hanging over him every minute of his life since he was a child, so it's all second nature to him. Without his expertise, we wouldn't know where to go or what to do.

Even watching it from my relatively safe distance as Sisi's best friend and de facto lady's maid is overwhelming. I can't imagine actually going through with all of this.

"You should've just married the potter's lad," I tease, as I'm doing her hair up for a state dinner with the Lord and Lady of the Second Quarter, who are Fifth and Sixth in the Kingdom, respectively. Although they're about to get demoted after Sisi's wedding. "You'll be lucky if these people don't spit in your soup."

"Ha ha," Sisi says, but then looks thoughtful, and I don't think it's about the possibility of becoming Daren's bride. "When your supper is brought up, save me a plate, would you? I might wait to eat till I get back."

Diplomatic dinners, though hardly Sisi's strong suit, are nothing compared with the real Test. If she is to become Queen of All, she has to be approved by all Three Powers of the Kingdom.

I have to have King Balion explain the whole thing to me.

He looks puzzled at first when I point at his crown and ask him, "So what are these Three Powers that Sisi has to deal with, exactly?"

"Right," he answers, looking embarrassed. "I suppose it's not the sort of thing that just anyone would know. I forget, sometimes..."

"Did you know I couldn't even read, before I got here?" I say, just to shock him. It works, as I knew it would. Shocking Lio has become something of a hobby for me, not least because it's so easy.

But I also get my explanation.

Just as the Kingdom is divided into Four Corners, and each Corner into Four Quarters, and just as Gaia's People are divided into Three Nations, power in the Kingdom too, is held in a careful tripartite balance. He shows me the three symbols on the crown—the Sign of the Three Powers.

"I'm one of them," the King says. "Well, rather, the King is. And the Royal Family. The whole Power of the Crown. We rule over things of the mind—laws, regulations, trade, culture. Our power often seems greatest."

Next is the Power of the Sword, represented (appropriately) by the sword in the symbol, which neatly pierces through the crown. This, Balion tells me, stands for the Guard. Even he—though he's been followed by a member of this silent order all his life—knows little about them. They train in secret, and their members are ruthless, deadly killers in the service of the Royal Family. They rule over things of the body—fighting, yes, but also healing, hunting, and much else. To my surprise, I learn that Balertius, the King's dancing mentor, is thus technically a member of this Power as well.

Finally, and even more mysteriously, Sisi will have to face the Power of Magic. This power, which governs things of the soul, all that is unseen and unknown, is dwindling in the Kingdom, down to just the last two konim—the elderly Garem, and his assistant Jehan, my former reading teacher. Once they had vast schools of knowledge. Balion frowns as he tells me this. "Maybe Sisi's right. Maybe I ought to do something about it."

"Worry about your wedding first," I council him. "There's enough to fret about on that score without adding to the list."

But it turns out that, other than planning the wedding feast itself, all the real trials are on Sisi's shoulders, not Balion's.

First, she has to deal with the first and greatest, the Power of the Crown. The authority of this power is invested in the King himself. Fortunately, the King has already approved of her, so she just has to speak with a panel of his loyal advisors. Unfortunately, the head of this panel is Lord Ricard.

Balion assures her that she needn't worry about anything. "None of them will go against what I want," he says. "I want you to be the Queen. They have everything to gain by supporting my choice and everything to lose by going against it. And none of them have any reason to oppose you."

"Except for your brother."

He shakes his head. "You don't need to worry about him. I've known him much longer than you have. He's my brother and, really, he's a good man. He might have had his feelings hurt, but I'm sure he's gotten past it. And the heart wants what the heart wants. He'll understand that."

Sisi rolls her eyes. She's reluctant to argue with her fiancé, it seems, but I can't deny that I tend to agree with her assessment of Lord Ricard. I don't think the King understands nearly as much as Sisi does about him—not that it's hard to believe a man might be biased in favor of his own brother.

She has to go in to speak with the council alone. Even the King isn't allowed to accompany her. Instead, Balion and I wait for her on a red velvet-covered bench in the long marble hallway outside the chamber. For all his assurances that she has nothing to fear, he is obviously too nervous to do much in the way of making conversation. He sits on the edge of the bench, tapping his foot insistently and rhythmically against the floor, his eyes fixed to the dark wooden door. We have no way of knowing what is happening in there, and the King himself is as powerless as I am to help Sisi as she faces strangers who must judge her, and at least one person who is openly hostile to her.

Perhaps the King was right about Lord Ricard, or perhaps—as I privately continue to believe—the Prince has some secret reason of his own for not wanting to stand in his brother's way in this. Regardless, Sisi leaves the room grinning. "I have the council's permission," she says. "One down, two to go." Apparently, she has few fears now that this first hurdle has been crossed.

The Second Power must have given Sisi her Test without any of us noticing it, because one day, she wakes up and finds she has a mysterious black-clad shadow of her own, a bodyguard just like the King's. She tries to ask the guard about it, to find out who he is and where he came from, but he will say only, "You have been chosen, my lady."

Balion tells her what little he himself knows, that their order is as ancient as the throne itself and that they have their own rituals by which they protect the King and Queen. He also tells her that she's unlikely to ever learn any more—he's had his own bodyguard since he was a boy of seven, and he's never so much as learned the man's name.

Uncharacteristically, Sisi seems willing to accept that. Perhaps she's distracted by the staggering amount of wedding planning that she has to do. Or perhaps she's nervous about her third Test, the Test of the Power of Magic, which won't take place until the wedding itself. Even without that hanging over her head, though, the logistics at play are staggeringly complex. I wouldn't have thought every single aspect of the minutiae needed Sisi's personal intervention, but everyone has questions for the Queen-to-be.

Emissaries must be sent to our house to bring back our family, and to the Four Corners to invite every Numbered man, woman, and child in the Kingdom, lest offense be inadvertently given to some House that turns out to be more powerful than anticipated. Plans have to be made, for a banquet grander than any in living memory, for gifts to be made to the populace, for elaborate and unheard-of sorts of entertainment.

Balion and Sisi, I am sure, would be quite contented to whisper their vows to each other in front of a single priest, or indeed with no company but each other's, but they don't seem to get much of a say in that. After all, as Balion says himself while hearing half a dozen tailors plead their cases about how they should be chosen for the honor of sewing the wedding napkins, he is the King, and sometimes that means he has no freedom at all. Their wedding is more about Sisi becoming the Queen than it is about her marrying the King, and certainly more than it is about her marrying Balion, the man she loves.

I wonder distantly if I ought to be jealous of her. So often in the past, I've hidden a secret anger that Sisi is always the center of attention, always the one so admired by others, when I am ignored. Surely, now that she is about to become the most powerful woman in the Kingdom, that she has fallen in love with a man who is handsome, kind, and devoted to her, that their union is about to be celebrated by an enormous ceremony where all the most important people in the Kingdom will celebrate them—surely now, I have something to envy.

Yet I don't. She has so little freedom now, and soon, when she is Queen, she will have even less. She may have power, she may even be able to make her dream of justice for the forgotten people of the Kingdom come true, but she'll spend most of her life confined to the palace, surrounded by people who wish her ill or see her as nothing more than a means to an end.

At the same time, it is becoming clear that I, as a poor and unregarded girl whom no one cares in the least about, am free to do exactly whatever I want. I can sit in my rooms all day and read; I can go down to the kitchens and eat sweets until my stomach aches; I can sneak about the palace and listen to people gossip about exactly what Sisi must have done to win the King's hand in marriage. I particularly enjoy one popular theory, which holds that she is a witch who has put a spell on him so he will die a bloody and terrible death if he looks away from her for longer than an hour. Honestly, speaking as someone who spends a lot of her time watching the King stare at Sisi, this claim seems to fit the evidence. But, jokes aside, I appreciate that I can do as I please.

No, jealous I am not. But in private, I must admit to myself that I am saddened to realize that Sisi has grown so distant from me—not because, as when we'd first arrived, she is driven by a fury, but because she is happier in her new life, happier with her fiancé, than she is when she's with me.

I don't want to talk to her about it. Because if I do...

If I do, I fear that nothing will change, even if I ask. And I don't want to have to accept what that would mean about me. About her. About our friendship.

About my future.

Whatever unspoken hope I might have had about Sisi's feelings toward me is gone now. It's obvious that she is entirely in love with the King, as he is with her. She can't, and never could have, shared my longings for more.

I try to put those thoughts out of my mind entirely and focus on what matters. That is, I try to be a friend to her.

I can do little to help Sisi plan the wedding, since I'm neither important nor elegant. She's going toward her new life, and it would be foolish to try to follow her there, where I'm unwanted and unneeded. Instead, I resolve to find a useful way to fill my days: spending time in the library.

CHAPTER TWENTY-ONE

unt Mae finds me on my way back from a long day of studying. My eyes are bleary and my head aching, but I have a new tidbit to share with Sisi: a report of some of the pahyat, those who cannot use magic at all, still possibly living up in the Northern Mountains as recently as ten years past, when the book was authored.

I won't have a chance to tell her that—not straight-away—because she isn't in the room when I return. Just my aunt, sitting on the couch, drinking a cup of tea and watching me.

"Where's Sisi?"

"With the King, of course. But I'm glad to see you. I hardly do, these days."

"I'm glad to see you too, Auntie." It's true, especially with the rest of the family arriving from home so soon. I dread the moment when I will once again be lost in the crowd, but for now, it's just us—me and the woman who raised me as much as anyone did.

"Your father is coming tomorrow, you know."

"And the rest of the family?" I confirm, somewhat nervous. Sisi can hardly marry without her brother there, and I'd hoped to see the rest of them—especially Merri and the baby—too.

"Of course. But before they get here...before they get here, there's something I wanted to talk to you about. Will you sit with me?"

I do as she asked, my heart fluttering in my chest. For a moment I'm afraid that she somehow knows about my research into the go'im, that she's going to forbid it—but of course, Aunt Mae, who can't read much more than I could a few months back, has no way of knowing what I'm doing when I'm in the library for all those hours.

"I've wanted a word with you for a while, Jeni, but since I hardly see you these days, and with so much to do, there hasn't been time."

I feel briefly guilty at the thought of my aunt waiting around in the hopes of catching me alone. I know what it feels like to be ignored when others are too busy to spend time with you, and it can't have been pleasant for her, with Sisi always with the King and me buried in my books, even if Aunt Mae has made friends with some of the other ladies in the palace.

"I don't know how to bring this up, quite, but it's about... well, it's about your cousin. And your friendship with her."

This isn't the first time I've had this conversation with

my aunt. When we were younger, people always used to tell Sisi and I that we spent too much time together, that it wasn't normal or healthy, that we ought to make other friends. Like it made any sense to try to trek into town to play with one of the neighbors' children, when we had one another so close by. Or like we would have any interest in sharing games with the boy cousins, when we had each other to talk to. "I don't want any other friends."

"That's... that's not quite what I'm getting at." Aunt Mae hesitates, and then says quietly, "When I was a girl, I had a dear friend who lived in town. Hana, her name was—more girls used their True Names back then. We were inseparable, just like you and Sisi are. From the time we were old enough to walk and talk, we went everywhere together. Did everything together. It was clear that my brother was going to inherit, that the whole farm would be his one day, and Hana had older brothers herself. We used to talk about running away together, about starting our own little shop in the City. About living together forever."

I've never heard Aunt Mae mention Hana before, and there's no one by that name in our town. That seems strange, if she was so important to Aunt Mae. I frown, unsure where this story is going.

"She grew up, met her husband, and married. Her farm is about a two days' ride. I haven't seen her in... in twenty years, probably. Do you understand what I'm saying?"

I shake my head.

"It's normal for girls to be close. Even for them to

fancy themselves... bound together, in some way. As I felt about Hana. As you feel about Sisi. But most girls grow out of that phase. They find themselves interested in men, soon enough, and in marriage and babies and all the things they're supposed to. Hana did. Sisi has." She pauses, and takes a long, slow sip of her tea. "I never did."

I stare straight ahead, unable to meet my aunt's eyes. It's something I've always known about myself, and never said aloud. I don't have the words for it.

The reality is, I've never thought about a man the way I know Sisi thinks about the King. I've never had the kinds of crushes I hear other girls giggling about. When I think about the future, I think about Sisi, not marriage and children.

When I think about beauty, it's her face I see.

When I imagine being in love, I can only imagine Sisi, or, if I really try, some other woman.

I blurt, "I've never been interested in a boy. Not like that."

"So I feared. I had hopes, at first, when we came here —your reading tutor—"

"I like Jehan. But... I think he has as little interest in women as I do in—"

"I thought as much." Aunt Mae sets her tea down and gently places one hand on my shoulder. "I hope someday you'll find someone to make you happy. Whether you grow into yourself and decide you *do* want marriage, and all of that... or whether you find a true friend of your heart and stay with her all of your days."

But Sisi is the true friend of my heart. I know as

much, even though I cannot say it. "It's not the same for her as it is for me," I say dully. "I know that. I've always known much more awaited her than the life that she and I shared in our little attic room."

That doesn't stop me from wanting it. From admitting now, only to myself, that it's the only future I've ever wanted.

I know in my heart that it's impossible. I always have, so much so that I haven't even bothered to admit that it's what I want. Why would I, when I know I'll never have it?

"Knowing doesn't make it any easier," Aunt Mae says. "But maybe there's some comfort in hearing that you're not alone."

"Is there even a word for... for this feeling?" I ask.

"I heard a story once that it was common among the adirim. They called women like us Gaia's Wives, and saw us as closer to the Goddess than those who let men into their lives. I think it's a pretty idea, even if we can't call ourselves that openly."

Gaia's Wife. I suppose it's nice to think of being married to the Goddess Herself. Though it only speaks to the fact that I'll almost certainly never find someone to share my life with here on Earth. I say as much to Aunt Mae.

"I've had a good life, in spite of never finding a partner to share it with. Maybe you will too."

Or maybe I'll end up bitter and miserable like my father. Or maybe I'll be found out for the freak that I am and turned out of society. Or maybe Sisi will grow closer and closer to the King, to her *husband,* and further and further from me, until our old friendship seems like nothing to her, the mere relic of her babyish past, best pushed aside and forgotten because it no longer matters in her new life.

"You need not look so glum, Jeni," Aunt Mae says. "It's not a death sentence to be different, you know."

"It feels like it," I admit, staring down at the ground. "That Sisi is marrying someone else."

"I know. How do you think I felt when Hana married?"

It was easier when it was Lord Ricard, I think, though I'm sick with myself for the very idea. At least then Sisi was just trying to save the family's future and learn about the Kingdom's secrets. She wasn't choosing someone else over me. With Balion, she's genuinely in love, happy with someone the way she never would be with me. She *wants* to be with him.

There's nothing I can do about that. I can't even wish it were different, not with how much I love Sisi, how much it means to me that she has found someone worthy of her, someone who loves her and who can give her a good life.

All my life, I've known Sisi would one day leave me behind. I just didn't know how unbearable it would feel to watch it happen and know I can do nothing to prevent it.

"But you made it through?" I ask, desperate for any reassurance Aunt Mae can provide.

"I made it through. And so will you."

"Don't...don't tell anyone else in the family," I ask, my voice breaking. I mean Sisi above all, of course, but also my father. "I don't want them to know."

"Of course not. It's between you and me," she promises.

"Thank you, Auntie."

My voice breaks, and Aunt Mae glances sadly at me, almost like she wants to say something more. Yet no words come, and I take my leave.

For once, I am relieved to be alone in my chamber, where I can cry in peace for the love I'll never be able to speak aloud.

CHAPTER TWENTY-TWO

"**M**urder! In my own palace! Murder!"

I jump up from my spot on the couch, waking baby Mali on my lap. She starts to cry, which seems only appropriate, given the circumstances. "Your Majesty, what's the matter?"

"Where's your cousin?"

Sisi sticks her head out from her bedroom. "Here, Lio. What are you shouting about at this hour?"

"It's Garem."

She enters the room fully, pulling a dressing gown over her shoulders as she does. She leans against the wall near her room, apparently unimpressed with the King's hysterics. "That old man? What about him?"

"They just found him dead," Balion says, still pacing back and forth. He looks furious, frighteningly so. He's such an even-tempered man usually, and I don't know what to make of this sudden rage.

"He was an old man," I say, hoping to calm him somewhat. "Sad still, of course, but it must have been his time."

Balion shakes his head, slowly. "No. No, I've been blind for too long. They found him at the foot of the Tower of the Konim, as though he'd fallen. I'm sure it was meant to look like an accident. First, he tells me only *he* can do your Test. Then, he disappears into his rooms and will see no one, not even me. Now, just before it's time for the ceremony, he's dead."

"You think he was killed," Sisi confirms, taking a casual seat on the chaise.

"Yes."

"To prevent me from becoming queen."

"I fear it."

Sisi shakes her head. "But surely someone else can perform the ceremony?"

Balion sighs, sitting down heavily on the couch next to her. "There's no one else. I've been so foolish, I—I let my brother convince me. 'The konim have too much power, they've done nothing for the Kingdom but take taxes from our hardworking people,' that's what he said. And I believed him. Maybe he was even right. But now there's nothing I can do. We can't be married, not without the spells, not without the blessing of Gaia's konim."

"What do you mean?"

"Garem was the last fully ordained member of the konim. There's no one else."

At first, Sisi doesn't even seem concerned. Balion is, since he's faced with the potential of Sisi's wrath, quite a bit more nervous. I would be too, if I were him. Yet Sisi only shrugs. "There must be a way. People marry without a ceremony every day."

"Not to the King of All the Earth, they don't."

"Come on now. Let's not just sit here and worry. Let's focus on the good, first and foremost. We have each other, do we not?"

"Of course we do, Sigranna," Balion replies, sounding a little shocked. "From today to the end of my days, I am yours."

She pauses momentarily, blushing, but then returns to the matter at hand. "And we're hardly helpless. You're the King! And I am resourceful, in my own way."

That's an understatement.

"Yes. Yes, we'll figure it out." He stands. "I should go talk to the counsel. See if they can be persuaded to make an exception."

"That's a good idea." Sisi kisses him goodbye. As he's headed out the door, though, she speaks again. "Lio?"

"Yes, my love?"

"I'm sorry about Garem. He seemed a good man."

"Yes," the King says, gratitude and grief shifting across his face at once. "He was."

Once the King is gone, Sisi turns to me. "Will you help?"

"I'm surprised you bothered to ask."

"What does that mean?" she demands. I don't meet her eyes, immediately regretting my sarcastic words. No matter what else there is between us, Sisi is still my dearest friend, and I would never want to hurt her. "Well, come then. We've work to do."

She leads me back down to the library. I start out happy to have her at my side, and to be able to share my newfound expertise with her. That fades quickly enough, as we dive into the actual problem. It becomes apparent that, no matter how skillful our reading or dedicated our attention, we may not be able to fix this.

The rest of our morning is spent digging through the law books of the Kingdom. Again and again, written everywhere she looks, Sisi finds a fact even she cannot argue with—the Queen of the Kingdom, just like the King, has to be bound to the land. The Ceremony requires an enormous expenditure of magic, one that could be fatal to even a practiced witch. Only a highly trained member of the konim or one of the adirim could do it. And there are no priests left. Garem was the last of a long-dwindling group.

I jump out of my seat as Sisi slams *The Code of the Nation* shut.

"Did you find something?"

She doesn't respond to my question, just leaps to her feet and walks away. The heavy library door slams shut behind her, leaving me alone to stare at the discarded pile of books. Once I'm sure she's really gone, I dare to peek at the book she's abandoned.

Opening to the back index, I find S, for succession, and turn to the appropriate page.

None shalle rule, neither as King nor Queene, neither regnante nor consorte to the regnante, unlesse that they be approved by all three powers: by the power of the Crowne that resteth with the King and his consel, by the power of

*the Swourd that resteth with the protectors of the Earthe,
and by the power of High Magicke that resteth with the
greatest people above all, and also with the chosen in the
lign directe of the First Queene, and also with the dedicate
religious of Gaia.*

I suppose that answers that, then.

I put the book down, a little more carefully than Sisi
had, but just as resigned. I can't see any way around
what's written in black and white on that page. I take a
split second to relish in the fact that I can now read this
archaic text in its fading print and understand every word
before I return to the problem at hand.

Sisi was so close to her happiness—about to marry the
man she loved, about to have her place in the Kingdom
finally settled. And now, all of that has been torn away
from her, suddenly, through this violent and tragic act.

It isn't right. Someone ought to be able to do something. Even the King can't, seemingly, intervene, he
admits, looking ashamed when he rejoins all of us for the
midday meal.

"How did you let this happen?" Sisi demands of her
fiancé over a very tense luncheon of roast chicken and
fresh-baked bread. "Surely you knew that we would need
to have a new king or queen sooner or later?"

"I didn't think. I mean, Ricard was so sure that there
was a way around it."

"Now do you see why I don't trust him?"

"I'm sure it was a mistake on his part. He would
never be involved with something so terrible."

Sisi stands up at that. "If you want to remain blind,

then that's what you'll do. I would have thought you cared enough about our future together to finally see what's right before your eyes."

She storms out of the room. The King is wise enough, at least, not to try to follow her.

The days that follow are tense. The King and his brother have an argument behind closed doors that ends with Balion's bodyguard pulling him physically from the room. Sisi won't see any of us. And I...

I am in the library again.

At first, it's just to hide from all the conflict. Jorj is in a private drawing room with the King, negotiating how he'll make reparations to Sisi's lost virtue if the engagement has to be broken; maids are scrambling to postpone the wedding plans; the stewards are in a panic over what to write to the guests. At first, I just want to stay out of the way.

But as I read through the old books, something occurs to me—or rather, someone. It's some time before I can begin to put this plan into action, though. I need an occasion where I can speak to Jehan, unnoticed and undisturbed. And that means waiting for a time when we'll be in the same crowd.

I'm not proud of choosing Garem's funeral as the venue for this conversation—I know it isn't exactly respectful of the dead—but I also know that I'm not hurting Garem, and this will give me the cover I need to speak to Jehan unnoticed.

Garem is buried in a state funeral, after the week of private mourning has gone by. We gather in the same grand ballroom where the King and Sisi met, where their wedding was to take place. Now, instead of enchanted snowflakes or flowers, it's draped with red curtains, red tablecloths, red carpets—everywhere, the color of mourning. Red for the heart's ache, red for the heart's blood. Red for death, and the rebirth that may follow it.

After the ceremony, I find Jehan in a corner. He's dressed all in red, looking sober and devastated.

"I'm so sorry for your loss," I say. "You must have been close." Jehan was one of the three mourners chosen for an honor in the service, and his hand is still bleeding from where it had been pricked to let blood fall into the grave.

"He was my mentor. Like a father to me. I believed I would follow him into the konim, until His Majesty..." But his voice becomes choked with tears, and he says no more.

"I hate to ask you for this now, but perhaps you know what has to be done? For the royal wedding?"

Jehan looks grave and sorrowful. "I'm sorry, Miss Jeni. I simply don't have the training."

"But the King—"

"It's not the wedding we should be worried about. It's what comes after. With no konim, there'll be no heir named. When the King is gone..."

"Surely you could learn, though. If you were trained to be one of the konim, you could figure it out. You're so clever, I always saw that in you. I think you could learn it, if you just tried." I sound childish and foolish even to my own ears, but someone must be able to do something. I just can't believe that Sisi's chance at happiness is gone so quickly. I can't believe everything is changing, again. That Ricard, however he's responsible for this—as I know he must be—is somehow winning.

"That knowledge died with Garem. Excuse me," he says, and his voice is cold as he walks away—but as he does, he leans close to whisper something. "Midnight, tonight. Find me in the library, and I'll show you."

I meet his eyes for a single second, to show that I've understood, and then let him go.

As I hurry back toward my family, I see Lord Ricard watching me. I meet his sharp hazel eyes for only a moment before breaking away.

CHAPTER TWENTY-THREE

J'm as quiet and as careful as the bird Sisi used to call me as I leave our rooms that night. I sneak past our maidservants without them noticing me. The fact that our entire wing of the palace is now occupied with my extended family might have something to do with it—no doubt the servants have more work than usual to do.

As I expected, Jehan is waiting for me in the great library, where we used to meet for our study sessions.

He speaks in a low whisper. "Thank you for coming."

"No problem. I'm just surprised you'd want to meet now. This must be such a hard time for you." I go to reach out for him, just to take his hand and offer him some reassurance, but he jerks away as though my touch might burn him.

"Please. We're in a hurry. I just wanted to tell you. There might be another way." His voice is clipped, short, not at all like his usual kind, stammering self.

"For the wedding?"

"For the Kingdom. Secret knowledge, perhaps written and preserved. Perhaps saved, somehow, from the ancient days—before the konim, before any of this was formalized. Your cousin might have almost found it herself, as she looked into the oldest secrets of the Kingdom."

"Do you know where it is?"

He gestures, widely, all around us, and I realize what he means. Somewhere in this library is the ancient knowledge, forbidden and forgotten. "But I can't help you. I'm being watched, I know it. I'm suspected. By both the King, who wants to find Garem's murderer—and by whomever the killer is. Wherever I go, I'll be watched."

And no one ever notices me. No, if someone is going to look for this secret, it's going to have to be me. "I see," I say quietly. "Do you know where I should start?"

"I have no idea. All I know is that the konim haven't always existed, that there have been kings and queens chosen by Gaia's will since long before our order was founded. And that if that knowledge survives, it is here." He stands. "I told my manservant that I'd eaten some bad fish and wanted the privy. If I'm gone much longer, he'll get suspicious."

And report back to Ricard, or some other player in this dangerous game I've suddenly found myself in the center of, I don't doubt. I am keenly aware of the advantage of the thing that has plagued me all my life. Because I am unremarkable, I am able to slip beneath everyone's notice. It's given me a lonely childhood. It's also given me a chance to help ensure Sisi's future.

He pauses before he leaves the library and looks me right in the eye. "Jena, before you do this, please make sure you know what you're doing. That's all I can ask. If you get involved, you'll be in the middle of the most dangerous situation in the Kingdom. And you'll be assuring that your cousin becomes the Queen."

He nods to me, and then he's gone.

And. Not but. *And* I'll be assuring that Sisi becomes the Queen of All the Earth. As if he knows how much that is going to cost me. As if some part of him knows just how little I want to see her wear that crown, take those vows, choose her husband and her future over me once and for all.

This is what I wanted. It's why I crept out of my bed in the dead of night to come here, why I asked for this secret, whispered meeting. I wanted a path to this very thing—to give Sisi her happiness with Balion. To give her a way to escape our quiet farmhouse life together.

And yet, if I can find the answer I'm looking for, if I can save Sisi's wedding, I'll lose her forever.

Surrounded by the weight of all these books, all these untold stories, I feel the weight of my own loneliness. I feel the absence of Sisi at my side, her warm, steady presence, and her inner fire. I think of the thousand jokes we will never laugh over together, the days that will go by without her, the sorrows we will mourn apart. And then I do what I know I have to do.

There's always only been one way for me, really.

Because no matter what else I may feel for Sisi, no matter what impossible desires I may have, she is still my best friend. And I want her to be happy.

So, I find *The Code of the Nation*, the impenetrable book Sisi was reading the other day, and I begin my quest to ruin my own life.

The Code of the Nation is several thousand pages long, and it's all as dense as the section I read earlier. There's no way around that. I figure at first that I'll have to read the whole thing from beginning to end, but I quickly realize that, no matter how carefully I think I need to look, there is simply not much of a chance that the answer to Sisi's problem lies in the midst of a dense chapter on the methods of agricultural water management most favored by Gaia. Furthermore, if I stick to that strategy, we'll all be old by the time I make it through the first bookcase worth of texts.

Every tedious detail in this dull and dense book goes back to the Goddess. No matter how minor, no matter how obvious it seems (that crops must be planted in the spring, and harvested in autumn, for example), every single thing needs to be attributed, not to common sense, but to the will of the Goddess.

I flip through the pages, looking for any sign at all that the Goddess might will Sisi to be able to get married. I'm dozing off in the midst of a description of the Goddess-favored method for planning a Royal naming when I finally catch sight of something promising.

The three powers being the branches onlee, and Gaia

being the trunke and the roote, yet might the kingdome be sustained without them if onlie Her Will were for it.

I read the sentence again. The Three Powers are the Power of the Sword, the Power of the Crown, and the Power of Magic, I know that much. I feel it's safe to assume this book is referring to the same thing. All three have to approve Sisi as the Queen. She's been through the Testing of the Sword and the Crown already, and still needs to be confirmed with the Power of Magic, to be followed by the ceremony of marriage and crowning. I knew all that.

But this seems to be saying there's something more than the ceremonies Sisi has already done—that the many things in the Kingdom that require their approval can exist without them. I'm not entirely sure how much I can rely on a sentence that spells the word "only" two different ways, neither of them correct, but it's all I have to go on.

Gaia being the trunke and the roote...

Again, it all comes down to the Goddess. But maybe that means that there's another way. A way around the approval of the konim, through some deeper magic.

I read the sentence over and over, but I still can't get any more meaning out of it.

The trunke and the roote...

There must be something there, but I can't make the words resolve into anything that would actually let me help Sisi.

Perhaps this isn't the book I need. I decide to find another, maybe one that will be more useful.

Unfortunately, the library is in a state of some disrepair. I don't think it gets used very much. There is no structure to the order in which texts are stacked on the shelves: I find collections of poetry sitting in between histories and travelers' tales. After half an hour of careful scanning of titles and indexes, I carry a heavy stack of texts back to the table and begin to skim through them.

Morning dawns, finding me with a fierce headache and no answers. I am beginning to wonder if this entire idea was nothing but folly. I'm only one girl, and a few months ago I was completely illiterate. It's stupid to believe that I could find something that the King and all the learned men of the Kingdom couldn't.

Still, I have to try. For Sisi's sake. Because no one else will.

Oh, Balion would try, no doubt, because he wants to marry her. And he could probably command any number of people to try to find a solution, on his orders. But I'm the only one who cares for nothing except Sisi's well-being.

I creep out of the library for breakfast, which I eat in our rooms with Merri and the boys. The rest of the family is still in bed, but I want to get this done with—have myself seen and accounted for, so no one will wonder where I am when I disappear back to the library. If, for once, I happen to be noticed, I know there could be danger. Jehan certainly seemed quite frightened, and I suspect, as Sisi does, that this murder was no random crime. It must have been Ricard's doing.

After all, he's the only person I can think of with a

motive to stop Sisi from becoming the Queen. Ruining her future with Balion out of sheer spite seems like exactly the sort of vengeful thing he would do.

At that thought, the image of Kariana's cottage in flames flashes before my eyes, as does Ricard's voice, whispering, threatening me and our whole family, even the baby, if he didn't get what he wants.

What he can't have, he destroys. Whether it's magic —or Sisi.

I may be equivocal about the idea of Sisi getting married, but I'm convinced of one thing. If I can stop Ricard's plans, with this or with anything, I have no choice but to do so.

"Jeni?" Merri asks. "You seem distracted. Is everything okay?"

"I was just in the middle of a good book. I think I'll head back to it now."

No one notices as I sneak back to the library, ready to search through more texts. I toss aside several volumes on the religion of the Kingdom, since they all seem to have the same depressing message: only one of the konim can admit a new member to their order. After five say the same thing, I finally get some details on what that entails.

In Ye True Faithe, only the High Priest may stand forth for the Coronation of the King and the Queen. And only one can be the High Priest. Therefore such a one can be made only through sacrifice.

Well, that's something at least, even if I don't understand it. I wish I could ask Jehan, since he knows more about this than I do, but I know he'll be in too much danger if I try to speak with him about this again. I have to figure it out myself.

Just after lunch, I find a book entitled *A Path to Priesthood: My Journey from Farmer's Son to Head of the Konim*. That looks promising, and it's written in language I can understand with ease. Relieved to at least have consistent spelling to count on, I flip through the pages and discover the story of a young man who had risen through the ranks to become a trusted advisor to the King himself.

On the cover is the author's name: Garem Linson.

I wonder if the author could be the same man whose body I saw lying in state so recently. I can imagine those gnarled hands, once young and smooth, writing these words and setting them aside, perhaps knowing that the knowledge he had, of a Kingdom filled with different peoples, would one day disappear.

My best friend in boyhood, he writes, *was Elric Ireith, a member of one of the Dar'fish People, one of those tribes called the Pahyat. There were several families of his tribe in our little town in the Eleventh Corner, and we made no note of his stature or the long beard he sprouted at birth. He was simply one of us, and my dearest friend.*

Yet when I was five and ten, he told me that his family had heard the call: they needed to retreat, from our town to a place of their own, far away, over the mountains. I knew even then, as I watched them walk away, that I would never see him more. Our Earth was changing, and not for the better.

It was the loss of this friendship that drove him to the

Capital, that made him leave his own family and his expectation of inheriting his father's bakery in order to pursue the secrets of the Kingdom. He had hoped, at first, to find out where the tribe had gone, so he could at least find his friend and say farewell. Instead, his journey led him to the konim.

Unfortunately, the book doesn't go into as much detail as I need it to about exactly *how* he went about becoming a priest. All Garem writes on the subject is:

As is tradition, I could take on the role I had trained to assume for so many years only after making a great sacrifice. It was not I alone that had to make it—my mentor, Tinius, who held the title before me, made a sacrifice of his own as well. He set aside his dream, and the title he had worked for as long and as hard as I myself had in his own time, in order to pass it on to me. Not for my sake, but for the sake of the Kingdom's good, did he do this, and it is only thus that such a change can be effected.

Well, that's a dead end if I ever saw one. Not only does the High Priest have to choose his successor, but he also must willingly sacrifice his role for a new priest to take his place. Garem is quite incapable of doing this, or anything else, as he now rests in his grave and has nothing left to sacrifice, even if he wanted to.

The rest of the afternoon is fruitless. I look for other books like this one, other memoirs of the konim written by men who, like Garem, have experienced life in the order firsthand. There are none. So, I try to read more broadly about the ceremony of royal marriage itself. Everywhere I turn I see the same hopeless words—the test must be blessed by the High Priest. The only exceptions I can find are from the ancient days, when there were adirim to perform the ceremonies with their great magic. No hope from that quarter, either. Well, there are still thousands more volumes in the library, maybe millions. I'll try again tomorrow. Today, my pounding head has gotten the better of me.

The entire next day is a useless, eye-straining, head-hurting waste of time. The only thing I find that seems even remotely relevant is a footnote in a thin volume about, of all things, court etiquette.

The well-prepared Numbered lady or gentleman may wish to familiarize him or herself with the contents of the ceremony. It is always easiest to be a gracious guest when one is prepared for what may occur at any event. The details of some religious rituals, as for instance the Third Test of the ascending King or Queen-to-be, may be shocking to the Numbered personage not familiar with these practices, and yet one surely would not want to miss such a momentous occasion! I recommend to the interested reader a direct source, c.f. Gaia's Booke, or other religious texts, which may be found in the royal library or by enquiring of a member of the Konim.

Well, at least now I have a title. *Gaia's Booke.* Although if I had run across anything like that in my searches, I surely would've pulled it aside to read based on the title alone. I spend the afternoon and evening searching for it in vain.

There's just one place I haven't looked. I'm going to have to go to the priest's tower and search for it there. I remember Jehan telling me about the hundreds of books lining the walls in Garem's office. Either one of those volumes will have the answer, or it doesn't exist.

I plan my trip up there carefully. I know it's dangerous. I know that Ricard is probably looking out for me, and that if I'm caught, the consequences could be dire, and not just for me.

But there has to be a way.

I decide that the easiest time is at night, though the silent, empty palace is terrifying. My footsteps seem to echo as loudly as falling rocks off the polished floors, however careful I try to be. It's painfully easy to imagine myself getting lost in these hallways and never being found, becoming just one more mystery of the royal palace, one more secret for a future explorer to discover.

As I turn the corner to the stairway at the foot of the Tower of the Konim, I see a single gold-cloaked guard. At least it's only one. I take a deep breath, rehearse the lie I've come up with in my head, affix the saddest look I can manage to my face, and approach him.

"Excuse me, sir?"

"Yes?" The guard is a young man with a friendly face. He looks a little bit like Daren, the potter's apprentice back home, with the same dark hair cut short around his ears, the same tan skin. Daren is friendly and not too bright, so I hope the resemblance between the two goes deeper than looks. If I imagine I'm with Sisi playing some friendly trick on Daren, and not breaking into a forbidden part of the royal palace against the orders of the Prince, this interaction is, at least, a little less frightening.

I gesture up at the stairway that he's blocking. "My lord sent me to fetch something from the tower."

"No one goes up, no one comes down. I'm sorry, miss." At least the guard is polite about it, so I should be able to sneak away and make my escape if I can't persuade him to let me in.

"Please, sir. It will just be a moment. My lord will be so angry if I come back without it." I let my nerves show on my face, though the reason I give is a lie.

"Who's your lord?"

"His Royal Highness, Lord Ricard. He wants some book."

The guard laughs, which is a promising sign. "Of course he does. Tells me he'll have my head if anyone gets up there, then sends you looking for something he's forgotten."

"I'm new to the service, and I can't risk my position..."

The guard steps aside slightly. "All right. Say I stepped away because I heard something in the far corridor, if anyone asks how you got up there. But I think I'm the only one on guard, so you shouldn't have any trouble. Just don't disturb anything, and be quick about it."

"Thank you so much," I say, a little shocked at my own success. This is much more Sisi's area of expertise than my own, and I don't know that I've ever managed to tell a convincing lie to anyone before in all my life. My hands are trembling from the fear, but there's no time to relish my victory.

I all but run up the long flight of steps and into the small book-lined chamber that was once inhabited by the unfortunate Garem. At the center of the room, laid out on a pedestal, I find it as if it were waiting for me. The volume is slender, perhaps a hundred pages. It is bound in black leather, the pages edged in gold. My hands hover nervously over the open book for a moment before I dare to flip it closed to see the words embossed heavily on the front: *Gaia's Booke*.

Carefully, I return to the library, my prize in hand, where I read all night and far into the early hours of the morning. I'd thought some of the other volumes were hard to read, but this book must be more ancient than anything else I've read. It's mostly in the Old Tongue, and I have to refer constantly to a dictionary in order to make any sense of it. But after a while, I think I've found what I need to know.

Hiding the book under my skirt, I creep out to the garden to watch the sun come up, waiting for the hour when I can find Sisi and the King and tell them what we must do.

I can't speak at first, so I just show them the book.

"These are the words you need," I tell them when my voice returns. "I'll say them, at the coronation, and then the Test should be able to go forward. It doesn't need to be a priest, just someone who..." I look for the right way to phrase it. "Someone who is willing to make the necessary sacrifice."

I show them the formula in the book. It's clear to all three of us that I meet all the requirements to make the sacrifice. As Jehan himself pointed out, I am giving up my dream so that Sisi can become the Queen. In this book, the most ancient and thus perhaps the most true of them all, there is no requirement that the person making the sacrifice be a priest, merely that someone forfeit their heart's desire in order to receive Gaia's blessing. She—it says *she* in the book—then speaks the sacred words of the Old Tongue, as laid out helpfully in the text, and then she is endowed with the power needed to represent Gaia's choice. Everything else—the konim, the ceremony, the pomp and circumstance—all of that came later. The actual magic is quite simple. It's just a trade, of one dream for another.

I know I have the power to do this for Sisi. If I can make myself do it.

Sisi stares at me for a moment, her dark eyes filling with tears. Then, silently, she pulls me into a close embrace. "Thank you," she whispers fiercely, too low for anyone else to hear. I hold her back and smile, ignoring the rising lump of misery in my throat.

CHAPTER TWENTY-FOUR

I peek over Sisi's shoulder to get a look at myself. The Jena in the mirror is grim and pallid, visibly miserable even in her lovely light-gold gown. I try to smile and fail. The color doesn't suit my sallow complexion at all, but apparently we're supposed to match the color scheme so we can dress up like the decorations to the room. It's not just the dress that is making me look so unhappy, though.

There's a question I've been aching to ask Sisi for the last lonely months, and now that the moment has come, even though it's on the tip of my tongue, I just can't. I bite my lip so I won't say anything, and focus on actually performing the duties for which I was brought to the Capital in the first place anyway—I am her maiden in waiting, and I have to help make her as lovely as she can possibly be.

Again and again, I've rehearsed this conversation in my mind, and now that the moment is here I can't quite bring myself to speak. It's not that I'm afraid of the answer. It's that I can't think how to even ask without hurting Sisi, and I love her so much that the idea of causing her any pain fills me with a sinking dread, worse even than the misery that's been building up in my chest for weeks.

For a long time, Sisi and I are silent as I twist her hair into an elegant pouf atop her head.

Yet as distant as we've become, whatever is between us, she still knows me well enough to know that all is not right. "What's wrong?"

"It's nothing," I say, focusing back on the work of my hands, trying to blink away the tears in my eyes without her seeing.

She turns around and grabs my hands, making me still then, looking right into my eyes. "Jena. Tell me. I've barely seen you for the last few weeks. I don't know what's going on with you. Talk to me."

And now the words fall from my lips like a flood, unhindered by any interference from my brain. "That's exactly what's going on. I barely see you. You hardly have time for me even now. Next week, you'll be the Queen of All the Earth. Do you think you'll have a lot more free time then?" The bitterness is leaking into my voice now, even as I try desperately to hold it back. I had no intention of letting my secret unhappiness spill out like this, and certainly not on Sisi's wedding day, on what is supposed to be the happiest day of her life. I chose to find the spell, chose to give it to her. I've made that sacrifice, and I ought to live with it.

I watch in the mirror, furious with myself, as her eyes fill with tears. "Jena, I don't—I just don't know what to say."

I wish I'd just kept my mouth shut. This will change nothing, and it doesn't help me at all to make her sad. It just saddens me as well. Everything that hurts her hurts me too. It always has.

"I don't know what I can do," she tries. "I don't want you to be unhappy, I don't—"

"I'm sorry. Forget it. I know you're doing your best. It's not like you had another choice. You didn't try to ignore me, you just... you have a lot of responsibilities."

"I'm growing up," she says softly, and her voice is sad. "I'm a bride now. About to be a woman grown, in truth as much as in name. And I am in love with a wonderful, kind, gentle man. And I am *happy* to be sharing the rest of my life with him, truly I am. It's what I want. What I want more than anything else. But that doesn't mean that my love for you is gone, cousin. It will always be a part of me, even if we're not together every moment the way we used to be."

"But when we're not that, not ever again, what will we be?" What will *I* be, without her? It's the question I've been trying hard not to ask myself. It's the answer I'm afraid of knowing. What are Sisi and I to each other, really? And what are we about to become?

"I don't know," she admits, always a hard thing for the prideful Sisi to do. "I'd imagined you'd go home with your father, but now I'm not sure that's a good idea. Maybe I was wrong, and you should stay here in the palace with me. Balion would find a job for you, if you'd like, or you needn't work at all. I need ladies-in-waiting. I choose them myself, you could be one. My companion again, but in an official capacity. You could live here in the palace with me and want for nothing, but..."

"But it wouldn't change the fact that you'd be far away. Your life will never be with me again. Not the way it was. I could stay here, but we can't go back."

"No," she says quietly. "I don't think we can, Jena."

"Well," I reply, not sure what else to do. She turns away from me, toward the mirror again, and I go back to doing her hair. I'm grateful for the fact that I don't have to say a word for her to know that I'm in desperate need of this distraction. Still, I try to find a jovial tone, one that doesn't match the deep-seated despair I can barely express even to myself. My voice comes out high-pitched, obviously false even to my own ears. "Well, it is what it is, I suppose. I don't imagine there's much of anything either one of us can do about it."

"That's the spirit!" she teases, obviously grateful for my change into positivity, however feigned it may be, and —briefly—I laugh.

I take the opening to change the subject, since I don't want to upset her again. I love her too much to want to see her sad, especially on her wedding day—no matter how I may feel. Instead, I ask, "Are you excited?"

"Yes, I think so. Nervous, too. Of course."

"For the wedding? The marriage? Being Queen?"

"Oh, you know. Absolutely all of it," she says, and laughs again, more genuinely this time. Then her voice grows serious. "I think it'll be all right, though. I'll have Balion at my side, and that's what really matters. We love each other, and as long as we're together, I think we'll be all right."

I wonder what it's like to feel that way about someone. About a man, rather, for it's how I've always felt about Sisi.

"That's good," I say weakly.

"Wait. Jena."

"What?"

"I just wanted to say..." She takes a deep breath and turns to meet my eyes. "I know it wasn't easy. The choice you made, the sacrifice. You gave me my happiness, and I know what it must have cost you. What it must have done to you, to know...you and I could have gone home together, if you hadn't found the secret. We probably would have. So, thank you."

"What kind of friend would I be," I ask her, "if I had taken my happiness at the cost of your own?"

"I just hope you'll find yours one day too. No—I know you will."

"How can you be so sure?"

"I didn't think I would ever be here. I didn't think marriage was in my future, or that I would find my place in the Kingdom through love. But here I am. About to be the Queen. And it's all because of you. If you can make that happiness for me, I know you can find it for yourself."

I don't know what to say in response to that, so I just kiss the top of Sisi's head and return to work on her hair.

Before we have to talk any more, a bevy of maids bursts in to help with everything: to fix Sisi's hair—apparently I did it wrong, which ought to be no surprise since I seem to do everything wrong; squeeze her corset tight, a task which takes four strong-armed women, two on either side of her to pull at each lace; bind her feet into tiny little shoes; arrange her necklaces in the most suitable fashion; drape her veil prettily over her features; and make sure her dress is arranged so that it won't stop her from dancing or get dirtied by trailing too much through the halls of the palace.

Of course, she looks stunning when they've finished. The gold tone chosen for her dress is much more becoming on her complexion than on my olive-tinged skin, and where my gown is relatively simple in its shape, hers is elaborate, with enormous tufted sleeves, a full skirt, and intricate beading all around the waist in a diamond pattern that emphasizes her voluptuous shape.

She's always been beautiful. What has really changed is in her smile, in the sparkling of her eyes, in the dimples that appear in her lovely rounded cheeks. She is happy in a way I never saw of her back home. When we arrived here, she was sulky and sullen and *angry,* angry at everyone, at the many wrongs of a Kingdom she barely understood and held no real hope of ever changing. Now she is smiling and lovely, radiant with joy and calm. Now she is in love. I know that in my heart, know that is the real difference in her, even if I wish it were something else, something there was any hope of changing.

If it were something else, then I could hope for things

to go back to the way they were. But, however saddened I am by being left out of her newly transformed life, I cannot wish for her to lose the love that has given her so much pure and genuine joy. I know I've made the right choice. As difficult as it was, as much as I fear I may be consumed with regret and resentment as I journey toward home with a father who I don't understand and a family where I have no real purpose, I know I've done what I must.

With that knowledge in my heart, and with a pit of dread in my gut, I take Sisi's arm. Together, we walk down to the grand ballroom. These are our last moments as girls together, and though we don't speak of it again, we both know it. She turns and smiles at me just before we enter, and I see it in her eyes, both the truth and, I hope, the future. Sisi will be happy with the King. She'll have a good life, and that's all I can really ask for, even if it's not what I wanted.

To my surprise, the herald leads us not back to the ballroom or some other splendid part of the palace, but down, down, down a set of steep steps hewn from rough stone.

At the base of the long flight of stairs, we are ushered through a doorway so low that even I have to duck my head. On the other side is the chapel.

It smells of earth down here, and mud, and things growing. There is already a crowd seated on low benches, shivering a little in their finery. The silken gowns most of the ladies are wearing for this Midsummer evening are much too thin to protect against the chill of the air underground. Everyone is dressed in light colors and opulent jewels, and quite a few of the ladies are obviously concerned with whether or not the damp floor of the cave might stain their voluminous and likely expensive skirts. The only light comes from a single flickering candle that Jehan holds in his trembling hands. I can't see much except the shadows that one light casts on the walls.

From within the crowd, the King appears and offers his hands to Sisi. She takes them with a small smile and allows herself to be led up to the front of the room. As I had read in the book, as I have learned that I must, I follow. Sisi and Balion both kneel, facing each other, and I take a moment to gather my courage. To speak in front of all of these people. To let Sisi go. I don't know exactly what my fears are, but they are writhing within me, blocking my throat so that it's hard to speak.

And then I suddenly realize, in that long and unbroken quiet, what is making this place so very special. It's not merely the fact that it is so oddly real, so quiet and still and *natural* where everything else in the palace is overdone and overdecorated. No, it's the sound here.

For even in the still and silence, when no one is moving at all, I can hear a long, slow rumble, as of breathing in and out.

I think I can hear Gaia breathing, the earth Herself alive beneath my feet and all around me.

I can feel the spirit I never gave any thought to before this very minute. Now I must believe it. I believe there is something here with us, some essential and unnamable force, a goddess in our Kingdom, of our Earth, beneath and around us.

A sense of peace fills my worried heart, lifts the tension that has been squeezing at me for so long. It doesn't matter what becomes of me and my small life, of Sisi and our friendship, of anyone in this room. We are only humans, and our lives are small and brief, and our mistakes are vast and weighty. But they will all pass from the Earth, even as we ourselves will, and it will not matter at all because the Earth herself will still be here, breathing and firm, ready to lift up new lives and raise them into the light.

Perhaps this is what magic is: this moment of connection, of certainty, of belief.

Jehan hands me the three-pronged Crown of the First Queen, and I lift it high above my head. Sisi and Balion steal wide-eyed and fearful glances at me. All the other Tests were mere precursors to this moment. I wonder if they're worried I might not go through with it, that I might somehow tear their happiness away from them when it's so close.

I could, of course. It wouldn't work if I couldn't, if the power weren't in my hands. Now, for the first time in my life, everyone and everything depends upon me.

I draw in a slow breath, in time with the Earth all around me.

And I begin the words of the ceremony.

The chant is all in the Old Tongue, and I know little of its meaning. I memorized the words by rote, Jehan and Sisi's brother Jorj taking it in turns to drill me on the lengthy phrases. It seems to have paid off though, as the words flow from my tongue as if drawn out by...

By... something. Thought fails me, replaced by something strange.

It's like what happened on the night of the Spring Festival, but much, much more so. My entire body feels as though it's humming, alive with a power I didn't know I had.

The words, which I'd so carefully memorized over those many nights, fall from my mouth. Each one tingles, and then burns. I hadn't been prepared for the pain, for the searing heat I feel on my lips and teeth as I quietly chant the words. Yet, as the pain increases, so does my sense of exhilaration, my excitement at what I can feel throbbing through my body. I forget all about why I'm doing this for a moment. It's all about the words themselves, all about the power.

I'm surprised when the dark cave flashes brilliantly with light for a moment. I'd forgotten that it was dark, forgotten where I was, forgotten everything but the words. Now my attention is drawn back into the space around me. I see Sisi and Balion, kneeling before me, their faces drawn with fear as they wait for the future. I see their expressions change to wonder as they realize the cave is illuminated and the ground is gently trembling.

And slowly, slowly, the crown begins to rise from my hands. It glows with light, getting brighter and brighter as it floats free from any touch, free from my grasp. It illuminates Sisi's wide eyes as it begins to drift forward and then settles, gently, on her head.

Sisi, her whole body shimmering in her golden gown under the magical light, and the bright crown resting in her dark hair, slowly rises and turns to face the crowd, her new people, and there is a long moment of silence as they regard their Queen.

"*Gaia volut rein et kol!*" I cry, and the whole assembly repeats it. I look out, seeing Elan, my father, my aunts and uncles, even our boy cousins, their faces calm and still. *Gaia wills it: Queen of All.*

I don't know who the first to drop to one knee is, but it happens as if it's a natural movement, a sweeping wave across the crowd. All thought of neatness and propriety, of keeping expensive clothes clean, of maintaining a dignified elegance, is quickly forgotten because it simply feels right to do this, to acknowledge the beauty and dignity of the woman in front of them, the sacredness of this moment that we're somehow fortunate enough to witness, to be a part of.

Sisi stands there in silence, looking down at us all, and then inclines her own head. The quiet draws on for a long moment, broken by nothing but the heartbeat of the Earth. It's as though we're all enchanted—I barely feel the passing of the minutes as we remain there, still and silent, looking at each other.

Slowly, Sisi—Queen Sigranna, Second in the Kingdom—straightens back up, and she and the King make their way across the room crowded with their subjects. We file back out in their wake, stunned and awed at the moment we've just witnessed. The gossip of before is gone. There's no murmur of speech, no sound at all, as we walk up and up the stairs and back into the grand ballroom. But I know that my work is done.

After the ceremony, there is to be a feast celebrating the wedding. It's the same tradition we have at home, where the wedding of the newly married couple is finalized with a great big meal for everyone present. Of course, it's a little fancier here at the palace than in Leasane.

There are sixteen courses, one to honor every Quarter in the Kingdom, and I'm seated between the Duchess of the Second Quarter and Jehan in his new role as the chief of the konim (well, the only konim, at present). It is not exactly the most relaxing meal of my life. I'm too uncertain of the etiquette to enjoy any of the delicacies that are served, and the meal drags on for hours that seem interminable given how weary I am after all the day's anxieties. Talk is subdued even among the guests that might ordinarily feel more comfortable with such feasts, since we're all—I must imagine—still in awe of what we witnessed beneath the palace.

And yet, when I look over at the High Table, where Sisi and Balion are staring into one another's eyes, not even glancing down at their plates or any of their guests, I wonder if I've ever been happier.

After the sixteenth course—a tiny piece of spun sugar made to look like a pile of purest snow—is served and eaten, the two of them are finally able to escape up to bed. There is much cheering, and several ribald jokes of surprising boldness, from the crowd. Sisi blushes at it all, but she also waves cheerily at everyone—for despite their jesting, the subjects do seem to love their beautiful new queen. Balion leads her out of the hall, her hand in his, and soon after that, the party begins. In his brother's absence, Ricard is responsible for hosting the dances, which he does with unsurprisingly ill grace. I make a hasty exit from the hall as soon as I think I can and retire up to my room.

In the dark, my dress unlaced and the familiar soft fabric of my nightgown against my skin, I can finally try to make sense of the startling truth. My cousin is the Queen.

I made this happen, I think, silently, gleefully, proudly. I'm only a girl, only a foolish young girl—but I do have this strange power.

I don't know where it came from. I don't know what it is. I don't know why I could do what no one else could. I don't even know if I'll ever be able to do it again. But I know that I did. Just once, I held power in my hands— and let it go when I needed to.

CHAPTER TWENTY-FIVE

I am still sleeping off the heavy dinner and rich wine—not to mention the exhaustion of the painful chant, which hits me hard as soon as I'm back in my room—when I am awoken by a knock on the door. I realize the sun is high in the sky as I force my heavy eyes open, but that does not make me feel any more ready to face the day. Still groggy, I put on my dressing gown and stumble to the door.

To my surprise, I find my father frowning in the doorway. "Papa? What are you doing here?"

Without any further commentary, he says, "We're going home."

Oh. For a moment I thought he had come simply to talk about Sisi's wedding. Maybe to *discuss* the plans for our future, for what we would do now that we were kin to the Queen of All the Earth. Or even, as foolish as I know the thought is, simply to see me. "When?" I ask.

"Tomorrow evening."

So soon. I should not be surprised, but I am. I imagined there was more time. I've been in the palace for nearly a year now and have made something very like a life for myself here. I wasn't expecting it to all end so soon. "We're—I have to go with you?"

He looks right at me. It's a strange feeling, having his calm brown eyes properly on me for once. It's almost as if he understands what he's asking of me. Almost like he understands *me*. "Yes, child. I don't think you should stay here with your cousin."

"She said I could be her companion. I could live like a Numbered lady. Stay here with her, have work to do..." I don't know what I'm saying. I don't even know if I want what I'm asking for. The words tumble out of me seemingly without my say-so. Though I never wanted to come to the palace, now I can't imagine suddenly returning home, a place I haven't missed, a place where there is no future for me. Not after what happened last night, and all the questions it raised for me.

In response, he only sighs. His face goes slack, and he suddenly looks not like my strong father, but like a tired old man. "You could certainly have the King intervene. Gaia knows I won't be able to take you home if the King and Queen both wish for you to stay here. I can only say what I hope for—and I hope that you won't decide to remain. I hope you'll come home, where you belong. There may be a title for you here, but your home will always be with us. We're your family."

The words, perhaps the longest speech I've ever heard my father make, sting me. Maybe they hurt most of all because I know that he isn't really wrong. There's nothing at all for me in the City. Sisi may be here, but she has a life now, with no need at all for me. I'd only be a reminder of the unpleasant time before she found her true love, her happiness. She might not even want me here. After all, who would want to spend her time thinking about her former days of being an orphaned farm-girl when she could focus on being the Queen? Would she have me stay only out of obligation—the memory of our friendship, the fact that it was I who found the spell to allow her marriage?

That thought makes me flinch. Perhaps I could accept that my cousin has moved on to better things, but it hurts more than I would have thought possible to imagine her remembering all our years together—maybe the best years I will ever know—as nothing more than an unpleasant hardship, the dark early days she had to over-come in order to win her King and her crown.

Strangely enough, my father seems to notice that I'm upset. He places one of his big, warm, callused hands over mine. I can't remember the last time he tried to comfort me with a touch. He embraced me before I left, that's true, but that lasted only a moment. And he must have held me when I was a baby. But otherwise, he has steadfastly avoided any contact with me through all my fifteen years.

Now, he holds on tight to my hand, like he doesn't want to let me go. He stays there while he looks for the right words. He doesn't seem to quite find them though, if they even exist. I'm not sure the most eloquent person in all Four Corners of the Earth, much less my taciturn father, could find anything comforting to say. In the end, he says only, "I'm sorry, Jeni. I wish that things could be different. I wish that we didn't...I'm sorry. I know that this is hard for you."

I'm surprised he's even noticed, though I don't want to say as much because I can imagine it will only hurt him to know that I have grown accustomed not to moments like this attempt at care, but to the silence that lingers between the two of us like an unhealed wound. There is so much we have never been to one another, so much we cannot say.

I wonder what he would do if I told him that I know his secret, know about my mother, know that he cannot love me and why he cannot do so. I wonder what he'd do if I told him how I feel about Sisi, that I'm afraid I love her the way I'm supposed to love a husband.

I wouldn't share the former secret, of course, because Aunt Mae made me swear a promise, and I wouldn't break that promise for anything—not least of all because if I did, that would surely be the last time I got any of the good family gossip from my aunt, and if we're leaving the palace to go back to Leasane, I'm going to need all the gossip I can get or else risk losing my mind entirely from sheer boredom.

And the latter is something I've still never quite said aloud, not to anyone, and I'm scared of how the words would change everything. Change me.

Yet I have to ask myself if honesty between us, at last, could do anything to heal the scars he still carries, the pain of my mother's loss, or if I would only be hurting him more. Perhaps if we talked about it, I could find the right words to make him forgive me for being my lost mother's daughter; to make him forgive himself for being unable to love me. Maybe he could see that we're the same, in some way, both loving those who were always going to leave us. But most likely, I would only cause more damage, and so what I say is not some perfect plea, but the whine of a petulant child. "Why do we have to go back at all?" I ask. "If we have everything now, what's the point of keeping the farm going at all?"

"It's what we have. It's my whole life. A man is nothing without his place in the Earth, and the farm is mine."

"And mine?" I feel a strange, overwhelming urge to slam the door shut and turn my back on him, or scream and stamp my feet, or anything, *anything*, that might somehow make him understand why I can't just go back, that could provoke a reaction from him at all.

"And yours," he says, though that isn't even slightly the answer I was looking for. It isn't true, and I think he knows that. Yes, I may inherit the farm when he's gone—though I suspect he'd rather leave it to his brother Willem, who has sons—but it's not for me that he keeps the land. It's for himself.

"Fine. Tomorrow," I respond. "I'll start packing." I cross my arms over my chest. If he wants to say something more, he'll have to be the one to do it.

When he does, his tone is quiet and calm, with an urgency undercutting the words.

"Listen," he says. "Jeni, we'll come back to visit. You'll see your cousin again, before too long. It'll be a bit of a change, of course. But it's not as though you'll never see Sisi again. We'll want for nothing now, and that means we can come back and forth to the palace, all right?"

I am choking back tears, though I don't quite know why. I feel his desperation in the words, his need to make me happy, make me understand that things will be all right even if he doesn't quite believe as much himself, and I wish I could put a name to the feeling that bubbles up in my heart as a response. I want to find the right words to say, want to be able to comfort him, just as he is trying— and admittedly failing—to comfort me, but I know I can't. I know there is nothing I can do to make this easier for either of us. So I say only, "Thank you, Papa."

Maybe it is at that moment that I first know what I am going to do.

He leaves without another word, though he gives one last sad look at me as he walks out of the room. He closes the door behind himself, and I let out a long, weary sigh. The tears still feel like they're just a moment away, bubbling up in my chest like a spring from the Earth, like something alive and wanting to burst to the surface.

I don't cry, though. I don't want to, even though I can feel the threat of it rising up. Something new is arising in me too. As intense as the tears, as much as the sadness, I sense something unfamiliar and a little frightening in my heart. There is a burning coldness rising up from my chest the way the tears won't, stinging in my throat, holding back the tears from my eyes where they well and stay and do not fall. It's like the fire from last night. It's like the humming within the Earth. It's so much bigger than me.

I am angry. I am frightened. But I am also ready. At first, I'm not sure what for.

But some impulse moves me to reach for the book I keep on my shelf, the book of maps that Sisi first read at the very beginning of our time here, that we used to share together, that I looked at before I could even understand a word. I haven't revisited it since, too busy in the library reading about the history of our Kingdom to consult these volumes that Sisi has already looked at and discarded, or studying to improve my own ability to read (not to mention my increasingly intense and time-consuming hobby of wallowing in self-pity.) Yet it somehow occurs to me that it might be a comfort to return to those pages, to revisit the shapes that fascinated me when I knew less and had more, when Sisi and I were best friends and more than sisters.

The thought compels me, consumes me, and before I know what I'm doing, I'm tracing my fingers over the gilt lettering. Now I can read the words on the cover easily: *The Earth Entire, a guide illustrated to the Four Corners of the Kingdom, with an examination of the major rivers, roads, forests, cities, towns, settlements, and etc.* I wonder why old books always have such long and peculiar titles, but for once, I feel too focused to lose myself in that or any other musing.

I open the book up and look back at the first map. I remember how it had fascinated me, how struck I had been with the idea that the entirety of the Earth could fit on those two pages, how Leasane—which I can find readily enough now, a small dot off on the far left side of the map —might be nothing more than a smudge in the fabric of the wide Kingdom I know so little about. My whole life, lived in that dot of nothingness. And now I'm going back there, when there is all this vast Kingdom I've never even seen.

I let my eyes trace across the pages, back toward the East. Aunt Mae told me my mother went East, I find myself remembering again. I wonder if there's any way of knowing if she's still there.

I remember how long I had looked at one spot, how I had let myself fantasize about a better life, a life with my mother, a life where I belonged, where I never felt as though I were slipping through the margins of a family that didn't truly want me there with them, but had to take care of me because I was, however little I seemed it, their own blood.

I see the mark I looked at for so long before, on the first night that Sisi met Ricard and this whole mad drama began. It's outlined in silver, and this time I can easily read the label that is written there in a careful and elegant script.

Iashome.

The two words leap out to my eyes. I blink carefully,

as though I can't believe what I'm seeing, but I know in my heart I can trust it. I know that what I've discovered, whatever I've discovered, is truth, and that I can rely on it. That I must rely on it.

I knew when I first saw it. Before I could even read the name, before I had any way of knowing, I felt some kind of connection with that place. Wherever it is, whatever it is, whatever it means, I felt as though I were drawn there. I looked at it, at that mark on the map, and I imagined my mother.

And then I learn to read, not thinking of this map at all for months, and when I most needed guidance, I somehow knew to turn to these pages again, and what did I learn? What did I find? One simple and clear truth. One thing that may very well, it seems, change my life forever.

This town has my mother's name.

And so, looking down at the paper, unwilling or perhaps unable to tear my eyes away from those words that look like something more than words, that look like a prophecy, that look like my future, I know what I have to do.

This is a sign. Maybe Gaia arranged it, maybe the universe itself, or maybe it is just chance righting the fact that everything that has ever happened to me up until this moment seems to have gone rather terribly and entirely wrong. I can't be sure either way, but I can know that it means something.

Iashome.

Ia's home.

My home.

This town has my mother's name, and I am going to find it, no matter what it takes. I am going to journey there, whatever it costs.

I'm going home.

I'm not quite sixteen years of age, but that doesn't matter. Merri was scarcely older than I am now when she was sent away from her family and everything she knew to find work with Jorj's family, and that much she did with our family's knowledge and blessing. Why, Sisi is only four years my elder, and she's just been crowned the reigning Queen of the entire Kingdom.

Running away from home can hardly be *more* difficult than what Sisi is being asked to do.

I don't have any illusions that what I'm doing is anything other than running off. My father would never give me permission. He's never so much as mentioned my mother's name in my hearing—that's how upset he still is with her for whatever happened between them at the end of their marriage. He'd never give me permission to go look for her.

And so I won't ask for it.

Instead, I determine to leave by myself.

My preparations have to wait for tonight, when no one will see me and suspect. First, I leave the room and find my family gathered around in the parlor. I need to allay any suspicions they may have, or I'll be caught before I can even set off.

"I'm sorry, Papa," I say. "I was upset. When are we leaving?"

I try to avoid lying to him outright as the plans are made. Instead, I stay silent as the rest of the family talks about the logistics of hiring carriages and how many guards will accompany us, as I wait for night to fall. Then I can begin.

CHAPTER TWENTY-SIX

I find, in the back of my overstuffed closet, behind all the fine gowns I've worn but once, a plain white petticoat made of solid and sturdy cotton. That will do as a travel sack. I tie it at the top and make some quick stitches across the bottom with a needle and thread. I've never been nearly as handy at sewing as, say, Aunt Mae is, but it should last for a while at least.

Then I ring for a maid. I tell her that that the entire family is planning on leaving tomorrow, and I ask her to bring me up a selection of cakes and dried fruits and hard cheese—things that will last for a long journey—as well as a skin for water. I'm sure the King has actually made provisions for our family's travel back to the farm, but the maid doesn't seem to know that, and I have to take the risk of asking. I will need something to eat along my journey, though I expect I'll eventually need to forage for food or trade for it, and I'd rather not actually steal from the kitchens if I can possibly help it.

I do hate asking for food. I know people look at me and assume that, because of my size, I must have an excessive appetite, and it always makes me self-conscious. But in this case, I can use it to my own advantage.

When she's been sent off, I begin packing some clothes. To my sorrow, all the loveliest of the dresses that have been made for me have to be left behind. They'll be no use at all while I'm on my journey, and most of them, being encrusted with gems and so on, are too heavy to carry even if I thought I'd find some opportunity to wear them along the way. Instead, I take simple things: the homespun I travelled here in, my new warm wool coat (since I'm not sure how long my journey will take and I fear that the warmth of summer may fade into fall long before I reach my destination), two spare day dresses chosen from the simplest of the ones I have, and my sleeping gown.

I do allow myself the luxury of shoving the silky pillow from the bed into my pack. I know that this trip won't be an easy one, that I won't be comfortable again as I am in this bed now for quite a long time. I want to take a small piece of that comfort with me, something to soothe the difficulties of the journey and remind me of how cloying even the greatest luxury can become.

There's one more thing I need with me. Wincing at the damage done to such a lovely and ancient object, I rip the map out of the book. I don't have time to trace the whole detailed map onto another piece of paper, and I know that I won't be able to bear the weight of the whole bound volume with me on this enormously long trip.

Instead, I will have to do my best with this single page. I trace out my route with one finger: from the star in the center, the Capital, over to the silvery dot in the distant East.

Iashome.

And mine too, I hope. I *believe,* with a clarity I've never felt except in the cavern when Sisi was crowned.

The maid returns with the pack of food I'd asked for. I thank her and send her back to bed. As soon as she's gone, I begin digging through the pack, eager to see how many supplies she's brought me. She was very generous: three paper rolls of two dozen hard-baked crackers each, a wheel apiece of two different kinds of hard cheese, a pound of dried cherries and one of dried apples, and even a log of dry beef sausage.

If I'm careful with it, this is easily enough food to last me for three weeks' journey, perhaps a month, even if I need more than usual to eat since I'll be walking so much. And it's now the height of summer, so hopefully I'll be able to find some berries and such along the way.

I tie everything up in my canvas sack, as neatly and carefully as possible, and then slip out of the room to find the last of what I'll need.

Luckily, my long weeks of wandering unseen through the palace give me an advantage. I am resolved not to take anything that isn't mine if I don't have to, but there are a few tools I'm certain are necessary. I return to my room with a compass, some rope, and a brick of matches pilfered from various supply closets before I imagine anyone has noticed I'm gone or could have seen me on my way.

All packed for my journey, I take up the pen, ink, and paper on my desk, and begin to compose my notes of farewell.

The first is to the family as a group. I know that not all of them will be able to read it for themselves, but I hope Jorj will agree to read it to them. I'm not sure if what I'm able to put down is right. I want to find words that will stem the feelings everyone will have when they find my bed empty in the night, but I'm not sure what that reaction will be.

Will they be furious? Upset? Devastated?

Or will they not even care?

I look to my pack as that thought crosses my mind and let it make my resolve even firmer. As frightening as it may be to leave everything behind, I can't stay here, where I have no purpose, no reason, and no one to care for me. Still, this last task has to be done. I can't just disappear without a word to anyone as to where I'm going and what I'm doing.

They have to at least have some reason to hope that I'm safe. I want to leave them with that much, in case they want it.

To all of you who are so dear to me: Aunt Mae, Aunt Sarie, Uncle Willem, Cousin Will, Cousin Merik, Cousin Belerd, Cousin Merri, Cousin Jorj, and little Mali:

There is no way to say this lightly.

There is no way to say this that will not hurt you, as much as that is the last thing I want, for I love you all dearly.

But here it is, for I feel I owe you the truth: there is no place for me back at Prinnsfarm. There never has been. You have loved me well, but you have never needed me there, and so there is nothing for me to do but to leave. I have to figure out who I am and where I come from.

I believe that my mother is out there. I'm going after her, however far I have to look. I hope I will come back with good news, and with a sense of who I am and what I ought to do.

I, like Sisi, am coming of age. I hope that I will find my place in life as she has found hers. You must think on the fact that, two years ago, none of us would have believed that she could find the happiness she has here in the palace. My own journey may seem just as unbelievable, and yet I know it is possible for me, too, to find my place, but not if I go back to the farm. There I will only rot, like fruit that has been left on the branch for too long. I must harvest myself now, while it is time.

I will miss you all bitterly, and our home near as much. Take care of one another for me. Tell the baby about me. Don't forget me, wherever I go.

All my love,
Jeni

IT ISN'T easy to write, but when it's done it feels right. It feels like enough. I've done the best I can to tell them of my plans, to let them know my reason for going, without giving them any hope of following me and making me come back. I try not to dwell on what their reactions will likely be. If I'm going, I should not let too many of my thoughts stay behind.

The next letter is to my father. I know I ought to write something just to him, even though it's hard to figure out what that is. He and I have never had much to say to one another, and so it's difficult to encapsulate everything that has been underneath all our long silences as I begin to put pen to paper. But I'm leaving, and I know this might be the last thing I ever say to him. I don't want to leave with regrets and questions, and I can't make him open up to me. I have to be the one to bridge the gulf between us now, at last.

Dear Papa,

Thank you for what you said to me tonight. It is the first time I have ever felt that you and I understand each other. That we know a little bit of what is in one another's hearts.

And I know there is love in your heart. Love for me. I wasn't always sure, but now, as I'm leaving, I know that it is there, unspoken and steady. Just like you. It isn't easy for you to show it. I know how much you miss my mother, how different I am from you, everything that stands in the way of us loving one another.

I wish that I could write more clearly of some kind of

forgiveness for that, but I don't feel it. I am terribly angry.
I believe that is part of why I am leaving.

My mother abandoned me. Did you have to do the
same? It was almost worse, since you were gone though
you stayed there right beside me all the time.

MY EYES well up with tears as I write those words. I
know I shouldn't say it. I've been *not saying* it as long as I
can remember. It's always been in my heart, on my mind,
but I've been avoiding ever putting it into words because
I don't want to hurt my father, and because I have no idea
what will come of it. I can't imagine that it would be a
particularly productive conversation to have face-to-face.
And, just like with Sisi, I can't face the possibility of
opening myself up, pleading to be seen and heard as I
never have been, and being turned away.

But here is my coward's way of making my feelings
heard. Everything I've ever not said, I will write here,
even though I'll have no way of knowing how my father
takes it.

I'M SORRY, Papa. I'm sorry that I am going, that I am
doing as my mother did and leaving you behind. I am
sorrier still that I cannot be more understanding as I do so.
I wished to leave with kind words, so that you remember
me with nothing but fondness if I do not return, but you
are honest enough that I doubt that is what you would

want. I think you would want the truth that has never been spoken between us.

I wish I could have told you to your face, plainly. I wish everything was different for us. But if it were, I wouldn't need to be going.

You said there's no place for me here at the palace, and I do believe that. I do know that, in my very heart. There's no reason for me to stay here.

But there's no reason for me to return home, either.

You don't exactly need me to make the farm run. I do have a job, but it's one that you could easily do without me there. I have been happy at times, sad at others, like any child. I know you have loved me, in your quiet way, but I must try and find my home, the way you have found yours on the farm. As you said, we are nothing without our place in this Earth. You have yours. I need to find mine.

I hope you will miss me, but not too much. I will miss you, and terribly so, but nonetheless, I know I must go.

I love you, wherever I am, whatever may happen. And whenever I think of you, know that I am thinking of the love you have shown me, and that I leave the bitterness, the anger, behind in this letter.

I hope beyond hope that you will do the same for me.
Jeni.

AND FINALLY, the saddest and hardest of them all. I don't let myself think of what this last farewell will cost me, or what it means. I've already chosen to make the sacrifice for her sake, to let her go. This is just the last formality. Or so I tell myself, but my hand is shaking as I dip my pen in the ink, set it to paper, and write out the words.

*D*EAR *S*ISI—
   My darling, my love, my Queen of All—

I CAN'T DO IT. I let the pen clatter back down and put my head in my hands. What am I *thinking?* I can't leave her, can't leave everything I know behind when I don't even know what I'm doing, where I'm going. I won't survive the trip, much less find my mother and whatever it is that I'm looking for. The whole thing is only a temporary madness, and I ought to put it all right out of my mind. I stand up to start putting things away, about to begin unpacking my bags when I hear a knock at the door. I assume it's the maid—I just won't answer, and soon enough she'll depart.

"Jena?" a voice calls.

It isn't a maid at all. It's Sisi. I would know her voice anywhere. And no one else calls me by my True Name.

I look around, desperate. There's no way to hide everything, the letters, the parcel of clothes, the sack of food, unless I'm willing to make her wait. And knowing Sisi, it won't be long before—

She lets herself in.

She stands in the doorway, arms crossed. Her unbound hair haloes her head, and she's wearing a white shift, simple and stark against the dark brown of her skin. She's clearly still half-asleep. She comes over to me, sitting next to me on our bed. *My bed,* I correct myself. This has never been ours, and we'll never share again, but that feels hard to believe as I look back at her and the almost-familiar picture she makes there. We could be in our bedroom back at home. I feel the tears in my eyes again, and this time I can't stop them from falling.

"I thought so," she says softly.

"Thought what?"

"You're running away." It's not a question.

"What? How do you know? I mean, what are you talking about?"

"You're a terrible liar, Jena."

"I know." I always have been.

"You were bound to, sooner or later." She sighs. "I could tell that you were becoming restless. I didn't know when you would decide to go, but I felt sure that sooner or later you would determine you couldn't stay here any longer. And you can't exactly go home, can you?"

"So you believe that too?" I ask, eager for her reassurance. "I thought so, but—" It made me feel a bit mad, to be so convinced my home wasn't really my home.

"Of course. You've never belonged at the farm."

"And now you won't even be there."

"So you have to go somewhere else. Where?"

"East. I'm looking for my mother."

She nods, unsurprised at my answer, though of course she has questions. She wouldn't be Sisi if she didn't have questions. "Why do you think you should look to the East?"

I show her the map.

"This is—"

"From one of the first books you brought up here. I always felt, I don't know, drawn to it. And now I see—"

"Your mother's name. You think she's there."

I shrug. "I hope so. I don't know. But it's somewhere to start. Somewhere to go."

Gently, Sisi takes my hand, lacing her fingers with mine. We sit in silence for a moment. I soak up the warmth of her touch, her familiar, steady presence beside me. I don't know how long it will be before I can feel it again, and I want to remember it perfectly if I never do. "I wish I could go with you, my dear one," she says.

"What? But you have Balion. Why would you want to leave?"

"Because you're going on the great adventure I never had. I probably never will have one, now." She smiles slightly, and I think of how she'd been when we set off for the Capital, full of anger at the way the Kingdom works, full of passion to change it for something better. She's somehow, silently, given much of that up for Balion's sake. I don't think she regrets it, but I realize in that moment that I'm not the only one who has had to make sacrifices.

Somehow that makes it all much easier, and some of the bitterness that has filled me up ever since we arrived leaches away, replaced with a glow of tenderness toward her. It's easy, suddenly, to find the right words to make her feel better, and to *want* to say them with a whole heart.

"You're a penniless orphan who fell in love with the King and *married* him! What could be a greater adventure than that?" I'm teasing, a little, but I mean it too.

"I suppose. But I'll spend most of the rest of my life in the palace or traveling on official business. My journeys from now on will take place in the royal library and around meeting tables. And if I change things, it will be through the slow process of law. No mysteries, no assignations, no revolutions. You, on the other hand, are completely free. You will go far, and you'll find what you're looking for."

"You think so?"

"I do. And I'll prove it, too. I can't go with you, but I can ease the way."

"Sisi?"

"I'm giving you some money. For your trip. It's in your bags, which are in the stables, ready to go. I had a horse saddled for you—consider it a wedding gift."

"Sorry," I say as I realize. "I guess I should have gotten you a wedding gift—since you're the one who got married."

She grins. "I got the most wonderful man of the Earth, and an entire Kingdom to call my own. I think that's agreeable enough, as gifts go. I wouldn't ask for more."

"And?" Because I know her just as well as she knows me, and I know that there's something she isn't saying.

"And I thought this might be good for you. I don't *want* to convince you to stay, Jena."

"Why not?"

"Think of the night we learned we were coming here. You were afraid to even go down to the kitchen after you were supposed to be in bed. You were such a timid little girl, always in my shadow and frightened to be even there. Now you are ready to set off into the Kingdom all by yourself, ready to become a woman grown and independent. I want this for you, as much as I wanted it for myself. I could never wish anything more for you than to find this bravery in yourself: the knowledge that you have to find your place, and the courage to go out looking for it. As I have. As I have found it with Balion, much to my own surprise."

"Sisi," I say, suddenly overcome by emotion. "I don't know what to say. I don't..."

It's the first time I can remember that I haven't been immediately corrected for calling her by her childish by-name. For so many years, she's been very insistent on being called by her True Name, ever since she was old enough to understand why women have True Names and by-names and why the former is forbidden. But this time, she doesn't correct me, only smiles at me.

"No one will call me that anymore, I've realized. How I used to hate it. But from now on, I won't be Sisi to anyone. It'll be Your Majesty, or Lady Sisi at the best. Maybe I can even make them all call me Queen Sigranna. I don't know that that's what I want. I don't know that I want to forget the girl that I was with you. Yet I have to let you go, little bird."

"Why do you call me that?"

"It's what your True Name means. Jena. Little bird. And you're going to learn how to fly."

She's always insisted on using my True Name, just as she wants me to use only hers. She's the only one that ever called me that before I came here to this palace, and I'd never been very fond of it. From Sisi though, this time, it sounds loving, affectionate. It sounds like a playful secret between us, the kind we will no longer whisper every night. Not ever again. I take her hand for a moment, and she leans in to kiss my forehead.

"Now, it's getting late. You should go, if you want a good start on your trip by the time the others wake in the morning. You should plan on being outside the City walls by then, in case your father comes after you. I'm sending a guard to the wall with you, since there can be a great deal of danger in walking around the City by yourself as a young woman. I can't ask a soldier to travel further than that without telling the King—"

"Don't. I don't need an escort. I want to travel alone."

"He'll go with you just as far as the Unplanned Regions just around the palace. It's dangerous out there, and it's changed since the last time there was a map drawn. Another thing I suppose I ought to have fixed around here once it comes time to govern. By morning, when you're in the woods and you're not likely to see anyone to bother you, he'll be gone."

I agree to that much, and Sisi nods conclusively.

The business is over. It doesn't seem right to end things at this moment, on this strangely mercenary note. We've been everything to one another for so many years, and now we're about to say goodbye. I don't know for how long, but certainly for long enough, and perhaps forever.

Finally, at that thought, the tears come properly, welling out through my eyes, rolling down my cheeks, hot and heavy. I fall into Sisi's open arms, pillowing my head on her breast, and I cry and cry. She weaves her fingers through my hair, holding me, and for a long time I think of nothing except this. Except the fact that, for now, likely for the last time, we are together.

After a long minute, I start to feel a little ashamed at the way I'm clinging to her, when I ought to be heading out on my own.

"I'm sorry," I say. "You thought I was so brave."

"There's no shame in weeping. I believe it makes you all the stronger. You are afraid, and yet you are going."

The two of us hold each other tight for a long moment, saying nothing. And then it becomes clear—the moment for our goodbyes has come at last.

I don't want that to be the case, but it is. I need to be able to accept that. I need to say the words.

"I love you so much, Sisi. Make sure that King of yours takes care of you, would you?"

She laughs. "I'll do my best, cousin."

"And thank you. Thank you for everything. Thank you for being the only person who has ever really believed in me. I don't know what to say about that, except that I'm grateful, and I love you more than I can say."

"And I love you, my little bird, my sweet Jena. You have brightened my childhood days. And you were here during the hardest hours of my life, and I never would have had my happiness without what you did for us. It's here now, for me. I hope that soon enough it will arrive for you too."

"If it does, Sisi, it will be thanks to you. Thanks to all this." I pull back from our embrace, knowing that the moment has come to say the last few things. "I wrote letters for everyone. The rest of the family, I mean. I want you to pass them along. Or read them. You don't have to say exactly what I did. I don't think I found the right words at all. I've always been the one who struggles to speak, and you're the clever one. If anyone can help them understand why, and what's happening...well, you understand, yourself. Maybe you're the one who can make sure they understand it too. Will you try, at the very least?"

"I'll do more than try, Jena. I will make sure they know why you're leaving. Because I think I do know, as perhaps no one else can. I know that it's hard to leave us all behind."

"It's harder than I can explain," I admit, though I'm trying to keep a brave face to impress her. "It's unbearable. And yet I can't help but feel like it has to happen. I don't know if I can go on living the way I have been up to this moment, in this palace, absolutely useless. And I know I can't go back to being bored and lonely at home. So, I will go on, alone, into the future of my life, even though it terrifies me to try and do that, to try and create something new for myself."

"You go with all my blessings, my darling. And if you ever can, send a message back. I would like to know if you find your destination safely. Does that sound agreeable?"

"Agreeable?" Oh, Sisi. How strange and formal you sound. How much like a woman you are. How you've changed.

How I will bear you with me, in my heart, in my thoughts, every part of you. From my childhood friend who laughed and teased me down the stairs while I grumbled and clung to my bed, to the Queen sparkling at her royal wedding and kneeling solemnly in the sacred caves of Gaia Herself. From the great beauty at the royal Midwinter ball, to this moment right here, as we remain together, the two of us looking into one another's eyes and trying to memorize the sight of each another, hoping to keep something we can carry through the rest of our lives even as we turn away from each other, knowing we may not see this familiar, beloved face again.

"Come," she says. "I'll walk you to the stables."

We say nothing as we walk through the halls of the palace together, silent and still in the night. We've said all we can say to one another. Once in the stables, we embrace one final time. She kisses me softly on the cheek, and I return the gesture.

"I love you, Jena. Ride safe."

"I love you, too. Rule safe," I reply. I mean it is as a joke, but she only gives me a small, sad smile as she watches me try to mount up on my mare.

Sisi has indeed found a horse for me to ride and a guardsman to help me find my way out of the City. Unfortunately, I don't know how to ride a horse. The poor guardsman, who is doubtless less than impressed with having been given the duty of taking a fifteen-year-old girl to the City wall, is nonetheless a fairly patient teacher in trying to get me up onto my horse so I can attempt to ride for a while.

Eventually, I manage to stop falling down. This is probably helped by the fact that they've chosen a particularly calm and steady horse for me, a mare who seems to be getting on in years, if I judge by the dusting of white hairs around her nose. She does all she can to stay steady —it's entirely my own fault that I can't seem to stay on her back. Yet, after about my third tumble helplessly off of her, I am able to keep a seat at least while the guard has a hand on the reigns to keep me moving forward.

Sisi watches us ride out of the stables. I look back at her for as long as I can, memorizing the sight of her: Queen Sigranna, Second in the Kingdom, the most beautiful woman on Gaia's Earth, wearing a white nightgown and a blue blanket wrapped around herself like a scarf, weeping small, silent tears as she watches me ride away. She looks so much like she did on that night when she shook me awake in the loft at my father's house, and told me she wanted to go downstairs and hear what the fuss was all about. I raise up a hand to wave at her, but it feels too heavy to say goodbye to all those moments, from our girlhood at my father's farm, to the long lonely months at the palace, to the coronation.

Just as when I sat to write my letter, there is nothing left to be said. All I can do, though it takes all my strength, is turn my face away from her and ride on.

I love her still. No doubt I always will. But I chose to give that hope up at the moment of her Test beneath the palace, to keep the love silent in my heart. To accept that I would never be more to her than a sister, and sisters grow apart with time.

I love Sisi. And I'm leaving her behind. Those two opposing truths lie heavy in my heart as the guard and I walk toward the stone wall of the City inexorably, at an even and slow pace. With every step, I feel my heart beat faster.

I don't speak to the guard. I don't even get his name. He just keeps his hand on the reigns, and I keep trying to balance myself on the horse.

No one bothers us, despite the odd sight we must be. I see many eyes watching us though, from around corners. This is the most I've seen of the City itself, strange as that is. How long ago arriving here seems, though it has been not even a full year.

It's only about a twenty-minute ride to leave it all behind, even at my spectacularly slow pace. The trip through the gate is much less intimidating this time; with the royal seal by my side, no one even tries to stop us or ask us any questions. When we arrive on the other side of the wide gate, the guard reaches up to shake my hand.

"Have a safe trip, wherever you're going, little lady."

I want to thank him for his kindness. I want to ask his name. I want to say anything at all. I turn behind me, wanting to draw out the moment before my departure just a little longer, wanting one more goodbye.

But he's gone, and I'm alone, looking out into an Earth I know nothing about.

It's the middle of the night. The sky is dark, though the moon and stars shine. I gently tap my heel into my horse's side and begin to ride.

We go slow at first since I'm still getting my grip on the bridle. I've no idea what I'm doing on the back of this beast, but I find it comes naturally to me. I start to loosen up on the reins, feeling a little less like I'm about to go flying off at any moment, and the mare seems to understand this as a cue to speed up. For a moment, my heart drops, but I quickly realize that the faster speed isn't truly frightening me at all. Instead, I find it exhilarating, this racing ride through the chilly night air.

As the horse gains speed, I find something is changing within me. I've held a deep sorrow within for so long, and suddenly it seems to be dropping away from my heart. The change comes over my body first, before I know what it is that I'm feeling. First, I'm smiling. Then, I'm laughing. Then—I don't know if there's even a word for it, but this *happiness* rises from my heart, as free and bright as I am. I gallop through the dark, cold night, my hair streaming behind me as black as the night itself, and my heart singing an old song in a language I do not know. And I am filled with a joy I have never felt before.

*T*he end.

For today, at least. You look wearied, and my throat is dry. I have talked for too many hours, for one as old as I am. And there is much more yet to tell.

Go home, dear one. Rest, and think on what I have said, and what I am going to say.

And if you believe me—enough to wonder if it is so— come back tomorrow and hear the rest.

GLOSSARY

- *Adirim:* a species of extremely elevated magical ability, who are rarely seen in the Kingdom. Sometimes, archaically, called the "great people" or the "greatest people"
- *Adirit:* a single member of the adirim
- *Annunciate:* a title within the konim
- *Behemoth:* a legendary monster supposed to dwell beneath the sea
- *By-name:* a nickname, usually ending in -i or -e, used by women, originally to avoid sharing their True Names with strangers but now to avoid the association with magic
- *Go'im:* a collective name for the Adirim and the Pahyat—all those other than humans—meaning "the people"
- *Golden Soldiers:* a militia formed by Lord Ricard. The only military force in the Kingdom.
- *konim:* an order of scholars and magicians, and one of the Three Powers of the Kingdom, intended to govern matters of the mind and magic.
- *milar:* a coin of moderate value.
- *Numbered:* any of the thousand people closest in line to the throne, typically those

who can trace their direct descent to the First King and his Queen.

- *Old Tongue:* the universal language of the Kingdom until the decline of the Adirim, now mostly unknown. Used by magical peoples and to name things of particular importance.
- *Pahyat-house*: a small altar, traditionally built by rural people in the hope of attracting go'im and the magical fortune they bring.
- *Pahyat*: any of several tribes of people with limited magical ability, who once had their own civilizations throughout the Kingdom but now survive mostly as servants to humans, tending to be shorter in stature than humans and Adirim (their name means "small ones").
- *Pavain:* a courtly dance, done in circles.
- *Ruak*: literally, spirit. The closest translation into the Common Tongue would be "magic".
- *Shekin*: the most valuable coin, made of pure gold.
- *tonne*: a unit of measurement, the equivalent of all the weight a strong man can lift.
- *Tannin:* a legendary island-dwelling creature with the face of a woman and the body of a bird.
- *True Name:* a name in the Old Tongue that carries spiritual meaning. For women, universally ending in the letter "a", and

generally kept secret or used only by their intimates.

- *witch:* a generally derisive term used for women who practice magic.
- *zizit*: an immense legendary bird, famously supposed to be able to block out the sun with its wingspan.
- *zuzam*: the lowest denomination of money in common use.

CAST OF CHARACTERS

PRINNSFARM AND LEASANE

- Jena (Jeni): a girl of fourteen
- Prinn: Jena's father
- Willem: Prinn's brother
- Sariana (Sarie): Willem's wife
- Maera (Mae): Prinn's sister, Jena's aunt
- Merrine (Merri): Willem's daughter
- Jorj: Merri's husband
- Malaria (Mali)m: Jorj and Merri's daughter
- Sigranna (Sisi): Jorj's sister
- Willem, Merik, and Belerd: Willem and Merri's teenaged sons
- Zenel: the town's inkeeper
- Daren: the potter's apprentice
- Kariana: a magic user who lived in the woods outside the village. Murdered by the Golden Soldiers before the story began.
- Lilane (Lili): a neighbor
- Kariana (Kari): Lilane's daughter
- Taric: Kari's husband

THE ROYAL FAMILY AND THE CAPITAL

- Balion: the King of All the Earth

- Ricard: his elder brother and presumed heir, Second in the Kingdom
- Elan: a *Pahyati* and steward to Ricard
- Patine: a lady and distant cousin to Sisi
- Ransi: another lady and distant cousin to Sisi
- Balertius: the palace's dancing master
- Karili: instructor of etiquette
- Mari: the palace's chief seamstress
- Garem: the Kingdom's High Priest
- Jehan: his assistant
- Padrig: a guard

THANK YOU FOR READING QUEEN
OF ALL.

Please consider leaving a review so that other readers can find
this title.

Your reviews help feed an indie author and help other readers
and booksellers find their next favorite novel.

**AND STAY TUNED FOR THE JENA CYCLE BOOK 2 COMING
IN 2022!**

OTHER ZENITH TITLES YOU MAY ENJOY

Exordium by S.N. Jones

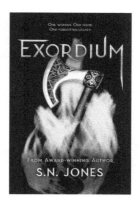

Sea & Flame by Tallie Rose

AUTHOR'S NOTE

Some of you may know that publishing this book is a near-lifelong dream of mine. I first conceived of *Queen of All* while playing a game of pretend as a kid—I might have been eight or nine. I started writing when I was twelve. I will be twenty-seven when the book is published.

That leaves me with about a decade and a half worth's of thank-yous saved up, so hold tight.

So, for a start, I'd like to thank the team that made this practically possible. To the entire GenZ and Zenith family, for taking a chance on an unknown debut author, for treating my story with so much respect and love, and for making my dream come true, thank you for this chance (and a special shout-out to Lauren for the gorgeous cover). To Beth Phelan and her hard work organizing #dvpit, the incredible Twitter event where I first connected with GenZ, thank you for everything you do for marginalized authors and our stories. To my fellow #21ders for your moral support, commiseration, and brilliance, thank you for creating such a special space for us to share.

Thanks to my teachers, from Duke Young Writer's Camp to Columbia to UCLA, who have guided me as I grew my craft and refined this story over the years. Thank you to the many people who have read *Queen of All* over the years and given such helpful feedback and encouragement: Kristen, Cynthia, Kersti, Elizabeth, Fiona, Emma, Katya, and many others I'm sure I'm forgetting. Thank you to Maureen for organizing our Fortnightly Writers' Group, and to everyone who has been a part of it. Thank you to Molly, who has been my rock during the querying and publishing process. It's your turn now, sorry.

Thank you to the many writers who have inspired me over the years, for your beautiful work and for welcoming me to the writing community with open arms. Thank you to everyone who shared, boosted, or blurbed my book so that it could find its way into readers' hands. Thanks especially to my fellow LGBTQ+ authors, for treading the ground where I now walk so that the path is a little easier.

Thank you to my family. To my parents: for always encouraging my love of stories, for answering random medical questions about things like medieval childbirth, and for raising me in a home where the arts were truly valued. And to my brother, for being this book's first fan and supporting Jena's story for all these years.

And most of all, thanks to you, dear reader, for making this dream come true. I hope you'll enjoy your first steps into this world, and stay tuned for the next adventure.

ABOUT THE AUTHOR

Anya Josephs was raised in North Carolina and now lives and works in New York City. When not working or writing, Anya can be found seeing a lot of plays, reading doorstopper fantasy novels, or worshipping their cat, Sycorax. Anya's writing can be found in *Fantasy Magazine, Andromeda Spaceways Magazine, The Green Briar Review,* the *Necronomicon Anthology, SPARK, SoLaced, Proud2BeMe, The Huffington Post, Anti-Heroin Chic,* and *Poets Reading the News. Queen of All* is Anya's first novel.

Twitter: @anya_writes
Facebook: @anyaleighjosephs

9 781952 919398